STAR CROSSED

THE SEDONA FILES: BOOK 4

CHRISTINE POPE

DARK VALENTINE PRESS

STAR CROSSED

ISBN: 978-0692358443

Copyright © 2014 by Christine Pope.

Revised version copyright © 2019

Published by Dark Valentine Press

Cover design by Lou Harper

Book formatting by Indie Author Services

STAR CROSSED

Copyright © 2014 by Christine Pope; revised edition © 2019

Published by Dark Valentine Press

Cover design by Lou Harper

Ebook formatting by Indie Author Services.

❃ Created with Vellum

CHAPTER ONE

Twenty-five years from now…

"Heading home, Grace?" Nate asked as I began to head out of the Lowell Observatory offices, although the question was pretty much superfluous, considering the weekender bag I held in one hand.

Unfortunately, yes, I thought. I knew if I dared to say such a thing out loud, though, I'd only be inviting more questions, and that was the last thing I wanted right then. It had already taken me too long to mentally prepare myself for this departure. So I shrugged and replied, "Well, I suppose the powers-that-be thought it wouldn't be fair to stick me on observation duty two Christmases in a row."

"Fair enough."

I could feel his cool blue eyes on me, watching me, and I wondered if he was finally getting the courage to make some sort of move. Never mind that we'd been working together for almost two years now, ever since I was lucky enough to be assigned to the weather station here at Lowell Observatory. Everything between Nate and me had always been proper, always been correct, but I knew he was interested. More than interested, although not enough to step over the line. After all, he was an assistant director at the observatory, and although he wasn't technically my boss, as I reported to the National Weather Service director in Bellemont, that didn't mean things couldn't get messy if our relationship turned into something a little more than professional.

In a way, I wished Nate would make that move. He was attractive, if not drop-dead gorgeous, and we had a good deal in common. I liked him. More to the point, if he spoke up now, asked me to go out for drinks, suggested that maybe it would be a good thing if I stuck around Flagstaff during the holidays, then I could avoid going back to Sedona altogether. Just another "sorry everyone, duty calls" kind of situation, like what had come up last year. But I knew that wouldn't happen. Nate was too cautious to ever instigate a first date during an emotionally charged time of year like the Christmas holidays.

"Well," I said, "I guess I'd better get going. That front is coming in faster than we'd first estimated, and I'd rather be down in Sedona before it hits."

A nod. "That would be safer." He hesitated, then

said, "Have a great holiday, Grace. See you in a week."

"You, too, Nate," I replied. What else was there to say, after all?

I gave him what I hoped was a friendly but noncommittal smile, then headed down toward the lot where my car waited. Normally, I would've left straight from my apartment, which was located just outside of downtown, but I'd wanted to take a few last readings here at the observatory before I headed down the hill. I wasn't taking that much with me, anyway—just the weekender bag I held now, and another smaller bag with toiletries and such, one that was already stowed in the trunk of my car. And since it had been easiest to put my laptop on top of my clothes in the weekender, that was why I had it with me now.

The smile I was wearing disappeared as I went to my car and dropped the bag in the trunk. I hadn't been looking forward to this trip at all, but there was no getting out of it. From the outside, my reluctance to go home probably would have looked pretty strange. After all, Sedona was gorgeous, a resort town that was a destination for people from all over the world. And it wasn't as if I had a horrible home life or anything. Yes, my stepfather Lance and I didn't get along all the time, but even so….

"Mom's house," I told the car after I'd buckled myself in. Immediately, the route popped up on the dashboard display, and the car began to back itself out of the parking space. Sometimes, I liked to disengage the auto-drive and handle things myself, but today, since I was feeling distracted, I thought it better to let the car do the driving.

Snow had fallen two days earlier in Flagstaff, and so, although the roads were clear, dirty drifts were piled to either side as I made my way down Mars Hill, where the observatory was located, through the downtown area, and onto the interstate. The sky, which had been a clear, clear blue that morning, had already clouded up to the north and east.

Right on schedule, I thought. The storm looked to be a nasty one, too, a deep low dropping south from Colorado. Most of northern Arizona was going to take a direct hit, which meant a lot more to the people in Flagstaff than it did to Sedona's residents. Down there, more than two thousand feet lower than the town I now called home, if it snowed at all, it would be just enough to make everything pretty and picturesque, but not enough that anyone would have to worry about plowing a street or shoveling a sidewalk. Sedona actually had several snowplows, but sometimes a whole winter would pass without them being pressed into service.

I knew why I was distracting myself by thinking about the weather. If I focused on that, on the observations and measurements I'd made before leaving work, then I wouldn't have to think about what Sedona meant, what being with my family meant. When I was away from them, I could almost believe I was normal. After all, I appeared normal enough. Two eyes, a nose, a mouth, ten fingers, ten toes. Nothing to merit a second look, really.

Except I wasn't normal. My family and a couple of family friends so close they might as well be blood relations knew the truth about my background, but that was all. No one who met me would even guess at the reality of my situation, probably because it still felt crazy to me, even though I'd had to live with that truth for more than half my life.

I looked human, but I wasn't. Not completely. My father had been an alien—or, more accurately, someone with both human and alien DNA in his veins. A construct. A hybrid.

If anyone had been paying close attention, they might have noticed a few anomalies. I never got sick, was one of those annoying kids with the perfect attendance record in school. Although people were still arguing over whether true eidetic memory actually existed, I had it, to some extent. I could read a book or article once and recall every detail of what I'd read, even years later. Almost without thinking, I could tell you that June 14, 2020, had been a Sunday. Things like that. It wasn't flawless, but I had to work to hide my abilities as best I could. I got straight As, but so did a lot of my fellow students—Sedona was that kind of town. Lots of overachievers there. What I doubted my classmates knew was that I'd spent a good deal of time purposely getting things wrong here and there, just so I wouldn't have psychologists and neuroscientists picking at my brain, trying to see how whatever made me tick was different from everyone else.

The car slowed as it approached the switchbacks that crisscrossed their way down the side of the mountain, taking me into Oak Creek Canyon. Here, too, there were muddy piles of snowdrifts on either side of the road, and ice gleamed in the shadowy sections of the asphalt, but I wasn't overly concerned. I'd specifically bought the car because, although it wasn't a full-blown SUV, it had all-wheel drive and the best traction control on the market. It was smart to be prepared when you could get hit with crazy monsoon rains in the summer and blinding snow in the winter.

Weather had always fascinated me, and so it had seemed logical for me to get my degree in meteorology. I think my mother had worried more than she should about me going off to the university in Tucson for five years, but I survived relatively unscathed. Kept my head down, got my B.S. in three years, my master's in two. And then the position at Lowell came up, and I returned to northern Arizona. Not Sedona, though, despite some subtle pressure for me to live at home, at least at first—"but it's only a half-hour up the canyon!" True, but even now the roads would get shut down occasionally if a storm was bad enough, and I couldn't risk having to take the long way around. Besides, I'd gotten used to my independence, didn't want to contemplate giving it up.

I was an adult. I needed to make my own way in the world. And so far, no one had learned of my secret. Then again, who would believe it? I didn't look any more alien than the girl next door…well, unless you stuck a blood sample under an electron microscope. Then you might find telltale signs that would raise a few eyebrows.

Despite the oncoming storm—or maybe because of it—traffic was fairly thick going down into the canyon. Maybe people were trying to get to town before it hit. In general, Sedona was quiet the week before Christmas. It was afterward, up to and including New Year's, that it could get kind of crazy. Now, with two days to go until Christmas Eve, I was sort of surprised by the string of cars both in front of and behind me. It could get really jammed going into Uptown, and I found myself a little glad that I'd agreed to stop in at the house first before going on to the cottage.

The cottage. That was what we called it, but really, it was just a two-bedroom ranch-style house that my mother and my Aunt Kirsten had inherited from a family friend, since he'd had no children of his own. By all accounts, when Michael Lightfoot passed away, the house had been anything but a showplace. But my mother and my aunt carefully remodeled it, clearing out all the tchotchkes Michael had liked to collect, and now it was a sort of crash space they used for visiting friends or people in their UFO groups or whatever.

Or for a prodigal daughter who didn't want to sleep in her old bedroom, even if said bedroom had at last been reluctantly turned into a guest room.

The car slowed, preparing to turn off the highway and onto the winding road that led to my parents' house. It wasn't paved, but every year, they laid down freshly crushed gravel, so it was in good shape. Dark pines and bare cottonwoods and sycamores passed on either side, and then I was crossing the bridge over the creek, going up the slight rise to the spot where the house stood. I didn't see any other vehicles—the house had a three-car garage, but with my siblings Kevin and Kelsey and Melissa still living at home, you usually always saw someone's car parked out front.

In a way, it was a relief. With everyone home, the place could be bedlam—I tended to refer to the old homestead as "the Nuthouse" in my mind, although I knew better than to use the epithet out loud in front of any family members. Now, if only my mother was at home, I could nip in and say a quick hi, pick up the keys to the cottage, and be on my way before anyone else came back. Maybe that was cowardly of me, but I found it always took some mental readjustment on my part to deal with being around my family after a prolonged absence. Because I'd had to work over Thanksgiving, and because things had been hectic even before that, I hadn't been home for more than two months.

The car parked itself off to one side, away from

the garage so it wasn't blocking any of the bays. I'd programmed it that way a while back, since it was only the polite thing to do. I didn't live here anymore. Then I unfastened my safety harness and got out, glad of the chance to stretch my legs.

A cold wind passed over me—not as cold as it would have been up in Flagstaff, but still cold enough that I was glad I hadn't taken off my coat or the wool scarf I had wound around my throat. Then I went up to the front door and let myself in. That door was never locked during the daytime, something I knew irritated Lance, but my mother always just laughed at his worries.

"No one's going to come in and steal anything, not here," she said. "Besides, I'm pretty sure most people know about that arsenal of yours, and how good you are at using it."

Not that having an arsenal was the sort of thing to raise eyebrows in Arizona. However, my stepfather was what you might call a serious collector. I'd never liked handling guns, although I learned to shoot, just as my sisters and brothers had. That's not to say I wasn't good at it; my alien DNA had given me great aim. I just didn't like it.

"I'm here!" I called out as I entered. Saying "I'm home" didn't feel quite right. This wasn't my home anymore. I wasn't sure whether my one-bedroom apartment in Flagstaff felt like home, either, but at least it was the place I went to every night—or morning, depending on which shift I was working.

"In the kitchen!" my mother called back, so I headed in that direction. I supposed I should have known she'd be in the kitchen, what with all the food prep she had coming up for the next few days. My mother took Christmas seriously.

When I entered the room, the kitchen did smell amazing, of sugar and cinnamon and warm bread. Two loaves were sitting on racks and cooling, and my mother was just pulling a sheet of cookies from the oven as I inquired, "So, what army are you planning on feeding?"

She set down the cookies and smiled at me, even as she shook her head. You'd think with all the cooking and baking, she might have gotten rounder with age, but she really hadn't. Not much, anyway. Her hair was so fair that you couldn't really see the strands of gray running through it, not unless it caught the light at exactly the right angle, and in a lot of ways she didn't look that different from the woman in an old picture she'd had taken with me when I was barely a year old, my dark hair a startling contrast to her bright blonde locks. No wonder it had been so easy to convince people I was adopted.

"Not an army," she said, "but the Olivers are coming over, since they're not going to California for the holidays this year, and then your Aunt Kirsten and Uncle Martin and Callista, and, well" —she waved a hand— "you know how quickly things can turn into a crowd."

"We're a crowd right in this family," I told her,

whereupon she gave me a reproving look before coming over and taking me in her arms for a quick hug. I didn't bother to protest, although generally I wasn't what you would call the huggy type.

"Grace—" she began. I could tell the quips about the size of our family had worn thin over the years.

"I know, I know," I broke in, then added, "Where is everyone?"

"Your father and Kevin are doing a tour, and Kelsey is working. Melissa is over at her friend Brian's house down the creek."

Your father. That was always how my mother referred to Lance to me, even though he wasn't my father. Not really. Yes, he'd helped raise me, had never shown his biological children preferential treatment over me...and yet there was always this distance. It wasn't even something I could really put my finger on, except that I somehow knew he did all those things not for my sake, exactly, but more because of how much he loved my mother. I couldn't even blame him for that. What it did do was make me stop thinking of him as my father a long time ago. In my mind, he was always my stepfather, had never crossed the intangible line that would have made him something more than that.

I shook my head and said, "I'm surprised you're not enjoying the peace and quiet by taking a bath or at least reading a book and having a glass of wine."

"Not with everything I still have to do." But then she smiled and tilted her head toward a stemless wine glass sitting on the counter. I hadn't noticed it amongst the mixing bowls and containers of spices and flour and whatnot. "But I did pour myself a little pinot noir. Care for some?"

"Not right now, thanks," I said. "I'm just popping in to get the key for the cottage."

She was disappointed by my reply, I could tell, but she only nodded and went to the key rack by the back door, then fetched the key I'd used many times before, the one with the silver fob inlaid with turquoise in the shape of a thunderbird. "Here you go," she said, pressing it into my hand. "Are you coming back up for dinner?"

"I'm not sure," I lied. Actually, I'd had no intention of eating here tonight, since I figured Christmas Eve and Christmas Day back to back were about as much family togetherness as I could handle in a short amount of time. Instead, I'd set up some tentative plans with a friend of mine. "I think I'm having dinner with Noelle. We haven't seen each other since I came down over Labor Day weekend."

"Well, then," she said, and paused. I could tell she wanted me here, but that she also wasn't going to interfere with my plans, not when they involved seeing my best friend from high school, who still lived here in town. "You say hi to Noelle for me, and we'll see you tomorrow night for Christmas Eve dinner."

"What time do you want me to come over?" I asked. "I'll help with whatever you need."

My mother made an off-hand wave with one hand. "Don't worry about that. Kelsey and Melissa will be here all day. You might as well take some time to relax—I know you've been working very hard lately."

"Thanks, Mom," I said simply, but I meant it. I'd been lucky to get the spot at Lowell after the National Weather Service decided they wanted a set of eyes up on Mars Hill in addition to the regular station over in Bellemont, but it meant long hours and not a lot of relief. That was why I'd worked Thanksgiving this year, and Christmas the year before that. I had Dave Aguirre, one of the meteorologists at the Bellemont NWS station, spotting for me over the holidays on this go-'round. Since he was in the middle of a protracted divorce, I got the impression that he was only too glad to be able to work during Christmas and not have to think about the breakup of his family.

"So, say, five-thirty or thereabouts," she went on. "If you want to come earlier, that would be wonderful, but not to help in the kitchen—your sisters and brother can take care of that."

"We'll see," I said, my standard noncommittal reply when I didn't really want to do something but also didn't want to say no outright. My mother knew that as well, so she just gave an almost imperceptible sigh before turning back to her bowl piled high with cookie dough.

"Have a good time tonight," she replied, her

expression a little sad. By that point, she was used to the distance I continued to put between myself and the rest of my family, but I knew she didn't like it.

"I will," I told her, managing to smile. And it would be good to see Noelle—she had a fifteen-month-old daughter and didn't get out much, but this time she'd promised she had a babysitter lined up, and the two of us could just have a girls' night out. That sounded fun, and normal.

I thought I could do with a little normal for a change.

It was not to be, however; my phone buzzed as the car was creeping its way down the crowded two-lane road into Sedona—the first manned flight to Mars was due to land in five days, but they still couldn't figure out how to widen that damn road—and Noelle was on the line, apologizing profusely, but her babysitter had canceled at the last minute and her husband was working that night.

"And I tried and tried to find someone else, but everyone's booked. All these holiday parties," she said. In the background, I could hear the baby crying and tried not to wince. That was a sound I did not miss. I'd heard enough of it while growing up.

"It's fine." The response was automatic, not really reflective of my feelings. It wasn't fine, but on the other hand, it wasn't Noelle's fault. "I'm feeling kind of tired anyway—it's been sixty-hour weeks lately. So I think I'll just hang at the cottage with a fire and a bottle of wine."

"That sounds relaxing," she said, not bothering to hide the envy in her voice. It had probably been a while since she'd been able to relax.

I made what I hoped sounded like a sympathetic noise, but actually, I still couldn't quite figure out why Noelle had had her daughter Becca when she herself was barely twenty-three. These days, most people waited until their early thirties until they started families. But she was madly in love and wanted a child with Pablo, her new husband, who was a chef at one of Sedona's higher-end restaurants, and that's how Becca happened.

"Well, I'm here until the thirtieth, so maybe we can figure something else out."

"Oh, great," she said. "Maybe right after Christmas would work. I'll be in touch—but I've gotta go now. Becca's pitching a fuss about something or other."

"No problem," I replied. "Merry Christmas."

"Merry Christmas to you, too," she said, then hung up.

And that was that. So much for my girls' night out. A bottle of pity wine sounded like a good idea, though, so on the way to the cottage, I stopped at the supermarket and bought a couple of bottles—hey, I was going to be in town for almost a week—and a few staples, like a box of croissants and some tea and fruit. I probably wouldn't be on my own too much, but it never hurt to have some noshing fodder around, just in case.

The store was packed with people getting last-minute items for their feasts on the following two days. I stood in the express line and tried not to look as out of place as I felt. Just a sad-sack singleton with her wine and her croissants, looking as if she was going to end up being the neighborhood cat lady at the rate she was going.

No, that was stupid of me. For one thing, most crazy cat ladies weren't part alien…and I didn't even have a cat.

I checked out and had the car take me the rest of the way to the cottage, then pulled up in the drive, belatedly realizing that I hadn't gotten the remote for the garage from my mother. Oh, well. The car was already dirty, and if the snow in Flagstaff turned into a good rainstorm down here, as I was thinking it probably would unless the temperatures dropped some more, then I might get a free wash.

After retrieving my meager luggage from the trunk, I took it and my grocery store purchases and let myself into the house. It was cold, so I said, "Set temperature, seventy-two degrees Fahrenheit," and went on into the master bedroom as the furnace quietly turned itself on and started blowing warm air through the vents. The living room did have a good fireplace, of local stone with a lovely carved juniper mantel, and Lance always made sure there was a handy stack of wood in the bin at the back of the house. In fact, there were logs already laid in the fire, just waiting for me to get settled.

Which didn't take very long. I hung up the clothes that needed it, set out my toiletries in the bathroom, and headed to the kitchen, where I'd left my groceries on the counter. All right, it was barely four in the afternoon, but that didn't mean I couldn't pour myself a glass of wine. I felt as if I'd earned it.

But even as I began to reach up toward the cabinet that held the wine glasses, I found myself pausing. Something about this didn't feel right. For some reason, I felt as if I should be doing something else.

Maybe it was just guilt over coming here instead of staying at the house. I could tell my mother wanted to talk more, but what would we have even talked about? "Hey, Mom, I'm thinking about sleeping with my boss, but I just haven't decided yet"?

Which was not just melodramatic, but also not true. Nate wasn't my boss. The situation might have been mildly weird, but it wasn't *that* weird.

No, something was pricking in me to get out, and I couldn't even say why. Unlike my mother's friend Persephone and her equally psychic daughter Taryn, I didn't get flashes of precognition or strange insight. There were a lot of things about me that might not be exactly normal, but that wasn't one of them.

Restless, I went to the window and looked out.

The skies were growing darker as clouds continued to move in from the north and east, but the rain wasn't here yet. My best prediction had put the real arrival of the front sometime around ten o'clock tonight, maybe as late as eleven if the winds stalled or shifted. And it wouldn't be fully dark until a little before six. I had some time.

Time for what? I asked myself, but I didn't have an answer. Instead, I picked up the remote for my car from where I'd dropped it on the kitchen counter, shrugged back into my coat, and headed out the front door, intent on something.

I just didn't know what it was. Not yet.

CHAPTER TWO

Because I wasn't sure of exactly what I was doing or where I was going, I pushed the button to disengage the auto-drive, then tried not to roll my eyes as the little tube deployed from the dash.

"Blow here," the car's mechanical voice said.

Blow yourself, I thought, but complied. The only way to drive a car unaided was to prove to it that you weren't impaired by alcohol or other some other illicit substance. It was kind of annoying, but it worked. Deaths in alcohol- and drug-related car accidents had dropped to almost nothing once the "sniffers" had been installed in the vast majority of vehicles on the road.

As I backed out of the driveway, I headed toward the main road, Route 89A. No big shock there, since it was pretty much the only way to get from here to there in Sedona. What did surprise me, though, was that I turned left, heading away from the heart of town. Almost without thinking, when I got to Dry Creek Road, I turned right, winding my way through residential areas, and then moving out to the more open land past them. There wasn't much out here, except the Enchantment Resort.

So, what? I asked myself. *Is this all a sudden yearning to hang out in the resort's bar and try to pick up rich retirees or something?*

But that wasn't the way I turned when I came to the fork in the road. No, I headed the opposite direction, and my heart sped up a little as I realized where I was going.

Secret Canyon.

The spot where the aliens had hidden their base, all those years ago. The place where my father had once been…well, grown or hatched or decanted or whatever it was the aliens did to bring their armies of clones into the world.

It wasn't something I'd known at first, of course. That's kind of a lot to lay on a kid, and I had to give my mother credit for handling it better than most people probably would have. She waited until I was old enough to understand, but not so old that I would blame her for hiding something so important from me for a good chunk of my life. I was eleven when she'd sat down with me and said she needed to tell me some things about my past, about my father. By then, I'd guessed that I wasn't adopted—or rather, I knew I was her child, if not Lance's. My mother and

I might not have had the same coloring, but there were certain things about my appearance that did echo her features, such as the shape of my mouth and chin, if you knew enough to look.

So, I'd already been wondering for a while as to who my father really was, and what had happened to him. On that day, she'd had Lance take Kevin and Kelsey and Melissa off to the movies so she and I would have the house to ourselves. And she'd taken a picture from inside an envelope and laid it down on the dining room table.

"This is your father," she'd said simply, and I'd lifted it up and stared down at it, gazing at the image of the man it contained, trying to see something of myself in him.

The dark hair, yes, and a little of the high, wide cheekbones, too. The photo was obviously something she'd taken with her phone and then had transferred to photographic paper later on; it was a little out of focus, but I could see them clearly well enough, see her happy smile and the smile he wore as well, which had an element of wonder in it, as if he was staring at things he'd never seen before.

Which made sense, considering that he'd spent what little there was of his life before that cooped up in a base somewhere in the mountains I was now approaching. He hadn't known anything of human life, even though he looked like a normal man. Well, an unbelievably good-looking man, that is. Even as a young girl, I'd recognized that he must have been very handsome. I suppose that begs the question as to why aliens who were creating hybrid soldiers would care enough about human aesthetics to choose genetic material from good-looking people to work with, but their motives were inscrutable most of the time. Besides the whole world domination thing, that is.

Then my mother gave me a carefully edited version of how she'd met him, how she'd taken him into her home. It wasn't quite the "well, when a human/alien hybrid super-soldier and a woman love each other very much" speech, but it was something along those lines. The upshot seemed to be that she'd pretty much given up on Lance, who at the time was doing everything he could to keep my mother at arm's length, and so she'd hooked up with the gorgeous stranger, and the end result was me.

My father had sacrificed himself to destroy the alien base, or at least put it out of commission long enough to give the people who were fighting the aliens—my parents and my Aunt Kirsten and Uncle Martin and Paul and Persephone Oliver—a chance for some breathing space, time to regroup. That might not sound like a particularly impressive collection of people to pit against a bunch of hostile reptilian aliens intent on taking Earth and its resources for their own, but Aunt Kirsten was sort of their secret weapon, since it turned out she was half-alien as well, and Uncle Martin not of this earth at all. Of course, they were of the "good" kind of aliens, the ones the UFO community generally referred to as Nords or Nordics. Still, it had been a shock for my Aunt Kirsten to learn she wasn't exactly as girl-next-door as she'd once thought. And it was probably even more of a shock for the Reptilians, since it sounded as if they really weren't prepared to face someone with her kind of powers.

At any rate, things in Sedona had been completely quiet since then. So why I was driving out here now, with the sky lowering and my car bumping along a road that had suddenly turned to gravel, I really couldn't say. The smart thing would've been to turn around, go home, and open the neglected bottle of pinot noir that was currently sitting on the kitchen counter.

But I didn't do that. Instead, I inched along until even the gravel road ended. A weathered sign indicated this was the Secret Canyon trailhead, although I didn't see any hikers out here today. The weather had most likely scared them off, which I thought was probably just as well.

I turned off the car and got out, then tightened the scarf around my throat. Since I'd been tromping around Mars Hill, checking weather stations, before I left Flagstaff, I was wearing jeans and sturdy all-terrain boots. As long as I didn't do any serious rock climbing, I should be okay with pretty much anything I encountered out here.

Well, almost anything....

Shaking my head at myself, I headed uphill,

moving to the north and east, toward the box canyon where the "back door" Persephone and Lance and Michael Lightfoot had found so many years ago was supposed to be located. There was another way in, farther north, through a narrow defile that extended to the actual rear entrance of the base, but I'd been told it was all caved in, due to the explosives my father had set off in his failed attempt to destroy the whole operation. I say "failed" because, although he did a lot of damage, he didn't get rid of the aliens utterly.

No, it had taken my Aunt Kirsten to manage that.

The cold, dry air seemed to catch at my throat, and I wished I'd thought to bring some bottled water along with me. Then again, when I left the house, I'd had no idea as to where precisely I was headed. Certainly not on a wild-goose chase like this.

A chill wind soughed through pine and juniper, and I could practically feel the light failing as the sun slipped farther west and the clouds moved in. I pulled my phone out of my pocket to check the hour, then slid it back in. Five-fifteen. I didn't have much time.

Time for what, I wasn't precisely certain.

I climbed upward, scrabbling over ruts left by torrential monsoon rains, avoiding abandoned branches and patches of cactus. The whole time, I kept thinking I really must have lost it, because only a crazy person would have come out here at this time of day in the first place, even leaving aside the dubious nature of my intended destination. At the same time, I was thankful for all the hikes my family had taken as I was growing up. I was used to this sort of terrain, and since I'd also done a good bit of hiking around Flagstaff after I moved there, I hadn't allowed myself to get soft.

But then I saw it—a metal door set into the hillside, so obscured by overgrown manzanita bushes that if I hadn't known it was supposed to be here, I probably would have passed right by it. I had a feeling that the protective camouflage was what had kept it from being discovered prior to this…or maybe it was simply that people avoided this obscure little corner of the canyon. The aliens were long gone, and yet I still felt something here, something cold, menacing. It was not a spot to linger in.

Given all that, logic suggested that the best thing to do was to get the hell out of there. Since logic had absolutely nothing to do with why I'd come here in the first place, I ignored those prickles of cold trickling down my neck and instead reached out to touch the wheel-like latch in the center of the door, to wrap my gloved fingers around it and attempt to turn it to the right.

I'd halfway expected that it would be rusted shut, or that it wouldn't budge at all. Instead, it turned easily enough, opening on a dark tunnel which led into the hillside. The air that emerged was far colder than the brisk wind currently blowing at my loose hair, and I shivered. Along with the cold came an acrid, bitter odor. Not decay, which was something I'd halfway expected, since a bunch of aliens and hybrid soldiers supposedly had died in there before I was born, but it was still unpleasant.

All the more reason that you should hike back down this hill and let well enough alone, I told myself. For some reason, though, my feet remained resolutely planted where they were. Worse, they began to move into the darkness, which was blacker than anything I'd ever seen before. Even on moonless nights in this part of the world, the stars were so bright that you could use them to navigate if necessary.

There weren't any stars down in that scary black hole, however. I dug my phone out of my pocket once again and switched on the flashlight app. The beam wasn't very wide, but it was bright enough to show me my footing, which was all I really needed. And at least the phone was fully charged, so I wouldn't have to worry about the light dying on me and stranding me somewhere in the bowels of the base.

I moved forward, feeling my boots touch smooth rock. With my free hand, I reached out to feel the wall, which was rock as well. The corridor sloped downward, and I recalled Persephone saying at some dinner or another years ago…when the adults were talking in hushed whispers and hadn't realized that I was sitting on the stairs and eavesdropping… that there had been both elevators and a stairway. I sort of doubted the elevators would be working after all these years, so I had to hope the stairs were still clear.

They turned out to be, the metal free of rust despite the quarter-century that had passed since anyone had set foot in the place. I paused on the landing for a few seconds, and then that strange pull or compulsion or whatever it was seemed to tell me to go down.

So that's what I did.

The clang of my footsteps against the diamond-plate metal of the stairs seemed to echo in my ears, and I couldn't help wincing. Maybe that was a foolish reaction, since there was no one around to hear me, but still it felt as if I'd awakened something here, something that had slept for far too long.

I went down one flight of steps, stopped at the next landing.

No.

The word sounded so clearly in my head, it almost felt as if someone had spoken it aloud. In fact, I was startled enough that I turned around, flashing the beam from my camera in all directions, making sure I was still alone. But of course, I was. I saw nothing, not even cobwebs in the corners, not even beetles scuttling away from the intrusive illumination of my camera's flashlight.

I made myself pull in a breath, and then another. After that, it seemed as if my racing pulse had slowed enough to allow me to descend another flight of stairs. Again, I felt that sense of negation, that this was not the place I was supposed to go. Down another flight, then another.

Persephone had said that the base had ten levels, so it wasn't as if I could descend indefinitely. And after I went down the fifth flight, I stopped. This was it. Whatever had drawn me here, it seemed to be on this level.

Without stopping to think, I reached out and grasped the handle of the door, pulled it in toward me. And then I gasped, because what met me wasn't utter darkness, but a corridor illuminated with what appeared to be glowing red emergency lights placed at regular intervals at the junction of the walls and ceiling. Supposedly, my father had blown the reactor in this place, so where the power was coming from, I had no idea.

But eerie red light was better than no light at all, and I slipped my phone into my pocket before moving forward again. The place was utterly deserted, empty carts tipped over, machinery I couldn't even identify strewn throughout the corridor. The aliens appeared to have left here in some haste. But there was no sign of them other than the artifacts they'd left behind, and although the equipment I saw now was unfamiliar, the architecture of the place was strangely prosaic, pale painted walls on either side and a cement floor beneath my feet.

The emergency illumination seemed to only be functioning in the corridor itself and not in any of the rooms that opened off it. No, those were yawning dark voids that I didn't care to peer into. Anyway, whatever had pulled me here so far wasn't in any of those chambers, but in something that seemed to still lie ahead of me. As I walked, I realized my destination apparently lay behind a set of double doors at the end of the hallway.

My feet seemed to move forward of their own accord. I didn't know if I could have turned around then, even if I'd wanted to. The doors had reinforced glass set into them, so I could see the chamber beyond was the only one on this floor that still had any illumination; it pulsed as redly as the hallway through which I'd just walked.

And then my hands were extending in front of me, pushing the doors open, and I entered the room. It was not all that large, its walls covered with a flat array of dully blinking lights. I didn't give them more than a second glance, however, because in the center of the room stood what apparently was the reason for my being there.

At first, I thought it was a coffin, gleaming and sleek and black, until I realized one section was clear instead of opaque. More lights flickered from a control pad at one end. I approached the coffin or pod or whatever it was, my breathing sounding hideously loud in the utter silence of the room around me.

For the longest moment, I just stood there, working up the nerve to look into the coffin-like object. What if it was one of the Reptilians in there, lying in stasis, just waiting for the opportunity to lure me down here and...what? Have his evil lizard way with me? I knew that wasn't outside the bounds of possibility, not according to some whispered conversations I'd overheard, or accounts I'd read on some of the more lurid UFO sites.

Then again, I could run pretty fast when the occasion warranted.

Finally, I drew in a breath before moving closer and looking down into the clear section of the pod so I could see what had been waiting there all this time.

It was a man.

All right, probably a hybrid, if I knew my aliens, but the first glance told me this man must have come from a different stock than my father, as they did not look all that similar, except for their dark hair. This man—hybrid...whatever—had a face that seemed a little narrower, his nose stronger, more defined. His lashes were thick and dark, and I could see a faint shadow of stubble against his jaw.

Even in repose, he was kind of spectacular.

Although I didn't understand quite what I was looking at, I glanced down at the control pad. A faint line with regularly spaced blips seemed to indicate his heart rate, or maybe his brain waves. They didn't seem to be very strong. No wonder, if he'd been kept in stasis here since the base was evacuated. Had he been left behind on purpose, or merely overlooked, something discarded because, after all, they could always make more?

Something in that thought angered me. Maybe this man was a clone, a hybrid, but he was still a living, breathing being, even if he wasn't completely human.

After all, I wasn't completely human, either.

On the control pad was a flat area that looked like a biometric scanner to take a thumbprint. I wasn't a Reptilian, but I had some of their DNA in me, somewhere. Whether it would be enough to fool the scanner, I didn't know, but I felt as if I needed to at least try.

So I took off my glove and stood there, hesitating, wondering whether I should just stop now and get out of this place, go up to the house and tell my mother and Lance what I'd found. They were the UFO experts, after all.

But the pull that had brought me here was still so strong, I had to think there was some kind of reason for it. Maybe the faint readings on the control pad meant he was failing, would die soon if he wasn't removed from the pod. It very well could end up being his coffin if I went running for help instead of attempting to free him now.

Well, that seemed to decide things.

I placed my right thumb on the scanner. At once, a ripple of color seemed to move over the control pad, as if my touch had activated sensors and readouts that had previously lain dormant. Within the pod, warm light began to emanate from all sides, moving over the man within.

And then he blinked.

Oh, shit.

I'd done it now, so I couldn't back away. *Would* not. It was probably the hardest thing I'd ever done, though...standing there and watching as he came alive, as his eyes opened, and I saw they were some light color, possibly blue. It was hard for me to tell for sure, since the lighting in the room was so strange.

At last, there came a hissing sound, and a split appeared in the previously seamless-looking pod. The "lid," for lack of a better term, lifted and moved to one side, rather like a clam shell opening, and then the man inside sat up, his gaze fastening on me. A look of utter confusion passed over his face.

I couldn't really blame him. I had no idea what his previous experiences had been—if he'd even had any—but I doubted his training or conditioning or whatever it was had prepared him to have a human-looking female be the first person to greet him upon his awakening.

Thank God he wasn't naked, or at least was mostly covered. His torso was bare, so I could see how well-defined the muscles in his chest and arms and shoulders were, but he did have on a pair of pants that were similar in construction to sweat pants, although the fabric appeared to be much finer.

We stayed that way for an interminable few seconds, both of us staring at the other, and then he spoke.

"Who are you?"

Perfect English. No trace of an accent that I could detect. So he must have received some sort of implants or something else that allowed him to have mastery over the language. But to what purpose? Did it matter, if he was just another clone working in a base run by aliens?

He was staring at me, obviously expecting an answer. I said, "My name is Grace Rinehart."

A second as he processed my reply. Then, "But who are you?"

Good question. If I told him my father had been a hybrid like him, would he believe me? Maybe he could sense it in me somehow, the way some dogs could smell cancer in a person. Somehow, this didn't seem like the time or place for those sorts of revelations, however.

"A friend," I said simply. "How do you feel?"

Another blank stare. I supposed that wasn't the sort of thing a hybrid super-soldier got asked very often. His dark brows drew together as he appeared to consider my question. "Hungry," he replied at last, sounding surprised, as if hunger was the last thing he should be feeling.

No wonder he was hungry, if he'd been stuck in that pod ever since the aliens had evacuated the base. I was already feeling hungry, and it had only been five hours or so since I last ate.

"All the more reason for you to get out of here," I said, trying to sound hearty and normal, as if I went around reviving people from suspended animation every day. "Can you walk?"

In answer, he planted his hands on the edge of the pod and swung his legs over. Immediately afterward, he straightened, pulling himself up to his full height. I was not short, standing five foot eight in my bare feet, but he was a good six inches taller than I was.

And big. And broad. And...gorgeous.

Somehow, I managed to keep my attention fixed on his face, and not his abs, which looked distinctly rock-like. No muscle atrophy there, that was for sure.

He took an experimental step forward, then another, moving past me. Then he stopped and nodded. "I can walk."

"Good," I said. My gaze fell on his bare feet, and I frowned. "Do you have any other clothes...any gear...somewhere in here? The terrain's pretty rough outside."

"Outside?" His head tilted as he appeared to contemplate the levels of the base above us. "We are not supposed to go outside."

"Maybe you weren't...once...but I really think it's for the best if you get out of here now. You're the only one left."

Those pale eyes, rimmed in a fringe of black lashes, snapped back toward me. "The only one?"

"The base is deserted. You've been here...a long time."

Silence as he took in that statement. He glanced away from me, down at his bare feet, at the analogue of sweat pants he wore. At last he said, "Our gear was stored down one level."

Exactly the opposite direction from where I wanted to go, but at least it sounded as if he wouldn't have to walk out of here barefoot. I gave him a nod before saying, "Okay, let's go check it out."

─────

It was surreal to have him padding along beside me in his bare feet, seemingly unconcerned about the icy floor against his skin...or the icy air of the base itself, actually. I was still wearing a heavy coat, a scarf wound around my throat, but all he had on was those sweatpant things. And I do mean all. I could tell from the...movement...underneath the fabric that he wasn't wearing any briefs.

Somehow, I managed to avert my eyes as I led him to the stairs, explaining as I did so that the elevators were no longer operational. He accepted that statement with a slight frown, as if he was trying to piece together what had happened here, why his masters and the other hybrids were gone, why the base itself was no longer operational. I knew that my biological father had blown part of it up, but I didn't know which section. Certainly, the parts I'd seen so far looked undamaged, if abandoned.

But the hybrid said nothing as we descended to the next level. He led me to a storeroom midway down the corridor, one guarded with a thumb lock.

Luckily, though, the door opened once he put his finger on the scanner, and we went inside. Here, there was no emergency illumination, so I retrieved my phone and turned on the flashlight again, shining it around the room so he could locate what he needed.

He did so quickly and efficiently, pulling a jumpsuit from a locker, buckled combat boots from another, socks and underwear from a set of drawers built into a wall. With absolutely no sense of shame, he stripped off the sweat pants, and I just barely managed to avert my eyes in time. Okay, almost in time. He turned around, so I did get a glimpse of a nicely muscled backside before I realized I should be looking anywhere other than at him.

But then he was safely dressed and saying, "I'm ready."

I shifted back toward him, noting how well everything seemed to fit his muscular physique. Well, that probably wasn't so strange, considering all these clothes had been left here to outfit an army of clones. It wasn't as if you needed to have a variety of different sizes. Maybe two, three at the most? Hard to say, since I didn't know how many different types of clones there had been. From the way my mother had talked about them, it sounded as there had been only one.

That made me wonder if this man was the same build as my father, although I knew their genetic stock had to be different, since their features weren't similar at all.

"Were there...others like you?" I asked as we moved out of the storeroom and back into the corridor. I also realized then that I was going to have to climb seven flights of stairs to get out of here, and bit back a sigh. It wasn't so much that I couldn't do it, only that I wasn't looking forward to that kind of a hike.

"'Like me'?" he echoed. After a pause, he shook his head. "I don't know."

Hmm. Curioser and curioser, as Alice might say. Had he been some sort of an experiment, one of a kind?

"How did you know the storeroom would be there?"

Again a hesitation, as if he was mentally thumbing through the facts he had on file in his brain. "I just...knew."

Definitely some kind of mental conditioning, then. Sleep training? Hypnosis? That sort of thing was more Persephone Oliver's field of expertise, but I could only imagine her reaction if I brought my "find" to talk to her.

She'd probably say, "Like mother, like daughter," I thought, somewhat amused myself by the irony of the situation. True, my father had actually shown up on my mother's doorstep, whereas it seemed I'd actively sought this man out, but even so, I wasn't exactly the first Swenson woman to find herself tangled up with a lost hybrid soldier.

Of course, thoughts like that only led me to realize exactly what had come of my mother's "tangling"—namely, me—and I had no intention of going down that path. True, this man was gorgeous, but he wasn't really a man at all. He probably didn't even have a name.

"Well," I said as we reached the doorway to the stairwell, went through it, and began to climb, "I'm not sure exactly what's going on here, but I figure the best thing to do is to get you out and back to my place. Then I can get some food inside you."

He nodded, although something in his expression told me he was still puzzled, that he still couldn't figure out exactly who I was or why I would be going out of my way to help him. I couldn't really blame him for that confusion, as I was thinking the same thing myself. But something had compelled me to come here, to save him, and since I'd set myself on that path, however crazy it might be, then I'd continue down it. Maybe it was the hybrid code buried in my own DNA that had brought me to him.

Or maybe you've lost it completely, I thought. *That's always a distinct possibility, too.*

We didn't say anything else as we climbed. I noticed that he didn't seem to get out of breath at all, despite the exertion, despite his being in what had basically been a comatose state for the past twenty-five years. He moved easily and efficiently, and even though I would've said I was in pretty darn good shape, I could feel myself puffing a little by the time we finally got to the tunnel that sloped upward, leading us to the door that was our exit to the outside.

"Here we are," I said, and pushed it open. "Careful—the ground's pretty rough out there."

But he didn't seem to be listening, only took a step past the door and then stopped on the little hillock directly beyond it. By that time, it was almost dark. A broody, bloody sun sat low on the horizon, framed by a bruised-looking mass of clouds. The wind blew over us, colder by several degrees than when I'd entered the base.

"Is this...?" He let the words trail off, then shook his head and started over. "Is this what the world looks like?"

I couldn't help letting out a small chuckle. "Honey, you haven't seen anything yet."

CHAPTER THREE

HE STARED AROUND IN WONDER AT EVERYTHING HE SAW on the ride home—the other cars on the road, the shops and gas stations and restaurants along 89A, the people coming and going, bundled up against the cold. Luckily, he didn't quite smash his nose up against the window, but I was still glad it was mostly dark by then. That way, it would be a lot harder for the people in the other cars or standing on the side-walks to notice the way he was gawking like a kid taken to the zoo for the first time.

I pulled into the driveway of the cottage and unlocked the car. "Come on," I told him. "Let's get inside. It's freezing."

He didn't move right away, though, but stood next to his open door, breathing in the biting air. "No," he said. "It is not freezing. It is precisely five degrees Celsius."

"Close enough," I told him. "Come on."

Having delivered his scientific observation, he seemed content to follow me up the walkway to the front door. It was dark, since I hadn't thought to turn on the porch light before I left, and I had to fumble in my pocket for the key before I got it inserted in the lock and let us inside.

Since this wasn't the first time I'd stayed in the cottage, I knew to flip the switch next to the front door to turn on the tall bronze lamp with the mica shade, the one placed in a corner so it would send a soft, warm light upward and out along the walls. The hybrid looked around, obviously trying to take in the idea of an interior that wasn't strictly utilitarian, one with red tile floors and Navajo rugs and sturdy oak furniture made by a local artisan over in Jerome.

"This is...where you live?" he asked at last.

"Not exactly," I said. "I'm just staying here right now. This house belongs to my family. My actual residence is up in Flagstaff."

Another one of those processing silences. Then he said, "Flagstaff, Arizona. Population, 69,000. Elevation, 6,910 feet. Founded—"

"That's enough, Mr. Wikipedia," I told him, breaking in. "And actually, the population is now closer to 80,000. Your info's a little out of date."

"It is?" He looked crestfallen.

"Well, it's—" Did I really want to go into all this right now? Sooner or later, I'd have to tell him that he'd been asleep for twenty-five years, but I thought it might be better to get some food in him first. Then I realized I only had some frozen stuff and those croissants I'd bought as comfort food. That didn't seem quite right for feeding someone who hadn't eaten in decades, but on the other hand, no way was I going to take him out to eat somewhere. That prospect seemed fraught with problems. Ordering in seemed the best alternative. "Do you like pizza?" I asked.

"Pizza is not an ideal source of nourishment," he pointed out.

"No, but it sure tastes good." As he hesitated, I said, "Come on—live a little."

That remark seemed to strike a chord, because he replied, "I think I would like that—to live a little, that is."

I'll bet, after being stuck in a pod for twenty-five years. But I only said, "Great. Why don't you go ahead and sit down, and I'll call in the order."

He did as I instructed, going to the stiff leather armchair under the lamp rather than the far more comfortable couch. Maybe he'd never seen a couch before. Anyway, that was something I'd have to puzzle out at a later date. Although I hadn't actually lived in Sedona for more than eight years, I still had the number for Moon Dog Pizza in my phone, in a contacts list that had already been copied over several times as I upgraded my devices. So I called up Moon Dog and ordered a large pizza and an antipasto salad, just to be safe. A lot of restaurants now had apps where you could make your selection right on the phone and send it in that way, but Moon Dog wasn't quite that technologically advanced. But at least they said they'd have it over in about twenty minutes, which seemed a pretty good estimate to me. Maybe people weren't that interested in ordering pizza right before Christmas.

I ended the call and set the phone on the little catch-all table near the door, then moved toward the fireplace, all too aware of the hybrid's eyes on me as I did so. "It's a little chilly in here," I said, trying to sound as casual as possible. "How about a fire?"

His gaze flicked toward the hearth, to the logs piled there. Someone must have come by in the past few days to get things set up. My mother? Maybe, although I guessed it was more likely that Lance had done it, or possibly Kevin. My little brother could occasionally be cajoled into doing something useful if you nagged him enough.

"A fire?" the hybrid repeated. Again, I saw a trace of confusion move over his features.

Well, it was entirely possible that the aliens didn't think open flames were a very efficient form of heating. In all truth, they really weren't, and various factions in the government had been wrangling for years over whether wood-burning fireplaces should be banned altogether, but luckily, no one had succeeded in implementing such a ban. I was all for saving the environment, but I couldn't imagine a world where I couldn't enjoy a fire, and wasn't sure I wanted to.

"Supplemental heating," I told him, bending over so I could pick up the long-handled lighter from the basket where it rested. A flick of the button to turn it on, and then I touched it to the kindling placed beneath the logs, watching as the flame caught and began to lick upward, already starting to crackle away.

The expression of puzzlement on the hybrid's face shifted to one of wonder, and he got up from his chair and paused next to me, watching as the fire gradually caught. He extended his hands, reaching out to feel the increasing warmth.

"It's...pleasant," he said at last.

"Glad you approve."

Then we lapsed into an awkward silence, both of us staring at the flames, as if we weren't sure what else we should say to one another. I was very conscious of him standing there, of his height, the width of his shoulders. It was strange, because normally I didn't find myself responding in such a way to a man. Sure, I'd note whether he was attractive or not, but I'd never felt this sort of... pull...before.

My alien DNA reacting to his alien DNA? Possibly. I had absolutely no frame of reference, and the very people I might be able to ask were the ones who were most likely to give me a serious ration of shit for reviving the hybrid in the first place.

The hybrid. I knew I couldn't keep referring to

him that way, even mentally. Risking a glance over at him, I asked, "Do you have a name?"

"Name?"

"You know…some kind of personal designation?"

He brightened a little at that clarification. "L-110."

I couldn't really see myself calling him "L-110" on a daily basis. "That's not very, um, user-friendly," I ventured. "Would you mind if I gave you a more… human…name?"

At that question, he shifted so he was facing me. His gaze seemed to flick over my face, as if attempting to read something of my expression. The light was a little better in here, so I could see his eyes were gray with no hint of blue or green, a pure steel color almost mesmerizing in their frame of dark lashes. I did my best to stand my ground, to not flush under that intense stare, but I wasn't sure how successful I was.

"Would you prefer that?" he asked.

"Well —" I floundered for a second or two, then said, "We don't normally go around referring to people by numbers, so I suppose I would prefer it, yes."

He didn't reply at first, only continued to watch me. "And…Grace   is   your   designation? Your…name?"

"Yes," I replied. "Grace Rinehart."

"'Grace,'" he repeated, seeming to study me. "Yes, I can see why someone would call you that."

Color flamed in my face, but I made myself

continue to look up at him, telling myself that he couldn't know that a remark like that might fluster a woman. Or at least, it had sure flustered me. "Okay," I said, keeping my tone as light as I could, "Since your designation was L-110, how about a name that starts with 'L'?"

"Such as?"

Well, there was a question. I'd never given the concept of names much thought, mostly because I'd always had in the back of my mind the notion that I wouldn't have children, and so didn't have much reason to study people's names. My mother would've been horrified to hear that, and so I'd done my best never to discuss the matter with her, but really, I thought it only prudent. After all, although I seemed stable enough, genetically speaking, who knew what might happen if I reproduced? All sorts of weird recessives might start popping out, starting with scales and ending up who knows where. Better to play it safe. If I ever felt the overwhelming need someday to be a mother, I could always adopt.

"Well…there's Lloyd"—*God, no*—"Lewis…Luke…Leonard…Logan—"

"Logan," the hybrid broke in. "That has a pleasant sound."

It could have been worse. "Okay," I said. "Logan."

He smiled at me then. The expression had something tentative about it, as if it was something he hadn't really attempted before, and was only doing so because he'd seen me doing the same thing. Even so, the smile seemed to light up those gray eyes of his, showed how straight and white his teeth were, and I had to keep myself from staring. It was like standing in the room with some megawatt Hollywood star, although I doubted Logan had any idea what kind of effect he was having on me.

To my relief, the doorbell rang then, signaling that the pizza had arrived, and I turned away from Logan and went to the door, pausing to bend down and retrieve my wallet from where I'd dropped my purse next to the catch-all table. When I opened the door, a blast of cold air rushed in, and I hurriedly handed my credit card over to the delivery guy so he could swipe it and finalize the transaction before the pizza went all lukewarm.

"Have a good evening," he said as he handed me back my card, and then the pizza and the bag holding the antipasto salad.

"Thanks," I replied absently, thinking I wasn't sure whether it was going to be a good evening or not…although I guessed it would at least be an interesting one.

After pushing the door shut with one foot, I said, "Food's here," and set the pizza and salad down on the table. We'd need plates and cutlery and such, so I kept going, on into the kitchen, where I looked with some longing at the bottle of pinot noir sitting on the counter before I decided that plying a recently revived hybrid with alcohol probably wasn't the best idea.

The hybrid—*Logan*—was standing by the table, sniffing the air with some appreciation but making no move to open the pizza box. "Here," I said, quickly setting down the plates, napkins, and forks and knives. "You can sit at the head of the table."

He seemed to note where I had inclined my head and took his seat there, pulling out the chair and then waiting as I hurried back to the kitchen to get a couple of glasses of water. I figured water would be safe enough, even if it came out of the door of the refrigerator. Lance was usually pretty good about checking the filter and making sure everything was up to date.

When I emerged, Logan was sitting quietly, clearly waiting for me to sit down before he touched any of the food. How or where he'd been taught manners like that, I had no idea, but it was sort of a relief to see that he hadn't just torn into the pizza without waiting. After all, he had to be starving, so that kind of behavior actually would have been somewhat understandable.

"Here you go," I said, pulling out the antipasto and using one of the serving pieces I'd brought with me to drop a hearty portion on his plate. "Let's start with this."

"What is it?"

"Antipasto," I replied, then realized he of course would have no idea what that was. "It's a kind of salad. The greens are lettuce, and that's salami and bits of mozzarella cheese, and there's oil and vinegar dressing—"

"You eat oil?"

"Olive oil."

He seemed to take that in and then nodded. No other questions seemed to be forthcoming, since he lifted his fork and scooped up a generous portion, then put it in his mouth. His eyes lit up, but it seemed he had enough self-control to finish chewing before he said, "It's very good."

"I'm glad you like it."

It was the sort of commonplace comment anyone might make in those sorts of circumstances, and yet he appeared to consider my words carefully, as if he'd never had anyone tell him they were glad about something he'd done. Maybe they hadn't. From the few things my Aunt Kirsten had let slip, it didn't sound as if the aliens who'd run the base were exactly the cheerful, supportive sort.

Logan and I ate in silence, partly because I could tell he was focused on everything he ate and concentrating on the taste, the texture, the combination of flavors. For all I knew, he'd never had real food before, had been given pills or shots or been fed through a tube. Well, I assumed a feeding tube of some sort must have been how he'd gotten his nourishment all those years he was in the pod, but before that? Again, I had a feeling there wasn't exactly a hybrid soldier mess hall where they all hung out and ate crappy stroganoff and talked about how they planned to get laid that weekend.

Okay, that was probably the wrong thing to be thinking about….

At length, I was feeling full enough, and Logan apparently was, too, since he ate one more piece of pepperoni pizza than I had and then shut the box. "You're finished?" he asked, which was sort of super-fluous, since I'd already pushed my plate away and wiped my hands on my napkin. Then again, he might not have recognized those cues for what they were.

"Yes," I said. "Thank you." Since doing some-thing, even if it was clearing the table, seemed infinitely better than sitting there with him looking at me with that half-curious, half-expectant look on his face, I got up from my chair and stacked the dishes, then took them into the kitchen. After a pause, he rose from his seat as well and gathered up the box with the leftover pizza—we'd effectively killed the salad, since he had second and third helpings—before following me.

He was obviously trying to be helpful, although I could have used a minute or two to gather my thoughts. I said, "You can put that in the fridge," and pointed toward the refrigerator.

Another one of those brief, puzzled glances, and then he nodded and went to the indicated appliance, wrapping his fingers around the handle and opening the door, appearing somewhat astonished that he had guessed correctly as to how to operate it. Sliding in the pizza box was no big deal, since the fridge contained only the few odds and ends that I'd bought at the grocery store, along with the ubiquitous half-used-up pack of bottled water that always seemed to reside on the lower shelf.

As he did so, I gave the dishes a quick rinse and slipped them into the dishwasher. That took a lot longer than putting away a box of pizza, however, and he leaned up against the tile counter, watching me. Being the object of such scrutiny was more than a little disconcerting, although I told myself he was just curious, that probably everything I was doing had to hold some sort of novelty for him.

I tried to make light of it, saying, "What, they never told you about dishwashers in some sort of training video about the crazy stuff humans do?"

But his expression remained serious, and he shook his head. "I did not have any...training videos. A good deal of factual knowledge, implanted." He pointed at his temple, as if to indicate the brain within. "I did not receive all of my training, however."

"Why not?" I asked.

He glanced away from me, seeming to take in the kitchen, with the cheerful Mexican tile on the countertops and the Saltillo tile floor. It was probably just as alien to him as the interior of a spaceship would have been to me, and so I waited, wondering what he was going to say next.

But he didn't speak, instead moved toward me. By then, I was done with the dishes, so I closed the dishwasher and waited, staring at him warily, wondering if I could move fast enough to get away from him if he made a sudden movement I didn't like. He did come very close, far closer than I normally would allow anyone I wasn't about to kiss...or something...but that didn't seem to be his intention. Instead, he reached up and touched his fingers to my brow, then shut his eyes.

I forced myself to stand still, even as I wondered frantically what on earth he was up to. His touch was very light, the tips of his fingers warm, and some-thing in that contact made a shiver go through me, as if he'd awoken something deep within.

Those gray eyes opened, a flash of molten steel. "You are his daughter."

"His who?" I asked, even though I thought I had a very good idea of who he meant.

"The traitor."

The word made me bristle. *Traitor?* I supposed from the aliens' point of view, that's exactly what my father had been, although it was through no fault of his own...not to begin with, at least. Something about the psychic blast Persephone had sent through the base all those years ago had affected my father differ-ently from all the other hybrids. Instead of falling down dead, he had staggered out into the desert, wandering until he found my mother. She'd taken him in, not knowing who or what he was, and had come to love him. Supposedly, he'd loved her, too, although the capacity to love wasn't the sort of thing normally programmed into a hybrid. And it was that love which had caused him to sacrifice himself to save her, and her friends…and her unborn child.

"You knew about him?" I asked, deciding I'd leave the fight about nomenclature for a later date.

"It is because of him that I exist," Logan replied, then removed his fingers from my brow. Oddly, I felt a small pang, as if I wished that he'd kept them there a little longer.

"How so?"

Although he'd stopped touching me, he made no move to step away. He stood so close that I could have reached out, pulled him to me, and—

And what? Kissed him? Was I crazy?

Probably.

Logan seemed to take no notice of my current roiled state, saying, "After what happened to the first generation of hybrids, and especially to the traitor, the masters determined it was best to make a new batch from fresh stock."

I decided to let the "masters" part go for now. "And you were the fresh stock, I suppose."

He nodded. "Yes. They would make one first, to determine whether it was viable. After that, they would move on to larger-scale production, but the base was attacked before that could occur. I was left there in the pod, in stasis."

"So—" My mind was reeling, attempting to take

in how he could speak of himself so casually, as if he was a product and not a person. But then, to the aliens, a product was exactly what he had been. "So that's what you meant back at the base when you said you were the only one."

Another nod. "Yes."

On the one hand, that was a good thing. At least we wouldn't have to worry about a new army of hybrids rising up to attack Sedona and moving outward from there. On the other hand, I couldn't begin to imagine the loneliness of his existence.

"And what would have happened if I hadn't found you?"

He tilted his head slightly, and then his shoulders lifted a fraction. I found myself fascinated by how he could use all those very human movements. Something else that had been programmed…implanted… in him, I supposed.

"My life support had become attenuated. It would only have held on for a few more days at the most, I believe."

"So you would have died?"

"I would have passed from this existence, yes."

He sounded so calm about it, as if dying was nothing to worry about, just another blip in your day. Maybe for a hybrid who'd been bred for fighting, for killing, death wasn't anything to fear, just another in a long list of inevitabilities.

I raised my eyes to his, fighting the sudden pain in my chest at the thought of him dying alone there in the dark, no one to mourn him, no one to even know that he'd lived. Was that foolish? I didn't know. I didn't even know *him*; after all, we'd spent a little more than an hour in one another's company, no more. But that was enough time for me to realize that he was a person, even if he'd been grown in a test tube or whatever. He lived and breathed, had stared out the car window at the last of the sunset, preferred antipasto to pizza. Wherever he'd come from, whatever his origins, certainly he deserved to live.

"You're leaking," he said then, and I startled.

"I'm what?"

Those steel-gray eyes were fastened on mine. "Moisture. Here." And he reached out and ran a gentle finger along my lower lashes.

"It's nothing," I said, turning away from him and searching for a napkin to blot my eyes. "They're called tears."

"'Tears,'" he repeated, then asked, a note of wonder in his voice, "Are you crying? Is that what it looks like?"

"Yes, that's what it looks like." The words came out more harshly than I'd intended, mostly because I was angry at myself for turning into a blubbering idiot for no reason.

"But...why?" When I didn't answer right away, his eyes narrowed, as if he'd had a sudden thought, and he asked, "Because of me?"

"Yes. Maybe." I pulled in a breath. "Look, it just

hit me the wrong way, I guess…thinking about you trapped down there in that pod…."

A silence then, as again he seemed to stop and consider. Then he said, his tone softer, "But you found me, and I am safe. So is there still a reason for tears?"

"Probably not," I replied. "But if you hang around us humans long enough, you'll find that we don't always have a good reason for the things we do."

"That is true. I have been trained to understand that human behavior is not always logical."

He sounded so Spock-like when he said that, I just had to smile, although I had a feeling that smile was a rather watery one.

In answer, he smiled a little as well, although it disappeared quickly enough as he seemed to consider me. "So, do you think of yourself as human?"

Talk about drilling into the heart of the matter. I glanced down at the floor, pretending to be fascinated by the pattern of the woven cotton rug beneath my feet. "My mother is human, you know."

"That isn't what I asked."

Great, a human/alien hybrid soldier who also thought he was a shrink. "It depends on the day. Most of the time, yes. I mean, as I said, my mother is human. And I don't know the ratio of human to alien in you hybrids, but since you certainly *look* human, I have to think the balance isn't quite fifty-fifty." I raised my eyes to his then, challenging him. "Do *you* know?"

"No," he said shortly. "That's not something it was necessary for me to know."

"Well, then," I replied, as if that was supposed to mean something. "Even if you hybrids are a perfect fifty-fifty blend, or maybe a little more, it still means I'm much more human than otherwise."

It was a reassurance I'd made to myself over and over again, although I didn't always believe it. Other than the perfect health record and the eidetic memory, though, I really wasn't that anomalous. After a spectacularly short gestation, I'd grown and developed just like any other human girl, along with all the inconveniences that entailed. It would have been nice if I'd been just alien enough that I didn't have to worry about getting a period and all that crap, but no such luck. And whether it was because my biology was more human than otherwise, or simply because I wasn't capable of getting pregnant, the once-yearly birth control shots I received seemed to work just fine. Not that I'd given them much of a workout lately.

"This is true...you are more human than not," Logan admitted. "And yet something in you knew to go to me, to come find me where I was hidden."

"Yes," I said with some reluctance. Before today, I'd never had any kind of psychic flashes, never shown any evidence of having that kind of ability. That was Taryn Oliver's thing, not mine.

Logan seemed to realize he was pressing too hard on that particular subject, so he let it alone then, saying, "And since you are a grown woman, you must have been conceived some time ago. How long exactly?"

There probably wasn't any good way to break it to him, so I said simply, "Twenty-five years."

A breath escaped his lips. "Ah. Well, that would explain why the pod's systems had begun to fail. That is at the very outer limit of their viability."

And if I hadn't come to Sedona, had instead stayed in Flagstaff and worked through the holiday the way I'd wanted? Would I have felt the pull of his need from that far away, or would he simply have slipped into the dark without my ever realizing he existed?

I didn't want to know the answer to that question. Anyway, what-ifs didn't matter. I had come here, and I had felt that pull, even though at the time I hadn't known what it was. When discussing the hybrids, Lance and Paul and Persephone had mentioned how they seemed to share some sort of hive mind, that they seemed to be able to communicate without speaking. Maybe some faint echo of that ability was what had called me to Logan, although it was clear enough that he wasn't of the same genetic stock as my father.

But you share some alien DNA, I thought then. I still didn't know what that meant, not exactly. If it really was that connection, like calling to like, then why hadn't I felt it before this? After all, I'd lived in Sedona for most of my life, only moving away when I was almost eighteen. I'd still come back here in the summer, had moved home for a month or two after getting my master's, waiting for my application with the NWS to get sorted out. That meant I'd had plenty of opportunities to hear that alien call, however it actually worked.

Then again, he hadn't been dying yet. He'd still had more time.

"Well," I said, attempting to sound heartier than I felt, "however it all worked, I guess the important thing is that it did work. You're here, and you're safe."

"I am," he agreed gravely.

"And you're okay with it?"

His brows pulled together. "'Okay with it'?"

"With getting assistance from the daughter of a traitor. With being here, in the home of a human." I gave a nervous chuckle. "I mean, I'm not going to have to worry about you pulling out your ray gun in the middle of the night and blasting me with it, am I?"

He didn't smile. Once again, those gray eyes with their rim of sooty lashes caught mine. Maybe he hadn't been taught that staring at someone in such a way wasn't generally encouraged, unless the people involved were already intimate. For some reason, though, I found I couldn't look away, couldn't do anything except gaze back at him.

"I don't have what you call a 'ray gun,'" he said. "But even if I did, I would not use it on you, Grace Rinehart. You saved my life when you did not have to. I am in your debt."

"Okay, then," I replied, feeling a weight I hadn't even realized was there lift from my shoulders. "In that case, let me show you where you'll be sleeping tonight."

CHAPTER FOUR

THE HOUSE WAS SMALL—THERE WAS A REASON WHY WE referred to it as "the cottage"—and so it didn't boast such amenities as *en suite* bathrooms, or even a spare bathroom. There was the master bedroom, so designated because it had slightly more square footage than the other bedroom, and the spare room, which was where I led Logan. I'd already put my things in the master, and besides, he might have thought it strange for me to give up what I'd already designated as my own space.

"It's not much, but I know the bed is comfortable, because I've slept in that one, too," I told him, flipping the light switch so he could see the place in all its glory. Not that there was much to see—a full-size bed, as a queen would take up much space, a dresser, a wooden chair in one corner. The closet in this room was tiny, but as Logan only had the clothes on his back, that shouldn't be too much of a problem.

However, contemplating his meager wardrobe made me realize we'd probably have to do something about that if I intended for him to hang around a bit. Yes, I'd rescued him, but I hadn't really stopped to think what that might mean long-term. I sort of doubted anyone would come snooping down here, at least not for a while, since they'd be consumed with holiday planning, but....

Christmas. I almost groaned aloud at the thought but managed to suppress the sound. Tomorrow was Christmas Eve. My mother...well, *everyone*...would be expecting me up at the homestead at around five o'clock. So what in the world was I supposed to do with Logan? I couldn't possibly bring him along, could I?

Never mind that I'd have to drag him to the mall to buy clothes on what was probably the most insane shopping day of the year....

Well, there wasn't much I could do about that right now, and as for Christmas Eve dinner, I'd just have to figure something out. I had approximately nineteen and a half hours to let my brain hack away at that one. In the meantime, I just wanted to get Logan safely stowed here in the guest room so I could decide what to do next. All right, so it was barely eight-thirty, far too early to really contemplate going to sleep. But I didn't know what else to do. We couldn't really settle down in front of the TV and watch a rerun of *It's a Wonderful Life* or something. Come to think of it, I'd always kind of hated that movie.

Since Logan was watching me, apparently waiting for me to continue, I said, "There's soap and shampoo and all that stuff in the bathroom, which is next door, and I'll be in the room on the other side of that if you need anything else. Okay?"

At first, he didn't say anything. He moved away from me, ran his hand over the colorful duvet cover on the bed, then stepped toward the window so he could push two slats of the blinds apart and peer outside. What he expected to see, I didn't know, since the bedrooms and bathroom looked out over the side yard, which contained a couple of bare willows and the enclosure for the trash cans, and not much else.

Finally, he turned back toward me. "All this…for me?"

"'All this'?" I repeated. "It's really not all that much. I mean, it's not as if it's a suite at the Ritz-Carlton."

His brow gave that funny little crinkle I'd already come to recognize as a sign of confusion. Probably the Ritz-Carlton reference had thrown him a bit. "It is a great deal. An entire room to myself? It's far more than I would have had if the base had survived."

I hadn't even stopped to think about that, but I realized he was right. What would he have been able to call his own as a hybrid soldier? A bunk and a foot locker? Most likely not even the foot locker, as those were for storing personal possessions, and I kind of doubted the aliens would have allowed their clones anything more than the clothing and equipment necessary to carry out their duties.

"Then I guess it's even better that I found you," I said lightly. "Anyway, I'm just down the hall, so if you need anything, let me know."

He nodded, and I went ahead and stepped into the hallway, then closed the door behind me. I didn't want to stop and ponder whether that was for his privacy...or mine.

If he needed anything in particular, he didn't ask it of me. I went into my own room and shut the door before retrieving my sleep shirt from the drawer where I'd stowed it. Although the house had a gas furnace, it was still drafty, despite the work my mother and my aunt had put into modernizing the place. No filmy lingerie here, that was for sure. Anyway, it wasn't the sort of thing I wore unless I had someone around to remove it.

I realized that was a dangerous train of thought and abruptly choked it off. As I was changing into my night shirt and putting away the clothes I'd worn that day, I heard the water running in the bathroom next door and realized Logan must be in there. When I'd said he'd find everything he needed, I wasn't exaggerating. My mother always made sure the cottage was stocked with guest supplies, just in case someone unexpectedly came to town and needed something, so there were toothbrushes still in their packaging, boxes of dental floss, face wash, soap, antiperspirant, lotion…you name it, you could find it there. Because of that, I tended to pack light when I came here, although I did bring my own shampoo, as it was the only one I'd found that really did keep my wavy hair from turning frizzy.

Once I didn't hear the water running anymore and a safe interval had passed, I went into the bathroom myself. Logan had been very tidy; the toothbrush he'd used was placed in the little bronze holder, and it looked as if he'd wiped down the counters, too.

Good-looking and *neat?* I thought then. *You're in trouble, Grace.*

Of course, I already knew that.

I did my nightly preparations in double time and then slipped back into my bedroom, shutting the door softly behind me. The sheets were nice and clean and rustled softly as I climbed into bed. It was a very comfortable bed…but that didn't mean I was going to get a very good night's sleep.

Could I sleep at all, knowing he was just doors down the hallway from me? I truly didn't think he meant me any harm, so that wasn't the reason for my restlessness. No, it was more that as I lay there in the dark, what I'd done that day really began to sink in. Bad enough I'd gone to the abandoned alien base, a place which had always been strictly off-limits. When I was in high school, I'd once broached the idea of going there to look around, to see if it was really as quiet as it appeared to be. Lance had immediately shot that notion down, saying darkly, "If something's been sleeping there all these years, do you really want to wake it up?"

Well, I'd definitely awakened it now.

How long could I reasonably conceal Logan's presence here? I didn't know for sure. A few days at least, until all the Christmas hubbub had blown over. But my mother would come wandering down at some point, ostensibly to make sure everything was still well-stocked, but mostly to make sure I was keeping the place tidy enough for her standards. Which I always did, because I was a neat person even without motherly urging. I couldn't say the same thing for my half-siblings, especially Kelsey. That girl was a walking disaster area.

All right, so even if I somehow managed to keep my mother away, in less than a week I was expected back in Flagstaff. This little holiday sojourn didn't include New Year's; I was due to return on the thirtieth. Would I take Logan back with me, introduce him to everyone as the boyfriend I'd suddenly acquired over Christmas?

Oh, yeah, that would work out perfectly, starting with my apartment in Flag not being big enough for me most days, let alone two people. When I'd rented it, I hadn't cared, since I'd known I'd be working long hours, and I'd just wanted something reasonably close to the observatory and low-maintenance. But if I had to stuff Logan in there? It would be awkward, to say the least.

And so my mind turned this way and that until I finally slipped into sleep. My last thought, before the blackness claimed me, was whether Logan would even need to sleep, or whether he'd been humoring me by pretending he needed the bedroom at all.

———

He was up before me, sitting in his black jumpsuit in the living room while the morning news blatted away. I'd slept later than I intended, probably because I'd had such a restless night. However, I still retained enough presence of mind to stuff myself into yesterday's jeans and top before I emerged, since I didn't think roaming around in front of Logan while wearing only a nightshirt was such a good idea.

"Are you really watching that?" I inquired, since he seemed fascinated by the broadcast.

"Yes," he replied, all seriousness. "I'm finding it very educational."

"Don't believe everything you hear on TV." With that parting shot, I wandered into the kitchen, knowing I needed a good IV of some coffee before I was fully functional. Like the other appliances, the coffeemaker was gleaming stainless steel, very high end. I found some Italian roast beans in the cupboard and poured them into the coffeemaker, then turned it on. At once, it started to grind the beans to the required texture, then began piping in water and heating it for the next part of the process.

Maybe it was my previous remark, or maybe it was simply the aroma of the brewing coffee drifting out to the living room that drew Logan in. Whatever the case, he appeared soon enough, sniffing the air.

"What is that?"

"Coffee," I said. "In other words, nectar of the gods. Want some?"

"I don't know…do I?"

"Well, it's a stimulant. It helps get you going in the morning. You already look pretty bright-eyed and bushy-tailed, so maybe you don't need it. But my brain doesn't really kick into gear until after I've had a cup or two."

Logan gave the swiftest of glances toward his rear, almost as if he expected to see a tail there or something, given my previous comment. But then his shoulders lifted. "I would like to try some."

I tried not to smile. "It'll be ready in a moment. In that cupboard behind you should be some mugs. Can you get me a couple?"

Again, he got that "processing" look, but he didn't reply, instead turning away from me so he could open the cupboard in question and retrieve the mugs. To his credit, he really did pull down two stoneware mugs and not water glasses or wine goblets, all of which were located in that same cupboard. "These?"

"Perfect." I took them from him, trying not to react when my fingers brushed lightly over his as he let go of the handles. Just then, the coffeemaker beeped, indicating the brew was ready. I filled both mugs, pausing to say, "I take a little milk in mine. Do you want anything?"

"Milk." He pondered that for a second. "It is a liquid from cows, correct?"

"Yes."

"I will try it."

Since I didn't want to get into a discussion of sugar-cane production as well, I doctored his coffee exactly the way I did mine—just enough milk to soften it a bit, the lightest little dusting of sugar. It took the edge off without making the coffee too wimpy.

"It's still pretty hot," I cautioned as I handed one of the mugs back to him. "So you might want to blow on it a bit. Like this." And I showed him by blowing lightly on the surface of my own mug of coffee.

He followed suit, although I could tell he wasn't quite sure why. I took a small sip of the coffee, just enough to get some caffeine circulating in my bloodstream, and then Logan did the same. I could see him try not to wince.

"It's bitter."

"It is not," I said indignantly. "That's some of the best Italian roast money can buy." Since he didn't say anything, only gave me a puzzled glance, I amended, "All right, I'll admit that it's something of an acquired taste. But once you've acquired it, you're hooked."

After sipping again, he nodded. "It is beginning to taste better."

"Well, there you go." We drank in companionable silence for a few minutes, and then I glanced up at the clock. Nearly nine, and we still needed to eat some kind of breakfast, get showered, and get moving. I could only imagine that the stores would grow progressively more crowded and chaotic as the day wore on. I sighed, just a little, and said, "Let me rustle up some food. We've got a big day ahead of us."

"We do?" he asked, looking surprised. I got the feeling he'd expected us to lie low and hang out at the cottage all day.

"Oh, yes," I said. "I'm going to introduce you to a human institution known as shopping."

As I'd feared, the parking lot at the Cottonwood Mall was packed by the time we pulled into it around eleven-thirty. I'd decided early on that shopping in Sedona wouldn't work at all; the town specialized in boutiques for women's clothing and jewelry and crystals and other New Age accoutrements. If you wanted gear for your guy and weren't willing to wait for mail order, Cottonwood was the closest place you could go.

At least there was a real mall. They started building it when I was around ten, capitalizing on the booming wine economy of the Verde Valley. Before that, you had Walmart and the world's teeniest JC Penney, and that was about it. But now there was a Kohl's, a Dillard's, and a cluster of smaller specialty stores. Not exactly the sort of commercial mecca you'd find down in Phoenix or Scottsdale, but it would do…especially since all we really needed was some jeans and T-shirts and pullovers, that sort of thing. Well, and underwear. And shoes.

I'd already warned Logan to not ask questions about everything, to follow my lead and shop quietly. That black jumpsuit of his would attract enough attention as it was, but I couldn't do anything about that. The cottage was supplied with a lot of things, but spare clothing wasn't one of them.

We circled the parking lot a few times before I spotted a banged-up Jeep exiting a space not too far from Kohl's. I swooped in—this was one maneuver I wouldn't trust to the car, and so I had it on manual —and snagged it just as someone else started down the lane, clearly intent on the same spot. They shot me the side-eye as they passed, but I'd gotten that space fair and square. Fortune favors the bold and all that.

Logan watched this exchange with some mystification, but did as I'd instructed him and remained silent as he followed me into the store. Luckily, we'd been able to park near the entrance that was closest to the men's department, so we didn't have to wander around too much.

Earlier, I'd debated with myself whether I should simply leave him at home and go pick up some items on my own, but I wasn't exactly an expert on men's sizing. I'd had a few boyfriends in college, but we'd never lived together or anything, so beyond the odd T-shirt or sweater here and there, I'd never bought clothing for a man. Not that Logan was all too much help, either; he stared up at the wall of jeans in obvious befuddlement, clearly unsure as to what he should select.

"Just try a few," I said in an undertone, scanning the signage. "Um...you're tall, so probably at least a thirty-two-inch inseam, and...thirty-four waist?"

I grabbed a few pairs of jeans, piling them up in his arms. That was good. They helped to hide that jumpsuit. Moving away from the jeans display, I found some stacks of T-shirts, both with long and short sleeves, and added those to the pile.

"Go ahead and try them on," I urged him. "The dressing room is over there."

He nodded and moved off in the direction I'd indicated, and I watched him with some relief. If we were lucky, at least half that stuff would fit, and I'd buy it and send him right back to the dressing room so he could swap out the jumpsuit for a T-shirt and jeans. Yes, he'd still have on the combat boots, but those weren't nearly as conspicuous.

"Is he on leave?" an unfamiliar voice asked, and I almost jumped. Then I turned to see a woman around my mother's age standing a few paces off and smiling at me. She wore a name badge that said her name was Joyce, so I figured she must work here.

"'Leave'?" I repeated, blinking at her in confusion.

"The jumpsuit," she said. "Is he in the Air Force or something?"

"Yes," I replied immediately, glad that she'd given me such a convenient lie to grab on to. "And wouldn't you know, the airline lost all his luggage as he was coming in from California, and now I'm trying to get him some clothes before we have to show up at my parents' house for Christmas dinner."

"Oh, wow, that is a nightmare," the saleswoman said. "You got him some jeans and T-shirts, right? Well, he needs something a little nicer than that for Christmas. Let me see what I can find for you." And she moved off, briskly scanning the racks and grabbing things here and there.

Thank God I had a hefty balance in my bank account. I had a feeling this little shopping trip was going to cost me more than I had expected. On the other hand, I should probably be glad that the men's section wasn't totally overrun. Yes, there were people around, but it wasn't the mob scene that the jewelry and children's departments probably were.

The saleswoman returned, carrying a couple of sweaters, several button-down shirts, and some pullover sweatshirts that were a little dressier-looking than your ordinary morning-jog kind of sweats. I took everything from her and was thanking her just as Logan emerged from the dressing room in a pair of jeans and one of the long-sleeved T-shirts.

"The other ones didn't fit," he said. "But these seem to be adequate."

That was one word for it. I probably would have said "amazing" or "spectacular," based on the way those Levi's fit his slim hips and muscular legs. And the T-shirt didn't exactly hide the way his muscles bulged under the stretch fabric.

"Wow," I could hear the saleswoman murmur under her breath, but since I was thinking approximately the same thing, I wasn't going to take her to task for making inappropriate comments about someone who was supposed to be my boyfriend.

"They...work," I said in somewhat strangled tones, then went over to check the label on the jeans. "Okay, I'll look for a couple more pairs in this same size, and you can try these on." I handed Logan the stack of sweaters and shirts, and a resigned look swept over his face.

"Are all these clothes strictly necessary?"

"Yes," I told him firmly. "This is nothing. You

should see Persephone Oliver's shoe collection." And I shooed him back into the dressing room, then went to scout for more jeans, even as I noticed Joyce the saleslady hanging around, probably so she could get another eyeful when he came back in a new outfit. Which he did a few minutes later, looking very respectable in a button-down shirt and a sweater over it. He gave me an uncertain glance, and I nodded.

"We'll take those, too," I said. "But that should be enough for now...." His expression brightened, then fell as I added, "...except for getting some shoes and socks and underwear, probably a jacket of some sort...."

Shaking his head, he went back into the dressing room. I glanced at my watch. Twelve-thirty. Obviously, hybrid aliens didn't have the same shopping stamina as we humans.

When he returned, this time back in his jumpsuit, I told him to wait so I could pay for his clothes and have him change into civvies afterward, as it were. I could tell from his expression that he didn't understand why I couldn't have paid for everything first so he wouldn't have to change again, but I didn't feel like explaining anti-theft devices. Those wouldn't come off until everything was paid for in full, unfortunately.

The tab was a little scary. However, I couldn't do much about it at this stage. At least my family had all come to a mutual agreement a few years back that we wouldn't exchange Christmas presents—it was too difficult to buy gifts for people who didn't really need anything—and so I hadn't depleted my account as much as some people might have by this point in December. Once everything was paid for and legal, I went back to Logan and handed over one of the pairs of jeans and one of the long-sleeved T-shirts, then waited while he changed.

"We'll need to get you a belt," I said, pulling the shirt loose so it would hide the naked waistband of his jeans. "But that should work for now."

"Your clothing is very complicated," he remarked. It was the closest thing to a complaint I'd yet heard from him.

"You think this is complicated? Be glad that Sedona isn't exactly three-piece-suit territory."

As he was puzzling out that remark, I led him over to the accessories department, scooped up a belt and a few packages of socks and underwear, then paid for all that before heading to shoes. Since I wasn't kidding when I'd said Sedona was less than formal, it seemed as if a pair of sturdy brown hiking-style boots and a slightly dressier but still casual pair of lace-ups would do well enough.

"Anything else?" he asked, once I'd added those purchases to the bags he was already carrying.

"I think that's it," I replied. "So we can go home now."

Even as I made the remark, though, I had to wonder at myself. The cottage wasn't his home...it wasn't even *my* home. Just a temporary place to stay. But it was home base for now, I supposed. I'd have to work out the rest later.

As we hauled our purchases back to the car, Logan said, glancing about, "This is a very busy place."

I shrugged. "It's Christmas."

"Christmas?"

Oh, boy. Talk about something I really didn't feel like explaining, especially when you considered that my family definitely leaned toward the more secular side of things. For them, Christmas was a reason for all of us to get together, and not anything particularly religious. "It's a…holiday. A special day. People get together with their families, eat, talk. Sometimes they exchange presents."

He appeared to think that over as we set the bags of clothing and other items in the trunk. As we were heading toward the front to get in the car, he said, "If it's a special day, why aren't you with your family?"

I didn't answer at first, mainly because I wasn't sure what to say. A little bit of the truth couldn't hurt, though. I got in and began to buckle my seatbelt, while he did the same. Only then did I reply, "Actually, on Christmas Eve, it's more a nighttime thing. My family isn't expecting me until around five o'clock."

"Ah." He didn't say anything for a bit, seemed content to watch as I put the car in auto-drive and let it back out of the parking space. We really didn't need to be in the front seats at all, but sitting in the back with him would have felt a little too...intimate...for my comfort zone. Once we were out of the mall parking lot and on the highway headed back to Sedona, he finally said, "But you are going."

"Going where?" All right, that was being obtuse, but I was floundering as to how I should best handle the situation.

His tone sounded infinitely patient. "To your family. For this...Christmas Eve."

"Yes," I said reluctantly. "It's sort of a command performance."

"You don't want to go?"

I hesitated. "It's not that I don't want to go, but...." I glanced over at him. He was watching me expectantly, but I didn't see anything resembling worry in his face. Clearly, he didn't seem to have a problem with me going off to my family party and leaving him behind.

"But?"

"But what about you?"

His head tilted slightly as he shot me a sidelong look. "What about me? I am not part of your family, so I would not expect to be invited to a family gathering."

That sounded so very logical. "Well, it's not always *just* family. I mean, the Olivers will be there, and we're not technically related to them. But they've been friends of the family for so long that they almost are just like family."

He seemed to ponder that comment for a moment, his gaze moving back to the scene outside, to the cars on the street around us, the bare limbs of the cottonwood trees as we passed over the bridge that crossed the Verde River. Although a good deal of rain had dumped the night before, it was partly cloudy now, shadows and light moving across the roadway and the hills above the town. Off in the distance, I could see a glint that must have come from sunlight reflecting off a window in hillside Jerome. "But you've only known me for less than a day," he said.

"True." Even so, it didn't seem right, leaving him alone on Christmas Eve. Okay, Logan probably didn't know Christmas from Arbor Day, but that wasn't the point. "What would you do, if I left you alone?"

"Watch some more of your television," he said promptly. "It is a fascinating way to learn more about your culture."

I reflected that it was probably a good thing the cottage's satellite service didn't include some of the spicier channels. That would have made things really interesting. But since he didn't seem concerned about having to amuse himself on Christmas Eve, I told myself I shouldn't be so worried about it. He'd watch TV until I came home, and that would be it. You couldn't feel left out of something when you'd never been in it in the first place.

"Okay," I replied. "But we'll stop at the grocery store on the way home and get you something decent to eat. I don't want you eating leftover pizza out of a box on Christmas."

He shrugged. "If it makes you feel better."

I wasn't sure it did, but it was the best I could do right then.

CHAPTER FIVE

ALL DURING THE DRIVE UP TO MY PARENTS' HOUSE, I kept fighting the urge to tell the car to turn around, to go back and either retrieve Logan so he wouldn't be at the cottage all by himself, or stay there with him and eat turkey breast from the deli department at Safeway, then watch *A Christmas Story* together and attempt to explain life in the United States in the early 1950s.

I didn't do either of those things, though. I let the car drive me through uptown, along winding 89A, until it pulled off onto the gravel road that led to the house. Of all my siblings, I was the only one who remembered the old house, the one that had been left to Kara by my great-grandfather. Not much, just flashes here and there, enough to remind me that we'd definitely moved up in the world when we came here, the twins less than a year old, and me barely four. And of course Melissa had been born after we were transplanted to the Oak Creek house.

It was because of the show, actually. Paul Oliver, because he was a bigwig in the UFO community... and photogenic as hell...was asked to host a TV show called *Paranormality*, something the producers had described as *Ghost Hunters* meets *In Search Of*, although both those shows were so old that I'd had to look them up on Wikipedia when I was older just so I'd understand the references. Anyway, the producers had been meeting with Paul here in Sedona, starting to lay the groundwork for the show, and then they caught a glimpse of Lance and my Uncle Martin when they stopped by. The producers decided right then and there that having three good-looking paranormal-chasers instead of one could only make the show that much better, and so that was how Lance got roped into the scheme. He wasn't thrilled by the whole thing, but I guess Paul and Uncle Martin talked him into it.

So the show ran for seven years, and everybody made a lot of money off it, enough that my mother and Lance had bought this piece of property by Oak Creek, razed the ramshackle cottage that was previously on it, and built the big five-bedroom house that stood there today. She'd kept the smaller ranch-style house her grandfather left her, fixing it up and using it as a rental property, mainly for friends in the local UFO group who wouldn't have been able to afford a house at all without the price breaks she gave them.

It still felt strange to come here sometimes, to look at the impressive house with its stone fireplaces and warm wood siding, and realize I'd grown up in this place. Now it felt doubly stranger, since I was carrying quite a secret with me. I had to hope I'd be able to keep it safely concealed while I was here…a prospect made a lot harder when you were sitting down to Christmas Eve dinner with a psychic and her daughter.

I spotted Lance's Jeep and Paul and Persephone's Land Rover in front of the garage, and Aunt Kirsten and Uncle Martin's Mercedes off to one side, so it looked as if I was one of the last to arrive. The clock on the dashboard said it was five-twenty. I'd headed out a little later than I'd intended, mostly because I was stressing about leaving Logan alone in the cottage. What if he wasn't there when I got back? What if his curiosity got the better of him, and he decided to go wandering around Sedona once the appeal of satellite TV had begun to pall?

After I'd said for about the tenth time that I wouldn't be late, that I'd be back as close to nine as possible, he actually smiled at me and shook his head. "Go. Be with your family. I will be fine," he'd told me, and practically shoved me out the door.

Even so, I was still running late. Cursing at myself under my breath, I gathered up the poinsettia I'd bought at the grocery store and got out of the car. Yes, we had a "no presents" policy, but I always brought my mother a poinsettia or a bouquet of flowers or something as a little thank-you for all the hard work she put into the holiday feast.

The door was unlocked, as usual, and so I let myself in, bracing for the hubbub I knew would greet me the second I crossed the threshold. I wasn't disappointed; I heard one babble of voices coming from the kitchen, and another from the family room, where the TV was tuned to a football game. Knowing I'd find my mother in the kitchen, I turned in that direction, only to almost collide with Michael Oliver, Paul and Persephone's son.

"Hi," I said, hoping I didn't sound too awkward. "I assume the moms are in the kitchen?"

"Yours and mine," he replied. "Kirsten's in the family room, trash-talking the Cardinals."

She would, mostly because she knew it irritated the heck out of Lance. Just one of the many reasons why I loved my aunt so much. "Okay," I told Michael, and hefted the poinsettia I held. "Guess I'd better deliver this."

He nodded and headed off toward the family room, obviously relieved that he'd survived the encounter with me more or less unscathed. It was too bad that we had to be so uncomfortable around each other, but that was really more our mothers' fault than anything else. They'd hoped, as friends did, that Michael and I would hit it off, make our own Sedona love connection, as it were. I wasn't quite a year older than he was, and we'd known each other for our entire lives. Which might have been the problem, come to think of it.

At any rate, even though he was tall and good-looking, with his father's friendly hazel eyes, his hair dark like Persephone's, I'd never been able to think of him as anything more than a sort of brother, and he'd never shown any signs of being attracted to me, either. We'd gone out on one disastrous date our junior year of high school, a date where we sat across from each other at an Italian restaurant that was supposed to be intimate and basically stared at each other the whole time, not knowing what the heck we were supposed to say. After that, our mothers apparently got the message, because I know my own backed off on the whole "why don't you like Michael, he'd be so good for you" thing. That incident was now almost nine years in the past, but we still weren't sure how to act around each other.

I entered the kitchen and spotted my mother just as she was pulling the turkey out of the oven. That was the tradition—turkey on Christmas Eve, ham on Christmas Day. Good thing I'd never decided to become a vegetarian.

She saw me just as she was straightening up. "Oh, you did make it!"

For someone of Swedish descent, she was awfully good at the whole guilt thing, especially since in this instance I was a whole twenty minutes late, which I wouldn't say exactly qualified me for "bad daughter" standing. Pulling a hybrid soldier out of an abandoned alien base? That was an entirely different matter.

I shut that thought off as quickly as I could, however, since I saw Persephone Oliver over to one side, tossing the salad. Yes, she'd always claimed that she wasn't telepathic, that her gifts were more of clairvoyance and clairsentience...but why take the chance?

"I got held up for a bit," I said, and left it at that. "Anything you need help with?"

She shook her head. "You know we've been over that. Anyway, we're good, right, Seph?"

"All handled," Persephone said with a smile. Unlike my mother, she'd put on a little weight over the years, but I thought it suited her, especially since she'd always been one to embrace the whole "boho psychic" look, with her ethnic jewelry and flowing skirts and wonderful curly hair. I'd always envied that hair, although Taryn had inherited it and hated it, spent hours trying to get it straight whenever a special occasion came up. "You're looking very well, Grace."

"You, too," I said sincerely. She had on a gorgeous embroidered jacket and the heavy miner-cut diamond and emerald necklace from India that I'd envied ever since I saw her wear it for Christmas about five years ago, after Paul gave it to her as an anniversary present. As for myself, well, I wasn't the dressy type, but I'd put on a dark red wrap sweater and a new pair of jeans to go with my knee-high boots. The ensemble had been enough to elicit a flicker of something in Logan's eyes as I emerged from my bedroom earlier that afternoon, although maybe I was just flattering myself.

My mother caught sight of the poinsettia, and she smiled. "That's lovely. There's some space on the sideboard—why don't you go ahead and put it in the dining room? We're just about ready here, so let the rest of the gang know that we'll be sitting down soon."

"Will do," I told her, and headed off to the dining room, where the table had been extended with several leaves to accommodate the crowd who'd be eating there. All the good china and silver and crystal had been set out, and there was a lovely centerpiece of fresh pine and red ribbon and gleaming brass candlesticks. And yes, the sideboard was already filled with bowls of stuffing and mashed potatoes and a basket of rolls and homemade cranberry sauce and green bean casserole, but in the center of it all was a single empty spot, as if my mother had known I'd be bringing the poinsettia plant and had reserved a special space for it. No psychic powers there, though—I'd been following this ritual for the past few years, so it wasn't that much of a surprise.

I set down the poinsettia, then hesitated. Persephone hadn't sensed anything out of the ordinary, so that was my first hurdle down. On the other hand, Kirsten and Martin, and their daughter Callista, while not what you'd call regular psychics, were still from a telepathically gifted alien race. I'd never seen any evidence of them reading anyone's thoughts... well, other than each other's...but what if they could somehow sense that I'd gone to the alien base, had saved its last remaining soldier?

Stop being paranoid, I told myself. *They're not going to sense anything, as long as you keep it together.*

Taryn, Persephone's daughter, was another matter, but even if she sensed something off, I knew she'd ask me about it later rather than say anything in front of the crowd. She was cool that way.

So I pulled in a breath and left the dining room, going down the hallway to the family room. It was fairly crowded in there, since everyone except my mother and Persephone had gathered in that spot, even my sister Kelsey, who hated football but had a serious crush on Michael Oliver.

"Hey," I said. "Looks like dinner is just about to hit the table. So that's it for football."

A few pained looks from the men, but my Aunt Kirsten grinned and said, "TV off." It switched itself off, and everyone got up and began heading toward the dining room. As she began to pass by me, though, my aunt paused and tilted her head in my direction. "Everything okay?" she asked in an undertone.

Damn. "Just fine," I said. "It's been kind of hectic lately, but that's all."

She didn't reply, only gave me a considering glance before she followed her husband and daughter into the dining room. I sighed in relief, but everyone had passed me by that point, and I didn't think anyone noticed.

Chaos could've reigned in the dining room, but we'd been performing this ritual long enough that everyone knew where they were sitting—Lance at the head of the table, my mother on his right, all of us kids ranged below her. Kevin and Kelsey were already sitting down, whispering and elbowing each other, blond heads bent toward one another. Mentally, I'd always referred to them as the "children of the corn" because they were just so darn blond, but I knew better than to ever utter that phrase in front of my mother or Lance. And Melissa, well, she was blonde, too, but a darker honey shade, not the pale, pale tow-color of the twins, or of my Aunt Kirsten and my mother.

Paul sat at the foot of the table, Persephone on his right and Taryn on his left. And in between were Michael and Uncle Martin and Kirsten, with Callista next to her. Altogether, we made quite a crew. Some years we weren't quite as many, since Persephone and Paul tried to get out to California at least every other holiday season to see her parents, but it was definitely a full house tonight.

In a way, I thought that might be a good thing, as it meant—with any luck—they'd be so occupied with all their various conversations that they wouldn't notice I was keeping conspicuously silent. And after Paul said grace, which was a duty that seemed to have fallen to him over the years, we were occupied for a while with filling our plates and our wine glasses. Melissa was the only one under age, but it seemed my mother and Lance had decided to let her have at least one glass with the rest of us, because Kevin obligingly filled her wine glass to about the halfway mark before passing the chardonnay to anyone else who wanted it.

Since I was more of a red wine drinker, I waited for the pinot noir to make its way over to me, and tipped some into my glass before handing the bottle off to Kelsey. And at first, the conversation did swirl this way and that without me—talk about whether the Cardinals would make it to the Superbowl this year, whether the cable station that had originally produced *Paranormality* was going to go through with the reunion special its execs had floated to Paul a few months earlier, whether everyone wanted to reconvene here to watch the Mars landing, scheduled for four days from now.

"It makes the most sense," my Aunt Kirsten was saying. "Kara has the most space—had to, to accommodate all these kids."

Kelsey giggled, while my mother shot her sister a very sour look. Sometimes, I'd thought it was exposure to my mother's brood that had made Kirsten and Martin stick with only one child. It did seem a lot less complicated.

"I think it's a good idea," Paul said in his thoughtful way. "This generation's moon landing, really. We haven't had anything like this to look forward to for a long time."

Well, that was true enough, what with the way the space program had languished for quite a few years before the current administration decided to forge ahead with the Mars mission. It was partly a PR stunt, partly a works program, and partly a very real need to reach out to explore viable venues for colonization. Climate change had affected us all, although here in Arizona and in other parts of the Southwest, we'd actually benefited, with cooler than normal temperatures and above-average rainfall. I couldn't say the same for the people on the West Coast, still baking in a decade-long drought.

"I'll stock up on popcorn," my mother quipped, and Kelsey asked, gaze fixed on Michael,

"When is it supposed to happen?"

"Seven o'clock our time, I think," he replied. He was also studying astronomy, was actually attending NAU to get his doctorate in astronomy...following in his father's footsteps, I supposed...so he would be up on all that stuff.

"That's right," Paul chimed in. "Of course, we can expect some variation in the actual landing time, so we should probably all bring our favorite snacks and settle in for the night."

Great, another opportunity for family togetherness. Not exactly the sort of thing I wanted, when I already knew I'd be spending the rest of my holiday time trying to conceal Logan's presence from my parents and anyone else who might be less than thrilled about one of the hybrids from the base actually surviving to the present day.

I told myself that the Mars landing was still a few days off, and I'd figure out something by then. Maybe a last-minute callback to Lowell Observatory for undetermined reasons. That might do it.

"…seem preoccupied, Grace," Lance was saying, gray eyes too keen on my face. "Anything on your mind?"

"No, not really," I replied hastily. "I suppose I was worrying about the new instruments I set up earlier this month. I'm not sure my relief pitcher up at Lowell is really up on the latest technology. I had to work hard to get the grant for that stuff."

All of which was true, except that of course I hadn't been thinking about my brand-spanking-new hygrometer and whether Dave Aguirre could handle it or not. Still, the excuse should have sounded plausible enough.

Hard to say whether he bought the lie, because Lance was the master of the original poker face, and I couldn't read anything from his expression. After a pause so slight I might have imagined it, he said, "I can imagine that might be somewhat worrisome," before lifting his glass of wine and taking a sip.

Relieved that he hadn't grilled me any further, I drank some of my own wine. Well, all right, I took a fairly large gulp. It didn't matter whether I got tipsy or not, since the car would drive me safely home.

And that might be just what I needed to get through the evening.

My mother did probe a bit, doing her usual thing of asking, in too casual a way, how my social life was. I saw right through that, of course, knew that she really wanted to find out whether I was dating anyone, which I wasn't. I knew it bothered her to see me spending so much time unattached, but even if I didn't have the whole "hey, my dad was an alien" baggage to contend with, I was working very long hours that didn't allow for much socializing.

Unless I caved and finally decided to start things up with Nate, co-worker dating issues aside.

Somehow that prospect seemed even less appealing than usual, though, and so I made some noncommittal answers about being really buried in work right now, giving the usual excuses I always handed her. In the midst of that grilling, another bottle came my way, and I poured some more wine into my glass. Thank God for self-driving cars.

Eventually, we ate our way to a point where we knew we needed to stop, or there wouldn't be any room for pie. The guys cleared the table—even my brother, the ever-reluctant Kevin—and came back in with the dessert plates and the pies: pumpkin, apple, and cherry, along with a plate of the Christmas cookies my mother made every year. I had no idea where I was going to fit all that, but I also wasn't about to miss having a slice of the cherry pie, which had always been my favorite.

At the same time, I couldn't help thinking of Logan, back at the house with just a slice of cherry cheesecake from Safeway to end his own solitary holiday meal. Everything else had been pretty much picked over at the store, and I hoped I might be able to take a slice of pie home with me if anything survived the ravening horde. I knew Kevin could eat his weight and never gain a pound. Quite a trick, and he didn't even have any extraterrestrial blood as his justification.

Again, I caught my Aunt Kirsten's gaze flicking toward me, and I pushed thoughts of Logan right out of my mind. Her sudden attention could have been because of something completely different—who knew how my expression shifted as I thought about him—but no sense in taking chances. Trying not to be obvious, I glanced down at my watch. Nine on the dot. I really needed to think about getting out of there, although, since everyone else had settled down with coffee or port or brandy or whatever other after-dinner poison they preferred, I wasn't sure of the best way to slip away gracefully.

In the interim, I pretended to be useful, getting up and gathering people's empty dessert plates, taking the mostly eaten pies into the kitchen, although I left the cookies behind in case anyone had a spare corner in their stomach that they hadn't yet filled up. My mother made a half-hearted protest, saying I shouldn't be putting myself out like that, but I just shook my head at her and kept going. It seemed the least I could do after all the work she'd done, and besides, if I was up and moving around, it would be that much easier to find a way to collect my coat and be out the door.

There was no cherry pie left, but the pumpkin had one slice remaining, so I scrounged the plastic wrap and covered it up. I heard people moving around and guessed the younger crowd had decided to relocate to the family room and channel-surf until the parents got around to calling it a night.

That sounded like the opening I needed, so I went out to the hall and got my coat. I was shrugging my way into it when my mother popped her head into the hallway.

"Sneaking off?" she asked, sounding half amused, half disappointed.

"I was going to come back in and say goodbye. But I'm tired and want to head back."

To my surprise, she didn't argue, only nodded and said, "Well, that's understandable. But we'll see you tomorrow, of course."

Christmas Day. There would be no ritual present exchange, thank God, but I still had that dinner to get through. It would be a little more intimate, since the Olivers wouldn't be here for that, although Gabriel—my Aunt Kirsten's father, and the man who'd become my adoptive grandfather—always came down from Flagstaff for the family Christmas dinner.

"Of course," I said automatically as I finished

buttoning up my coat. "I'm stealing the last piece of pumpkin pie. Is that okay?"

"Better grab it fast before your brother does," she replied, smiling, which was her way of saying yes.

So I went and got the pie, and stopped in the dining room to make my farewells there, and then in the family room to do the same, although my siblings didn't seem to care one way or another, and Michael only smiled in my direction without quite meeting my gaze. Taryn and Callista were a little friendlier, but still, I was glad to get out of there.

The wind blowing down the canyon was icy, and I wished I'd brought a scarf with me. Still, it was only a quick walk to the car, and I climbed into the back seat, then told the car, "Home. And heater on, seventy-eight degrees."

Warm air began to blow out of the vents even as the car maneuvered its way around the other vehicles in the drive, then pulled out onto 89A. Sometimes, you'd have to wait a long time for an opening on the highway, but not tonight—everyone was already where they planned to be, since it was Christmas Eve.

And I'd done my duty, and could now go home to the human/alien hybrid soldier who was waiting for me while eating cherry cheesecake and watching *A Christmas Story* on "repeat." Or maybe he'd moved on to something a bit edgier, like *Scrooged*.

Or possibly *Bad Santa*? That one would take a bit of explaining. Most of the Christmas movies that had come out after that had been treacly kids' stuff, nothing particularly memorable, but who knows what the satellite stations were lobbing through the ether this particular Christmas Eve....

I realized, as the car moved through the mostly deserted Uptown area and on into West Sedona, that maybe I shouldn't have had that last glass of wine. Everyone had been passing the bottles around, and I hadn't been paying that much attention. I certainly wasn't anywhere close to drunk, but I was probably a little tipsier than I should be. Oh, well, maybe some of it would wear off on the twenty-minute drive back to the cottage. If it would even take that long. The streets were fairly deserted.

All during that drive, I kept wondering what I was going to find when I got back. Logan had seemed nothing but well-mannered so far, but I knew I'd taken an enormous risk in leaving him alone. What else I was supposed to do, I didn't know, since dragging him along on Christmas Eve had been out of the question. But still, he could've gotten bored with the TV and hacked into my laptop, which was sitting on the dresser in my borrowed room. Or, as I'd feared earlier, he could have headed out to poke around the neighborhood. I just didn't know for sure.

As the car pulled into the driveway, I saw that the light in the living room was on, just as I had left it, which had to be a good sign. I scrambled out of the back seat, paused to pull the fob out of the ignition dock, and then headed up the front walk. The car would lock itself, so I didn't have to worry about that. I pulled the house key from the depths of my purse, then let myself in.

At first, everything looked normal. The TV was on, tuned not to one or another holiday movie, but to a cable news channel, which tonight was going on about above-average snowfall in the upper Midwest. No big surprise, since an enormous front had been expected to sweep in right on time for the holiday. Besides, the "average" all those shows talked about was ancient history. The weather hadn't been average for a good many years.

When I focused on the couch, expecting to see Logan sitting there, it was empty. And he wasn't in the chair under the lamp, either, although I saw he'd gotten a fire going in the hearth. It crackled away happily, indicating it hadn't been neglected for very long.

"Logan?" I called out.

"Here," he replied, his voice coming from the kitchen. It also sounded strangely blurry around the edges, but I hoped that was simply because he was on the opposite side of the house.

No such luck. After I had paused to take off my coat and throw it over the coat rack next to the door, then dropped my purse near the rack's base, I hurried into the kitchen, only to find Logan leaning against the counter, a half-drunk glass of wine in one hand. On the counter was the bottle of pinot noir I'd set down there the day before and had completely forgotten about. From what I could see, he'd drunk almost all of it.

"Leave any for me?" I inquired, attempting to keep my tone light. I didn't even want to think about what effect that much alcohol would have on the system of someone who'd just been revived from a twenty-five-year catatonic state.

"A little," he said, and pushed himself up from the counter. "Should I get you a glass?"

"Um…sure," I replied. The last thing I wanted then was any more wine, but at least if I drank it, he couldn't.

He did seem steady enough on his feet as he went over to the cupboard, fetched a wine glass and set it on the counter, and then dumped the remnants of the pinot noir into it. That was barely half the glass, so he really had drunk a good deal.

"So…what prompted the sudden exploration of viticulture?" I asked.

His head tilted toward the living room, apparently indicating the television. "I saw some people drinking this liquid on a show, and they were talking about pairing it with food. I recalled how I had seen a similar bottle here on the counter, and so I came in and got some to go with my meal." A puckering of his forehead as his gaze sought mine. "Was that wrong?"

"No," I said at once. "I mean, lots of people drink wine with dinner. It's fine. But…."

"But?"

I went and fetched the wine he'd poured for me, more to keep it out of his reach than because I actually wanted it. "Alcohol can be hard on your system. I'm not sure it's the best thing for you to be drinking. We have no idea what it might do to you."

"Does it affect you adversely?"

No more than the average person, I thought, but I just shook my head. "Not really, but remember, I probably have a good deal more human blood than you do."

"I feel fine," he said, and something about the way he looked at me then made my heart begin to beat a little faster. Those clear gray eyes weren't blurry at all. In fact, I felt as if they'd never focused on me so directly as they did now.

"Well, that's good." I lifted the wine glass to my lips and drank, partly because I wanted to break that piercing eye contact, and partly because I wasn't sure what else I should do.

Logan drank as well, emptying his glass, which he set on the counter behind him. Then he turned back toward me, taking several steps in my direction. "You're a very beautiful woman."

Suddenly, my mouth was dry, despite the wine I'd just drunk. I blurted out the first thing that came to my mind. "Um…I didn't know that was the sort of thing hybrids were supposed to notice."

"Your father noticed your mother, didn't he?"

"Well, yes, but that was different. *He* was different." My hands had begun to shake, so I took the

STAR CROSSED   103

wine glass and placed it on the counter behind me, hoping Logan hadn't seen how I was trembling.

"I'm different, too," he said, still moving toward me.

I could see that. He seemed very different from the man—hybrid, whatever—I'd left here a few hours earlier. True, he'd just drunk almost an entire bottle of wine on his own, and that was certainly a good way to loosen your inhibitions. "What exactly were you watching while I was gone?"

"A number of things."

He stopped then, less than a foot away from me. It had been a long time since I'd been this close to a man, unless I counted the way he had reached out to touch my forehead the day before. There hadn't been anything particularly intimate in that gesture, though. Now I saw the shadow of dark stubble on his cheeks, felt the heat of his body, smelled the sweet-sharp scent of wine on his breath. My pulse continued to pound, and I told myself I should back away, should put a safe distance between us. The problem was, I had the counter at my back, and so any evasive maneuvers I made would be painfully obvious.

"Whatever you watched, it must have been educational," I quipped, but the joke fell flat as he continued to watch me, gaze moving from my eyes down to my mouth.

"It was," he said, and then he was right there,

only inches separating us, and then nothing at all as his mouth came down on mine.

Maybe I should have tried to push him away, done something to stop him. The problem was, the second his lips touched my mouth, it was as if someone had set a match to a pile of kindling. A sudden wild heat rushed through my entire body, and I could feel a warm ache beginning between my legs, unlike anything I'd ever experienced with anyone else. I pressed up against him, felt his arms go around me, pulling me against those rock-hard muscles, his mouth opening to mine, and I tasted sweet wine on his tongue, sending a second heady rush through me.

"Logan," I gasped, but that was all I could manage, because his mouth claimed me again, and his hands were on me, moving down my body as if he knew exactly what he was doing. Only...how could he?

That was about the last rational thought my mind could entertain. Because he was lifting me, carrying me out of the kitchen and through the living room, on into my bedroom, his lips pressed against mine the entire time. And then he set me down on the bed, reaching for the ties on the wrap sweater I wore even as I grabbed his T-shirt and pulled it loose from the waistband of his jeans. He let go of me just long enough to yank the shirt over his head, and then he was grabbing one boot I wore, followed by the other, tossing them into a corner, where I heard them thud against the chair that stood there.

Oh, God, I'd seen his bare torso earlier, back at the base, but then I'd been trying not to stare. Now, staring seemed to be the only thing I could do as I gazed up at him, at the heavy muscles of his arms, the flat stomach with its hard, defined ridges. I'd never been with anyone who looked like that. Sure, my previous boyfriends had been in good shape, but with the lean, light muscles of the kind of guy who liked to hike and snowboard. Logan looked like he could easily have put any of them through a wall.

He, apparently not content to just stare, was busy, undoing the button and zipper of my jeans and sliding them off, pulling my socks with them when he got the pants down to my calves. Then I was sitting there in my bra and panties, glad that I'd packed the Christmas red ones, even though at the time I hadn't thought anyone would be seeing me in them except me.

Letting out a breath, he said, "You are far lovelier than any of those women on the television."

Ah, well, that explained where he'd learned some of his moves. Apparently, he hadn't just been watching cooking shows and weather reports while I was out. But we could discuss all that later. Right then, since we'd gone this far, I only wanted things to progress to their logical conclusion.

"Come here," I said, my voice husky, rough, sounding nothing like myself. He moved toward me, and I undid his belt and then his jeans, grasping the waistband of the briefs underneath so I could pull them away all at once.

I had no idea whether the aliens who had designed him were hung up on size or not, but he was certainly not lacking in that department. In fact, he was so large that I wondered how exactly this was all going to work, but the throbbing heat between my legs told me that probably wasn't going to be much of a problem.

Then he was sinking down on the bed next to me and pulling me against him, and I felt his fingers fumbling with the hooks of my bra. It loosened, and he tossed it onto the floor, next to the rest of my clothes. His warm hands closed over my bare breasts and I moaned, more heat pulsing through me as his fingers found the hardness of my nipples, caressing them. I closed my eyes, gasping, and in that instant, his mouth closed on one, licking, teasing, while at the same time, I felt him pulling at my panties, yanking them down my legs, only for them to be added to the pile of discarded clothing on the floor next to the bed. The next thing he pulled down were the bedclothes, so we could slip under the sheets and the blankets and the quilt; it was cold in that room, away from the fire.

And oh, then his fingers were slipping into me, into the wet heat at my core, strong yet delicate, seeming to understand exactly how to touch me. How he knew that, I couldn't begin to guess, and in that moment, I wasn't going to worry about it. All I could do was lie back as he touched me, feeling that wonderful tension coiling low down in my body, rising toward the inevitable release.

I cried out as the orgasm rolled through me, but he didn't stop, kept stroking me as I writhed against him, feeling his muscles hard against my cheek. And though I was panting and gasping, held in place as the ripples of one wave of pleasure seemed to get caught in a feedback loop when yet another climax began to build within me, I managed to reach out and take him in my hand, feel his shaft as rock-hard as the rest of him. I moved up and down, pumping him gently, and he let out a moan deep in his throat, his eyes closing, lashes thick crescents against his cheeks.

Even as I touched him, I felt my body release again, spasming around his fingers. He lifted them to his mouth, licked my wetness from them, and sighed. That was enough for me. I loved his touch, loved touching him, but I wanted to feel him inside me. So I rolled over onto my back, guiding him into me, gasping at the size of him, even as every nerve ending seemed to come alight at that sensation of being filled, of having the two of us fit like perfect puzzle pieces kept separate for too long.

And then we began to move together, bodies in sync, his thrusts meeting the upward pulses of my hips, and I could feel it once again, that blazing heat in my core, the sensation of every part of me focusing on that exquisite joining, only us and our mingled breaths and the realization that this was what I had been missing all along, that nothing had ever precisely worked before this because he was the one I'd been waiting for my entire life.

The climax hit him a second or two before I came again, and I could feel the heat of his orgasm filling me, feel him come with a strangled groan, almost as if the sound had been torn out of him. I clung to him, even as another orgasm shuddered its way through me, this one sharper, more intense. Closing my eyes, I could only ride it out, let the last of the tremors find their away along every limb, until at last I felt his gentle lips on my throat, on my mouth.

I clung to him, not wanting to let that sensation of warmth, of closeness, go away. At the same time, I didn't know what to say. This wasn't me, to sleep with someone I'd only known for a day. And certainly not a man who wasn't even exactly a man, but far more…or less, I supposed, depending on how you looked at it.

He solved my conundrum, murmuring, "Thank you," against my hair, his arms tight around me. It seemed he didn't plan on going anywhere, and so I huddled against him, even as a chill found its way through the warmth of our lovemaking's afterglow.

What the hell had I just done?

CHAPTER SIX

H<small>E WAS STILL THERE WHEN</small> I <small>AWOKE, TOO.</small> F<small>OR SOME</small> reason, I'd thought he might slip out in the middle of the night, go back to the bedroom that was supposed to be his, but he was here with me. "Hello," he said as my eyes opened and took in the half-familiar room, morning light slanting through the wooden blinds, clothes still flung this way and that.

"Good morning," I replied, pushing myself up to a sitting position. My mouth felt gummy. Passing out like that without brushing your teeth is not recommended. But even with that, I couldn't help experiencing a thrill as I glanced up at Logan, who looked just about as spectacular in the morning as he had the night before. Maybe a little more so, since he had that whole rumpled morning-guy thing going on, and I'd always been a sucker for bedhead and stubble and the warm, half-droopy look of a man who'd been spectacularly laid the night before.

How was it possible for him to be so...human? I couldn't begin to wrap my head around the whole situation, so I decided it was better not to try, at least until I got some caffeine inside me. "Coffee?" I ventured, and Logan nodded. He seemed to understand that I wasn't ready to talk about what had passed between us the night before.

"Coffee would be very good," he said, then slipped out of bed so he could pick up his underwear from the floor. He looked just as amazing from the back as he did from the front, and a flare of heat told me that some parts of me were less interested in caffeine than my mind was.

But I pushed the tremor of arousal aside, more because it was one thing to fall into bed and do something as crazy as having sex with a hybrid when you were working on your fourth glass of wine, and the evening was framed in firelight and a little blurry around the edges. Now, in the cold light of day, I needed to do some serious thinking, and that required caffeine.

I grabbed my own underwear, but instead of climbing into the rest of my discarded clothes, I went to the closet and plucked my sleep shirt and flannel robe off the hook where I'd left them the night before, then padded out to the kitchen in my bare feet. Maybe that wasn't such a good idea; the tile floor was cold. Since I didn't feel like going back for my slippers, not with Logan continuing to put on the rest of his clothes in the bedroom, I just gritted my teeth and hurried for the kitchen, where most of the tile floor was covered by various rugs.

Could you do the walk of shame in your own house? All right, it wasn't precisely *my* house, but there also wasn't anyone around to see me hurrying away from the bedroom where I'd spent the night with Logan. Even so, some part of it felt like that, although I'd never really done such a thing myself. I'd heard girlfriends talk about it, but I'd always been careful. Before last night, the soonest I'd gone to bed with a guy was after a month of dating, when things had begun to more or less coalesce into a semi-formal boyfriend/girlfriend kind of relationship.

Last night…I still couldn't quite figure out what had come over me. Was it simply being with someone whose biology more closely matched my own? I'd always known I looked perfectly human from the outside, that there was no way you could tell I had some alien DNA winding around my double helixes, and yet it had always created a distance. Although I wasn't someone who fell quickly into relationships, I had had them from time to time, mostly because I just didn't want to feel so damn alone. I'd never really clicked with anyone, however. Not the way I had with Logan last night.

Frowning, I got out the coffee beans, started the whole morning ritual. In a way, following that familiar routine helped calm me down a little. There was something so very prosaic about making coffee.

But then Logan wandered into the kitchen, and I could feel my heartbeat begin to speed up again. It wasn't fair that he could have that effect on me, simply by walking into a room.

"It'll be ready in a minute," I told him, mostly because it seemed as if the silence would get too awful if I didn't say something. Anything.

"Good," he replied. He gave me an uncertain smile, and I wondered what he was seeing in my expression. "You are...all right?"

"Sure."

An eyebrow lifted and he waited, seeming to know that wasn't the end of it.

I took in a breath, then got down a couple of mugs and set them on the counter. I'd have to remember to run the dishwasher soon. The cottage wasn't fully stocked with a service for eight; you could get by for a day or two, but that was about it.

"I'm just...." I let the words die away. I was just what? Freaked out? Frightened? Worried the birth control shots that had protected me so far were going to fail miserably, just like the pill had failed my mother a quarter-century earlier? Wondering if I'd lost my mind?

Make that all of the above.

The coffeemaker beeped, and I busied myself with filling both our mugs and then putting a splash of milk in each, followed with just a sprinkling of sugar. After that, my delaying tactics seemed to have been exhausted, so I handed Logan his mug and said, "I guess I'm confused."

"By what?"

"You." It was far too soon to drink any of the coffee, so I settled for blowing on it, then went on, "I suppose I'm trying to understand why you would even have any interest in women. Wouldn't your… masters…see that as a distraction?"

At first, he didn't reply, but appeared to ponder the question, gray gaze turned inward. His fingers were wrapped around the mug he held, but I noticed he didn't attempt to drink any of the liquid within. After a long, uncomfortable pause, he said, "I can see why you might think that. On the surface, it makes sense. Remember that I did not have all my training, and so perhaps there are nuances I am missing, but from what I can tell, it seems that was what they first attempted—to have soldiers who were neuter, who did not possess any sort of sex drive. But it turned out that they did not make very good soldiers, since they were lacking the very aggression so often linked to males of your species."

"Low testosterone," I remarked, and he nodded.

"Something like that. At any rate, when they started over, they made their new generations of hybrids fully functional in the sexual sense. It was thought it should not be much of an impediment, since they were never intended to interact with human females, except…."

Something about the way he let those words trail off sent alarm bells ringing in my mind. "Except what?"

"Except...certain experiments. I don't know anything else. I'm sorry."

Experiments? That didn't sound good at all. I almost asked him if he'd been involved in any of those "experiments," but I doubted he had. From what I could tell, his masters had baked him up and stuffed him in that pod, piped whatever experiences and memories they thought he'd need into his head, although the mental conditioning hadn't been flawless, since there were obvious gaps in those memories. Certain *sotto voce* conversations I knew I'd never been meant to hear surfaced in my own mind, things my Aunt Kirsten had let slip. She'd had her own run-ins with the Reptilians back in the day, and although they'd never touched her, never done anything to her physically, it was fairly clear that they'd wanted to... intended to...if the opportunity arose. I knew I was fooling myself if I thought they were safely asexual the way the Greys, the standard big-eyed aliens of popular culture, seemed to be.

Still, I had to ask. "Did you participate in any of those experiments?"

His response was immediate, and emphatic. "No. Besides the requisite muscle stimulation to ensure that I was functioning properly, I had no experience of anything except that pod. I was placed in there to receive the rest of my training, but, as you already know, that didn't work out quite as they had intended."

True. Getting part of your base blown up and then your entire complement of fellow Reptilians blasted from the face of the planet a few months later would sort of throw a monkey wrench into things. I could tell from the feel of the mug in my hands that the coffee had cooled enough to be drinkable, so I took a sip, trying to figure out the best way to ask my next question.

"So…last night wasn't part of the masters' master plan or anything?"

At once, Logan set down his own coffee and came toward me, then plucked the mug from my hands so he could twine his fingers with mine and pull me closer to him. Those clear gray eyes seemed to bore into mine. "No. I didn't plan for any of that to happen. I will admit that when I first saw you, I felt…something…but if you'd asked me then, I couldn't have even said what it was. But after spending some time with you, and after seeing what is supposed to pass between a man and a woman…."

"And after drinking most of a bottle of wine," I inserted dryly.

"That did help to remove some inhibitions," he admitted. "It helped me to understand that I wanted you. If you did not want it…if you did not want me…why didn't you stop me?"

"I did want you," I said. God, it sounded so bald, so unvarnished, when said that way. I cleared my throat. But I wasn't going to lie to him, make him think I'd been unwilling. "I *do* want you. I suppose I'm trying to understand why. I'm not the kind of person who just jumps in bed with a man. But I did with you. And yes, you're gorgeous" —he didn't blink, although I saw one eyebrow lift slightly— "but that can't be the only reason."

"I don't think it is." He let go of my hands, pushed a stray lock of hair back away from my face. "I think it is because we are alike, or at least as alike as either of us would ever be able to find. I am a hybrid, and you are the daughter of one. I can't imagine it has been easy for you, having to live with that secret. At least, I assume it is a secret."

"Oh, yes, it's a secret," I replied, my throat tight. How had he been able to drill to the heart of the matter, to know things about me I had never admitted to anyone else? "I mean, my family knows, and the Olivers—our closest friends—but that's all. Even the people in the local UFO group don't have a clue. They all still think I'm an adopted Romanian orphan."

In response, Logan bent and kissed me, very gently, on the forehead. The caress was so tender, so at odds with everything I knew about who he was and where he had come from, that I melted a little more inside. Had anyone ever kissed me like that, as if I was something precious and fragile, someone to be infinitely cherished? I didn't think so.

"But I know the truth," he said. "Just as you know

the truth about me. So we should be comfortable with one another, I think."

He made it sound so easy. I *wanted* it to be that easy.

Who knows…maybe it could.

We went into the living room after that, taking our coffee with us, splitting the piece of pumpkin pie I'd brought home the night before. Logan started another fire, and I flipped through all the channels on the TV until I got to a music-only station, this one playing old holiday standards.

Christmas. It was Christmas morning, and I had possibly the last gift I would have ever asked for sitting next to me…and the only one I had really wanted, even without knowing it was what I needed.

I tried to tell him about the holiday, but when you sat down and really attempted to explain it, you could see all the cognitive dissonance, how one singular event more than two thousand years earlier was sort of hard to connect with a fat man in a red suit who flies around delivering presents. Still, I did my best, stopping partway through to heat up the croissants and bring those out on a plate, along with some butter and strawberry jam.

Logan ate quietly, seeming to think over what I had just told him, which included my own family's small traditions. "And so you need to return to your parents' house, although you were just there last night." His tone wasn't even close to accusatory, but I still felt a pang of guilt ripple through me.

"Unfortunately, yes. That's how we've always done it, although Christmas Day is an earlier get-together. We usually sit down for dinner at around three." I picked up the last morsel of my croissant from the plate and ate it, wishing I'd had the brains to get some bacon or at least a half carton of eggs when I'd stopped at the store. My body was craving something a little more substantial than the carbs I'd just consumed.

Logan nodded, not looking at me, but gazing into the fire. It definitely made the room more cheerful, and because my mother had bought a fresh pine garland to drape over the mantel and had adorned it with a few red velvet bows, it did actually feel like Christmas in the living room, although there were no other decorations in the cottage.

I couldn't believe the words that came out of my mouth next. "Come with me."

At once, Logan turned back toward me, expression startled. "To your parents' home? To...Christmas Day?"

"Yes," I said.

"Wouldn't that be...dangerous?"

Most likely. Or maybe it wouldn't. As far as I could tell, Persephone Oliver was the only one of the group who could literally sniff out a hybrid, and she wouldn't be there today. Aunt Kirsten and Uncle

Martin and Gabriel, Kirsten's father, were not exactly human stock themselves, but I'd never heard anyone in our group say that any of the trio had the ability to distinguish a hybrid from a regular human being. At least, when my mother had recounted the story, it didn't sound as if Kirsten had noticed anything out of the ordinary about my father.

This actually could work.

I brushed the croissant crumbs from my hands. "Not necessarily dangerous. I can say…you're my friend Logan, who I'd just started dating, but we didn't think we'd be able to see each other at Christmas because you were supposed to be going home to see your family. But something came up at the last minute— family illness, maybe?—and so you stayed in Flagstaff."

Logan looked dubious, to say the least. "That is a rather…elaborate lie."

"It's not that bad. I heard on the news that the flu is really making the rounds in the Midwest. We can say you're from Chicago or something, and your family all got the flu and told you to stay out here, since there was no point in flying all the way back there just so you could get sick, too."

"Possibly," he said, although I could tell he still wasn't convinced. "And how do we know each other?"

"You're…." I paused, trying to think it through. "You're newly assigned to the National Weather Service bureau in Bellemont—it's about twenty minutes west of Flagstaff. Anyway, that's how we met. I'm a meteorologist. Do you know anything about the weather?"

"No," he said flatly. "Not much need for that when you're stationed at an underground base."

Of course not. I considered the problem for a moment. The NWS had a fairly extensive operation in Bellemont, so of course they weren't all meteorologists. "What about computers?"

"Yes," Logan replied at once. "That is, I did receive training on the computerized systems that ran the base. They are probably far advanced beyond anything you would have at this National Weather Service."

"Perfect. No one who's going to be at Christmas dinner is much of a tech-head, except my Aunt Kirsten. That is, everyone knows their way around computers, of course, but she's the only one who specializes in working with them."

"And what if she attempts to question me on the subject?"

"Even if she does, it shouldn't be that big a problem. You'd just be posing as an IT guy, not someone who's an uber-hacker or something."

"Uber...what?"

The puzzled expression on his face was so adorable that I wanted to reach out and hug him. "It means someone who's really good at breaking into secure computer systems and stealing their data. But an IT guy—information technology guy, that is—just makes sure everything keeps running, maintains the networks, that sort of thing. I'll send you to a few websites today so you can read up on it." I paused. "You do read English, don't you? You certainly speak it well enough."

"I do," Logan said promptly. "And also Spanish, if necessary."

"Useful, but nothing you'll need tonight." I reached over and took his hand in mine. His fingers felt very warm, although I wasn't sure whether that was from the fire or whether his regular body temperature was a bit higher than normal. "I don't want to leave you alone again. Will you please come with me to Christmas dinner?"

Silence for a few seconds. Then he nodded, although I noticed his mouth looked grim. Well, that was understandable. I knew I was taking a big risk, but there was also something to be said for taking the bull by the horns. Sooner or later, someone in my family would discover I wasn't staying at the cottage alone. Wouldn't it be better to be bold, to present Logan as my new boyfriend, and pray they'd be so startled by the revelation that they wouldn't ask too many questions?

Well, a girl could hope, anyway.

He certainly did look very presentable in his new jeans, with a white button-down shirt mostly concealed by the dark green sweater he wore. "Are you sure?" he asked me, expression worried, even though I noticed a flicker of admiration in his eyes as he looked me over. After I'd showered, I'd put on a slim-fitting black skirt, a gray sweater, and a pair of knee-high boots, and I could tell Logan approved of the change from the jeans I'd worn previously.

"I'm sure," I told him. "You look perfect." And he did. As long as he didn't say anything too outrageous, I didn't see how anyone would find anything strange about him. And really, I had a feeling that the women in attendance would probably be so dazzled by his looks that they wouldn't even think to start giving him the third degree.

Lance was a different matter, but I'd just have to hope for the best there. Maybe he'd be happy enough that I was dating someone...especially someone with a real job...that he'd take it easy this evening. And Gabriel would be there. Gabriel was always a leavening influence. In fact, I think part of the reason why my mother didn't pressure me too hard about living in Flagstaff was that Gabriel lived there as well, and so she knew I'd have some kind of family close by, even though technically he and I weren't blood relations.

But with him there, and Persephone the hybrid-sniffer safely at home with her own family, I thought Logan and I stood a fighting chance. And if the worst happened, and his actual identity was revealed?

Well, if nothing else, it would be a very memorable Christmas dinner.

The two of us exited the house and went to the car. I glanced upward, casting a wary eye at the clouds overhead. They were heavy and gray, and I could practically smell the snow in them. That would actually be lovely, to have it snow on Christmas Day, but I wasn't sure if the storm was quite organized enough for that yet. I'd been so preoccupied with other things that I hadn't had time to check the latest updates the NWS had put on the web, especially since Logan had spent most of his free time that day reading up on computer networks and weather software and anything else he could think of that might pertain to his pretend job.

No worries about sitting too close to him this time. We both climbed into the back seat and let the car chauffeur us out of the modest West Sedona neighborhood where the cottage was located and through town, up into the semi-wilderness of Oak Creek Canyon. He took my hand and held it, although whether that was to reassure me or himself, I didn't know.

When we were a few minutes from the turn-off to my parents' house, I said, "It's going to be fine."

"So you say." His fingers tightened on mine. "I have studied as best I could, and I am fairly confident of my technical knowledge. But I haven't spent time with any humans except you. I am not sure how well I will do in a crowd."

True, that was an untested factor. "Well, since I'm introducing you as a computer guy, no one's going to expect you to be the life of the party. It's okay if you're quiet. I'll do as much of the talking as I can."

He nodded but didn't reply, so I wasn't sure if that was tacit agreement, or simply his uncertainty preventing him from saying anything. At any rate, there wasn't much I could do about it now, so I sat quietly with him as we drove the last half mile to the house, then turned down the gravel driveway. Once again, it seemed I was the last to arrive, as I saw Kirsten and Martin's Mercedes, and next to it the dark gray Beemer SUV Gabriel had bought just last summer.

The car parked itself next to Gabriel's vehicle, and Logan and I unbuckled our seatbelts and got out. At least his presence wouldn't be a total surprise, as I'd called my mother earlier that afternoon and said my boyfriend Logan had canceled his trip to Chicago because of illness in the family, and would it be okay if we squeezed an extra place setting in at the table?

Naturally, she'd started asking questions, but I'd only told her Logan and I had been dating for a few weeks, and that I hadn't said anything to her before this because the relationship was so new. That would also help to cover up any inconsistencies in what we knew about one another, since it wasn't as if you could possibly be that familiar with someone you'd only been dating for a few weeks.

"I just didn't want him to be alone on Christmas,"

I told her, and that sealed the deal. My mother was very big on Christmas, and the thought of someone having to spend it alone because his whole family was in bed with the flu was something she wouldn't allow herself to contemplate.

"Of course you can bring him," she'd replied. "I can't wait to meet him."

But even though I'd laid all that groundwork, I couldn't help feeling a teensy bit apprehensive as we approached the front door. All right, I was so tense I could feel a trickle of nervous sweat make its way down my back, even though the day was chilly enough, barely fifty degrees, and a brisk wind was blowing down through the canyon. Beside me, Logan stood straight and tall, looking so handsome in the dark gray overcoat I'd gotten him the day before that I couldn't see how anyone would notice anything strange about him.

With that thought to bolster my courage, I reached out and pushed down on the door latch, then called into the house.

"We're here!"

CHAPTER SEVEN

A CHORUS OF VOICES GREETED US, MOSTLY COMING FROM the family room, although as usual, I heard my mother chiming in from the kitchen, Kelsey with her. So at least Mom wasn't being left to handle everything herself. Dinner on Christmas Day wasn't quite as labor-intensive as the turkey feast of the night before, but it was still a good deal of work.

"Go on into the family room," my mother called. "I'll be there in a minute."

"Okay," I called back, and began to take off my coat, nodding at Logan to indicate that he should do the same. We both hung our outerwear on the coat rack, and then I led him down the hall, past the formal living room where the enormous nine-foot Christmas tree held sway, and on into the more welcoming family room, where a fire crackled away in the hearth and everyone seemed to be talking at once.

That conversation died away abruptly as Logan and I entered the room. My little sister Melissa's eyes seemed to bug right out of her head as she looked at my "date," and I could tell from the lift of her eyebrows that Aunt Kirsten was impressed despite herself.

"Hi, everyone," I said. "This is Logan Myles. I guess you could say we're sort of co-workers, although he's at the main NWS office in Bellemont, not up at Mars Hill."

"Hi, Logan," they all said, more or less in unison, although I could see Lance giving Logan a cool, appraising look.

"Hello," Logan replied, clearly taken aback by the crowd that now confronted him. Even though I'd told him how many people would be there, I didn't think he'd quite absorbed the reality of that number until it was staring him in the face.

Quickly, I said, "Logan, this is my Aunt Kirsten and Uncle Martin, and their daughter Callista, and this is my youngest sister, Melissa" —she blushed as Logan smiled at her— "and this is my grandfather, Gabriel, and my…father, Lance." I hoped no one would notice the slight hesitation as I made that particular introduction. Mentally, I'd stopped thinking of him as my father some time ago, but there was no point going into all that right now. "And my brother Kevin."

"Hey," Kevin said.

Not sure how to respond to that off-hand "hey," Logan gave my brother a lopsided smile.

"So you're a meteorologist, Logan?" Lance asked, gray eyes keen. They were a shade or two lighter than Logan's, sterling silver instead of stainless steel.

"Actually, no, sir," Logan replied. "I work in IT."

"Really?" My stepfather gave Logan another one of those piercing stares. "You don't look like a computer guy."

From across the room, Melissa gave an exasperated sigh, followed by a commiserating glance sent in my direction. "Dad, seriously?"

Since Kirsten and Martin were sitting next to her on the sofa, I could see them share a quick smile, one that disappeared quickly, as if they didn't want it to appear as if they were amused by the interplay between father and daughter. And Gabriel only sat there, looking serene, the way he always did. Somehow, though, I could tell he wasn't surprised by the way Lance had started in with the questions right off the bat.

"No, it's all right," Logan said. He even managed to smile. "You're right, sir—my line of work is somewhat sedentary. So, a few years ago, I began a weight-lifting regimen, and I try to run three times a week as well, weather permitting."

Where he'd pulled all that from, I had no idea, but it certainly sounded plausible enough, and I could see Lance nod slightly. If there was one thing he could respect, it was staying fit. Even though I knew he was close to seventy, he was still tall and trim, in better shape than a lot of guys half his age. In fact, I sometimes got the distinct vibe that my mother would have liked to relax a bit and become comfortably round like Persephone, but didn't quite dare to because of Lance.

"Anything else?" I asked dryly. "I don't think he has his resume on him, but we could probably pull it up on CareerLink if necessary."

Lance shot me a narrow-eyed look at that remark, but his tone was mild enough as he replied, "I don't think that's necessary." His attention shifted back to Logan as he went on, "Sorry to hear about your family all being laid up, but Kara and I are glad we could give you someplace to go on Christmas."

"Thank you, sir. It certainly wasn't my attention to crash your family's party, but Grace said it would be fine."

"It *is* fine," came my mother's voice from the entrance to the family room. She stepped in a little further, and I could tell from the brief startled glance she gave me as she finally got a good look at Logan that she was surprised, and impressed. I had to admit he didn't look much like your standard IT guy, but the story about his workout regimen was probably enough to stop any rampant speculation as to why his physique and his profession didn't exactly line up.

My sister Kelsey had also come in with my

mother, and I saw her give Logan a quick look up and down, blue eyes appraising. Certainly, I'd never brought anyone that good-looking home before, and she was probably trying to figure out how I had managed it. But she didn't say anything, only leaned up against the lintel, nowhere near as animated as she'd been the evening before. Then again, Michael Oliver wasn't around, so she didn't have nearly as much to hold her interest.

"Logan," my mother went on, "we're very glad you could come. There's always plenty of room at our table. Speaking of which, dinner is ready, so let's migrate."

At those words, everyone started to get up from their respective seats, and I took Logan's hand so I could help guide him through the organized chaos to a spot at the dinner table, one safely separated from Lance by a few seats. With any luck, they wouldn't have to talk much at all. I was a little concerned about my Aunt Kirsten being directly opposite him, but I doubted she'd start picking his brain about IT stuff at a holiday dinner.

Actually, in a way it might be just as difficult for my family as it would be for Logan, since it wasn't as if they could start discussing the activities of the local UFO group in front of him, or anything else controversial. Not that our poor MUFON gang had had much to occupy it for, well, years and years. The aliens had been driven out when I was barely a month old, and although there were still reports of activity in other parts of the globe, Sedona had been conspicuously quiet all that time. But the UFO believers still hung on, the only difference being that they made pilgrimages to Roswell and the Superstition Mountains outside Phoenix and anywhere else in the Southwest that still could boast the occasional sighting.

But there were still enough commonplaces to keep us all occupied as the food was passed around, such as Aunt Kirsten and Callista sniping in a good-natured way about whether Callista should move out or continue to live in the little casita, or guest house, on her parents' property. Naturally, Callista wanted to get out, and Kirsten wanted her to stay, but it seemed kind of moot until Callista figured out what she was going to do for work. She'd gone to NAU and graduated this past June with a degree in English, but hadn't quite decided what to do next. At the moment, she was working two part-time jobs, one at the UFO Depot, the store my mother still owned, although she hadn't put in hours there for years, and the other at a wine-tasting shop in Uptown, which sounded like a fun part-time gig to me, although maybe not a real career choice. Anyway, it seemed clear enough to me that Callista wanted to strike out on her own, even if she wasn't completely ready, and Kirsten was doing the typical mom thing in wanting to keep her at home.

I knew they'd figure it out eventually, but I could sympathize. Yes, I'd made a pretty clean break, since

I'd gone to school halfway across the state, but my mother had kept hinting that I was welcome to come back anytime. On one occasion, I'd remarked that it was a little silly for her to be getting all concerned about her empty nest, considering she still had three children living at home. She hadn't appreciated that comment very much, but it was only the truth. Melissa, at eighteen, was most likely not going anywhere anytime soon, and it would probably take a few pounds of C4 to dislodge Kevin from his room. Kelsey I wasn't so sure about; she'd gotten her associate's degree from the local community college but had been waffling about where to go to continue her education. I had a feeling she'd end up at NAU, not just because it was the closest university to Sedona, but because Michael Oliver was doing his post-grad work there.

Good luck with that, sis, I thought. He hadn't shown much interest in her, but then again, he didn't seem interested in much of anything lately other than getting his doctorate, and who could blame him? If he actually did want to settle down at some point, he had plenty of time after he was finished with school. No point in causing himself any unnecessary distractions right now.

"...going to the spa the day after tomorrow?" my mother was saying, and I blinked.

"What?"

She lifted an eyebrow at my obvious woolgathering, but only said, "We're all still meeting at Sedona

Rouge the day after tomorrow, right? When do you have to be back in Flagstaff?"

"Not until the thirtieth," I replied. The girls' spa day out had completely slipped my mind. It was another tradition, one where all of the "womenfolk," as Kevin liked to refer to us, would get together and go to one of the numerous spas around town for a day of pampering. I'd always enjoyed it, although I'd never been much of one for the whole massage thing...I had issues with someone I didn't know touching me. But I'd still get a facial, and my nails done, and we'd all have lunch and have a good time relaxing after the holiday was over.

The guys would all go out, too, although not for pedicures. No, they'd pile in Lance's Jeep and go four-wheeling, then find a remote spot where they could play target practice with empty cans and bottles. I never saw the appeal, but then again, they probably didn't understand why we needed to take a whole day to have our nails painted and get photo-facials or whatever.

Would they try to get Logan to come along on one of those shoot-'em-up testosterone-fests? That could be awkward....

"Then that should work out just fine," my mother said, and I had to remind myself that she was thinking of my return to Flagstaff, not what might or might not happen if I left Logan alone with my step-father and the rest of the guys for a whole day.

Beside me, Logan shifted in his chair, and I could

almost feel a pulse of worry coming from him, as if he was wondering what he'd be doing while I went off with the girls. I reached under the table and gave his leg a quick reassuring squeeze, and he nodded slightly. Thank God he knew enough not to start asking questions now, in front of everybody.

Across the table, my Aunt Kirsten gave a quick flicker of a glance at Martin, and he responded with the smallest shake of his head, one I probably wouldn't have even noticed if I hadn't been watching for it. I had no idea what that was about, and had to hope it was completely unrelated to anything Logan or I might have done.

"Oh, sure," I said. "I'm really looking forward to it." And I actually had been...up until the day before yesterday.

But if anyone noted any falseness in my reply, they didn't seem to give any indication of it. The conversation ebbed and flowed, and Logan was quiet during most of it, responding when someone asked him a question directly, but otherwise just listening to what everyone else was saying. It didn't even feel strange, because I thought most people in a similar situation would have done the same thing, even if they didn't also happen to be hybrid soldiers attempting to masquerade as mild-mannered IT professionals.

At last, though, we'd all stuffed ourselves on ham and my mother's to-die-for potatoes au gratin, and asparagus and pear compote and everything else that guaranteed I wouldn't want to look at another holiday dinner again until next year. I noticed that Logan was very careful with the wine, having only a glass and a half...and I also noticed that Lance had watched him closely to see how much he was drinking, and seemed somewhat impressed with my date's temperance.

Good thing he hadn't seen him last night....

Dessert was black forest cake, rather than pie, and I could tell Logan was impressed by that, too. After finishing his slice of cake, he asked, "Do you all eat like this all the time?"

I knew his question was more general, that after seeing what people were whipping up on the cooking shows on TV and then eating one of my mother's holiday meals, he probably had the mistaken impression that humans feasted like this every day of the year. Luckily, though, my mother didn't take his question that way at all, but only laughed and said, "Oh, hell no. I like to cook, but after Christmas is over, I don't go near the kitchen for about a week. I make Lance bring us takeout."

Logan smiled a little uncertainly, and I stepped in, saying, "That's kind of an exaggeration, Mom. Yeah, we would live on pizza and leftovers for a couple of days, but after that you were generally right back in the kitchen, worried we were all going to suffer some kind of nutritional deficiency if you weren't making us stew from scratch or whatever."

She didn't bother to protest, because it was the

truth. My Aunt Kirsten grinned. "I don't know where she got that cooking gene from, because I know I definitely didn't get it."

"That's for sure," both Callista and Martin chimed in, and everyone laughed.

Gabriel shook his head. "You can't blame that on me, though. I've managed very well for myself all these years."

Which he had. After being banished to this world because of having the temerity to interfere with human events and father a child on my grandmother, he'd managed far better than anyone had probably expected. During his exile here on planet Earth, he'd acquired some halfway decent skills in the kitchen. I knew that because he'd gotten in the habit of inviting me over for dinner once a week, probably to make sure I got at least one solid meal in me now and then.

"That must have been our mother's fault, Kirsten," my own mother remarked, and although I could tell she was trying to keep her tone light, a hint of bitterness crept in nonetheless. "I don't remember her ever fixing us anything other than Kraft mac and cheese and the odd peanut butter and jelly sandwich."

"Well, I love *your* mac and cheese," I said, thinking I'd better steer the conversation away from my grandmother, who wasn't exactly an example of maternal devotion. I'd never met her; none of us had ever heard anything from her. Most of the time, I doubted whether she even knew she had grandchildren. Just one more complication she didn't want to deal with. "Of course, that's probably because you make it from scratch with brie and white cheddar, but...."

Everyone chuckled a little at that, and Logan shot me a small, questioning look. All I could do was offer a quick smile in return. He seemed to have realized that he'd asked a question he probably shouldn't have, but it hadn't steered anyone too far off course. Even so, I thought it best to get us out of there before he suffered a worse case of foot-in-mouth disease.

I pushed my chair away from the table and got up. "Dinner was amazing, Mom—as usual. But I'd rather get back before that storm really starts dumping on us."

She nodded, looking resigned. I was never one to hang around forever, lingering over coffee or what-not, but I think she hoped each year that I'd stay a little longer, wouldn't rush off as soon as the meal was over.

"It was looking pretty threatening," Martin said, rising from his own seat so he could go to the window. He pushed the curtain aside and shook his head. "Looks like we've all left it a little too late. The snow's already started."

Of course, we all had to go to the window after that, while he good-naturedly moved aside so we could get a look. It was already full dark, but the lights flanking the front door were on, casting a warm glow that illuminated everything enough to show that, as Martin had said, soft white flakes had begun to drift downward. The ground wasn't quite covered yet, but you could see that it was well on its way.

"Well, you all have four-wheel drive, or at least all-wheel drive, so it shouldn't be too much of a problem," Lance said. His gaze flickered toward Gabriel, who had the longest drive of us all, back up to Flagstaff along the switchbacks on 89A. "You're welcome to crash here, Gabriel, if you'd rather wait until morning."

But Gabriel only shook his head and offered one of his gentle smiles. "It's not coming down that hard yet. It is probably best if I get on my way, though."

After that, there didn't seem to be much else to do except for all of us to get into our coats, retrieve our purses, and then say our goodbyes. I hugged Kirsten and Martin and Gabriel, and Callista as well. I could've been imagining things, but it almost seemed as if Lance shook hands with Logan for just a second or two longer than was strictly necessary, and a chill went down my spine. But then my stepfather was saying, in quite normal tones, that it had been very nice to meet him.

Then it was my turn to give Lance a quick hug, and a longer one for my mother, along with the promise that I'd see her on Thursday. At last, Logan and I made our escape to the car, Gabriel and the others trudging through the snow to their respective vehicles. One last wave, and then the two of us were safely ensconced in the back seat of my car, buckling up as it slowly backed us away from the garage and then turned so it was pointing in the right direction to get onto the highway.

"We actually did it," I said, and reached over and took Logan's hand in mine.

"Do you think they suspected anything?"

"I don't think so. Lance had me a little worried at the end there, but...."

"I didn't think anything of it. That sort of thing can be an assertion of male dominance, can it not?"

I hadn't really considered that angle, but Logan was probably right. That extended handshake was most likely a "don't screw with my daughter" sort of warning rather than a hint that he'd realized my date was a little more than your standard IT nerd. I had to hope so, anyway.

"It can," I admitted. "Up until recently, I've been able to avoid bringing my boyfriends home, since I went to college hundreds of miles from here. Ever since I moved to Flagstaff, though, the whole avoidance thing has been a little more difficult."

"So how did you solve that problem?"

I grinned. "By not dating anyone."

Logan's mouth twitched. "I suppose that would be one solution."

"The safest one, I assure you." I'd dated a guy my junior year of high school who had his ears pierced multiple times. When he came to pick me up for a night out at the movies, Lance had taken one look at the poor guy and asked, "What's with all the earrings? Don't you have enough holes in your head?"

Needless to say, I didn't bring anyone home after that unless there was absolutely no way of avoiding the confrontation.

"Then…thank you, I suppose," Logan remarked, and I gave him a startled look.

"Thank you for what? Subjecting you to Lance?"

"I wouldn't put it that way. Simply that I'm honored you would bring me home to meet your family, even with the risks such an action might bring with it."

Instead of answering, I rested my head on his shoulder, and he took my hand in his and held it. I hadn't really thought of it as an honor, more that I didn't want to leave him alone, not after what we'd shared. Strangely, I felt closer to him now than I had with men I'd spent weeks or even months with. What that said about us, about the connection we shared, I wasn't sure. Maybe it was just as he'd told me, that like was drawn to like.

The car moved along the mostly empty highway, adjusting its speeds to the snow-slick roads. Outside, I could see snow drifting down, not heavily, but in delicate ripples and waves, dusting the familiar landscape, transforming it into something not quite earthly. Even a winter in Flagstaff hadn't dulled my appreciation for snow, and I was glad of it now, glad of this little present Mother Nature was giving us.

When we pulled into the driveway, I said to Logan, "Let's not go in the house right away. There's something I want to show you."

He appeared a little startled by that request, but then he nodded. "Of course."

So we got out of the car, and I led him around to the side yard, then into the back. Out here, the yard was cut into several terraces, all paved, although the landscape had otherwise been left minimal, allowing the trees that had already been there to grow more or less unfettered. The pines and fir were already dusted with snow, the bare branches of the cottonwoods and sycamores and oaks given their own traceries of white.

The property ran all the way down to Oak Creek, and a path wound its way through the trees. It was there that I took Logan, moving through the still, almost breathless night while the snow fell all around us. We were both bundled up well enough that I wasn't worried about catching a chill. Besides, I didn't intend for us to be out here too long.

We came to the water's edge, the creek splashing and dancing its way over the stony bed. It never got cold enough here for the water to freeze. Above, a gibbous moon glowed ghostly pale as the clouds thinned for a few seconds, then disappeared as a bank of heavier cloud cover moved over it.

I stopped there, then said, "This is what helped protect my mother and my aunt before. When the base was still active."

Logan's head tilted slightly as he considered my words. "How did it protect them?"

"I don't know exactly. There's some power in the creek, in the land itself. From the way they tell it, Sedona itself wanted to keep them safe. And it did… for a while."

A silence fell then. He glanced away from me, looking at the glinting waters of the creek, watching as the light snow fell, drifting this way and that. A few flakes were caught in his hair, giving it a faint dusting of white. At last he said, "It amazes me that anyone would want to destroy something so beautiful."

"Well, from what I heard, I don't think your masters were trying to destroy it—control it, more like."

"That's not what I meant." He shifted back in my direction, but I noticed that his eyes didn't quite meet mine. "I was speaking of what your own people have done to this world. Perhaps it isn't so odd that my masters thought they might do a better job of it."

"It's better than it was," I protested. "We've cut back carbon emissions, are using more and more renewable energy sources—"

"But it is still not all the way better, is it?"

I shoved my hands in my coat pockets. Even though I had gloves on, the chill was beginning to seep into my fingers. "It's better enough that I don't think being overrun by the Reptilians is an acceptable alternative."

At once, he came to me, his arms encircling me as he drew me close. "That is not what I meant. I was speaking of what they thought, not what *I* think." His lips brushed against my cheek. "You're cold. We should go inside."

"We will," I said. "I just wanted you to see this place, to know that I think you'll be safe here. Your masters are gone, but even if they came back looking for you...I think the creek would protect you."

He didn't answer immediately, but pulled away so he could look back over his shoulder at Oak Creek, flowing smoothly over the water-worn stones and the deep red silt of its bed, dust washed down from Sedona's red rock formations. Then he nodded. "I think it might."

His hand found mine and pulled it out of my pocket, and he led me back up the path and to the house. There, I had to fumble for a minute to locate the key, but eventually, I pulled it out of my purse and opened the back door, glad that the same key worked in both the front and back locks.

Inside, it was warm and dry, and even back here, in the service porch off the kitchen, I could smell the faint lingering traces of wood smoke from the fire we'd had earlier that day. Without speaking, I took Logan through the kitchen and out to the living room, where we pulled off our coats and draped them over the back of the sofa.

I couldn't be sure which of us reached for the other first. I only knew that I was in his arms again, and he was kissing me, lips warm against mine, casting away the chill of the cold, snowy night.

After a minute, though, I pulled away from him, just enough so I could say, "Let's have another fire."

He seemed to understand what I meant, because he went to the hearth and began stacking logs in the grate, then got the long-necked lighter and set it against the kindling at the bottom. At the same time, I went to the linen closet in the hall and pulled out two heavy quilts. There was always extra bedding on hand here at the cottage, since the house tended to be drafty, and we could still drop below freezing in Sedona as late as April.

Now, though, I took the quilts and spread them on the floor in front of the fire. Logan turned from what he was doing to watch me, the lighter still in his hand. As his eyes met mine, I bent down and deliberately unzipped one boot, then the other, and stepped out of them. The tights I wore came off next. After that, I undid the ties on my sweater and removed it before pulling down the zipper on my skirt and climbing out of it as well. Then I stood in front of him in only my bra and panties, black this time, with silver-edged lace.

For the longest moment, he didn't do anything, didn't say anything, but only stared at me, eyes fixed on mine. I could see the Adam's apple in his throat move as he swallowed. At last, though, he set down the lighter and stepped toward me, his form silhouetted by the flames of the growing fire at his back.

When he did speak, his voice was barely a whisper. "I never thought I could want anything—could *need* anything—the way I want you."

He crushed me against him then, hands running down my bare arms before moving on to rest on the curve of my hips. His fingers curled around me, holding me close. Even through his jeans, I could feel his arousal, and I needed him then, needed him to be free of his clothing the way I was. I undid his belt buckle, then pulled his shirt out of his jeans, and yanked both his sweater and his shirt over his head. There was still the matter of those lace-ups he wore, though, so I sank to my knees and untied his shoes as quickly as I could. He kicked them off, and then I was able to pull down his Levi's, maneuver his briefs over the bulge of his erection so he was at last gloriously naked, smooth skin warmed by the firelight.

Since I was already on my knees, it seemed the most natural thing in the world to take him into my mouth, run my tongue over his silky skin and feel how very hard the flesh beneath was. He groaned, one hand running through my hair, the other tightening on my shoulder.

"Grace."

It was something between a moan and a sigh. I glanced upward and saw how his eyes had shut, how thick his lashes were against the high cheekbones. I knew I could take him all the way with this if I wanted, but that wasn't my plan. Only to please him, maybe tease him a little bit, and then....

He seemed to guess what I was thinking, because after a few minutes, he gasped and pulled away from me, then sank down onto the quilt, bringing me with him, lifting me so I was straddling him, sinking down onto him, letting him fill me even more completely than he had the night before. And I was riding him, letting out gasps of my own with each thrust, my hands planted on the quilts beneath us to steady myself.

I'd never been very noisy during sex before, but now I could hear myself crying out as we moved together, as I felt the heat and the pressure and the need building in me. Maybe at some other time I would've worried about the neighbors overhearing us, even though the house was shut tight. Not now. Now I could only move with Logan, with each thrust and each drawing out, until the climax burst through me with volcanic heat, my body shaking as I sobbed his name over and over again. And then I could feel him coming as well, his rhythm faltering as he shuddered through his own orgasm.

My strength seemed to leave me, and I pushed myself off him so I could collapse on the quilt, my breath coming from me in little heaving gasps. He lay there without moving for a second or two, and then he reached over and pulled me against him.

"You are perfect," he whispered.

"So are you," I said, and in that moment, I knew it was the simple truth. Or at least, he was perfect for me.

We dozed off in front of the fire, still wrapped in each other's arms, and then an hour or so later woke up enough to put on some underwear and get cleaned up and ready for bed. No discussion of where we would sleep; he crawled into bed next to me as if he'd been doing the same thing his entire life. And if I had any say in the matter, he would sleep next to me for the rest of his life.

The next morning, we got up and puttered around like any ordinary couple might—making coffee, eating the last of the croissants, making plans to go to the store so we could get some real food. Afterward, we squeezed into the shower together even though it really wasn't large enough to accommodate both of us, and laughed as we tried to soap up one another and not get an elbow in the ribs or an eye full of shampoo, or whatever.

By ten-thirty, we were dressed and ready to head out the door. Logan had acquitted himself well enough last night and at the shopping expedition the day before that I wasn't too concerned about going out in public with him…*really* going out in public, to a grocery store where the clerks actually knew me and my showing up with an eye-popping specimen like my hybrid soldier was sure to raise a few eyebrows, if not elicit even more than a few questions.

I thought we were both ready for it. Or at least, I hoped we were.

Just as I was gathering up my purse, though, the doorbell rang. I paused, wondering who it might be, then shrugged. Possibly my mother, coming by with a care package of leftovers. Since she knew Logan was staying with me, I didn't think her dropping by was that big a deal. Also, because we were on our way out the door, we had a good excuse for not lingering and chatting.

When I opened the door, however, it wasn't my mother waiting on the doorstep, but Aunt Kirsten and Uncle Martin, both of them looking dead serious and not very holiday-ish at all.

"Um…hi," I said, too surprised to come up with anything more eloquent than that.

"Can we come in?" my aunt asked, and I saw her gaze slip past me to Logan, who was standing a foot or two behind me in the entryway. "We need to talk to you…to *both* of you."

CHAPTER EIGHT

WE ALL SAT IN THE LIVING ROOM, LOGAN AND I ON THE couch, Aunt Kirsten in one of the armchairs and Uncle Martin in the other. He, too, looked businesslike, almost grim, and I knew this wasn't exactly a social call.

Still, I attempted to hold off the dreaded discussion as long as I could. "Would you like any water, or coffee?" I asked, beginning to rise from the couch.

"Nothing," my aunt said. "We're fine."

I didn't quite sigh as I settled back down on the sofa. Beside me, Logan sent me the faintest of questioning glances, but I knew I didn't dare say anything to him in front of my aunt and uncle. "So…what's this about?"

Aunt Kirsten raised an eyebrow. Because she was half Nord, she was aging very slowly and didn't look anything close to her actual age of forty-eight. People who didn't know them were always mistaking her and Callista for sisters, not mother and daughter. Thank God anti-aging treatments were so advanced now that no one really raised an eyebrow at her appearance, except maybe to wonder how much she was spending to keep herself looking that good. Only the family knew she wasn't spending anything at all...that her youthful appearance was just one side benefit to having a father from a highly advanced alien race.

"I think you know exactly what this is about," she replied, her gaze moving from me and stopping at Logan.

Martin fixed me with a piercing blue gaze of his own. Like my aunt, he still appeared to be in his thirties somewhere, although none of us—maybe not even Kirsten—knew exactly how old he was. "We weren't going to make a scene last night, not in front of your parents, but I think we need to get to the bottom of this."

"So they don't know?" I asked, a wave of relief washing over me despite the current situation. If my mother and Lance were still clueless, I could let myself cling to the hope that maybe they wouldn't have to learn anything of Logan's true identity.

"No, they don't...yet," Kirsten replied. "We wanted to hear what you had to say first."

What *did* I have to say? Should I tell them the truth...all of it? I figured some things could be left out, since I wasn't about to go into detail about *all* the activities Logan and I had been participating in during the past forty-eight hours. Anyway, my aunt and uncle weren't stupid. I was sure they'd already put two and two together. Or six and nine, as the case may be.

To my surprise, Logan spoke then. "How did you know?"

Something in Aunt Kirsten's stern expression softened as she regarded him, and I allowed myself to feel a tiny flicker of hope. Maybe she only wanted to know the truth of what was going on, and wasn't hell-bent on exposing me to my parents.

"Little things," Martin put in, leaning forward slightly in his chair. "Your command of English is very good, Logan, but you don't use enough contractions."

"Maybe he's just an ESL student," I said, but my uncle shot me such a derisive look that I subsided.

"And his clothes are brand new," Kirsten added. "I can understand buying new clothes for the holidays, but even his shoes didn't look as if they'd been worn before. It's one thing to have a new piece here and there, but an entire outfit of new clothes?"

"That's still circumstantial evidence," I said.

She and Martin exchanged a glance. "And also that we—and Gabriel—could tell right away that Logan wasn't simply a computer guy from Chicago."

"You could?" I demanded. "But…how?"

"They are not human, either," Logan said quietly. "Their race possesses many special gifts, one of which is knowing when their enemy is near."

"I don't want to call you an enemy," Martin said. "I have a feeling it's not quite that black and white."

"Well, that's good to hear," I told him. "But that still doesn't explain how Kirsten could know. You didn't notice anything strange about my father back in the day, did you?"

A flicker went through her eyes as I referred to that long-dead hybrid soldier as "my father." I was sure that to her and everyone else, Lance was my only real father. But she seemed to let it go, saying, "No, I couldn't. But that was before I met Martin, before he helped awaken the powers that had been dormant up until then. Yesterday, I felt it even before Kara opened the door."

"And you didn't say anything, didn't react."

"Of course not," my aunt snapped, sounding annoyed for the first time. "What, was I supposed to ruin my sister's Christmas dinner that she worked so hard on? I could tell Logan was not human...but I also could tell he wasn't harboring any evil intentions. Were you, Logan?" Her clear blue eyes, a few shades lighter than Martin's, seemed to drill into the man who sat next to me.

"No," he replied, meeting her gaze without blinking. "I don't know why Grace was able to find me, or exactly how I managed to survive so long, but my last intention is to hurt anyone, or anything."

Those words should have served to reassure my

uncle and aunt, but if anything, they appeared even more troubled. They turned and looked at one another, and I guessed they were communicating with each other using the psychic bond they shared. They could only do that with one another, but it was still disconcerting to watch.

It's probably even more disconcerting for Callista, I thought. *Parents are hard enough to manage even when they can't read each other's thoughts.*

After a long, awkward moment, they appeared to stop their mental exchange, and shifted so they were facing Logan and me again. "I think it would be better if you told us exactly what happened," Kirsten said, and although her tone was mild enough, I could tell it wasn't a request.

So I explained how I'd come to the cottage and felt that strange restlessness, then found myself going to the abandoned base and discovering Logan there. "He would have died," I said at last, sounding a lot more desperate than I'd intended, as if I expected them to tell me I should have left him there to his fate. "I had to do something. I couldn't just walk away and pretend I hadn't found him."

"It's fine," my aunt replied. "We're not suggesting you should have done that."

"Of course not," Martin put in.

"But this whole thing is very strange, and so I think" — she paused, and I could tell she was having another unspoken convo with her husband— "I think it might be best if you took us out to where you found Logan. Maybe we'll see something you didn't."

"To the base?" I asked in bewilderment. That place had always appeared to be anathema to my aunt; she never even wanted to go out and have drinks at the Enchantment Resort, which was located the next canyon over from the spot that housed the alien base. "What do you think you'll find?"

"We don't know," Martin said grimly. "But there's only one way to find out."

The four of us went in their SUV, a blocky Mercedes all-terrain vehicle that I knew had to have cost them in the low six figures. Even after all these years, I still hadn't quite figured out my aunt and uncle's finances. True, Martin was still getting residual payments from his stint on *Paranormality*, but that shouldn't have been enough on its own to support their lifestyle. Although Martin had been exiled here, the same way Gabriel had, it was clear they weren't completely cut off. Maybe the Nords kept funneling money to them out of guilt or something.

Anyway, the Mercedes forged on past the trail-head where I'd parked two nights earlier, absorbing all the shocks from the rutted earth and the various rocks strewn everywhere as if we were driving over freshly laid asphalt. Logan and I sat in the back seat, not speaking. I desperately wanted to hold his hand, but worried that even such a minor public display of affection as that might attract too much attention. So I sat stiffly next to him, one hand gripping the safety harness I wore while the other clutched my jean-clad knee, until even the Mercedes couldn't go any farther and we had to come to a halt.

We all climbed down out of the SUV, and Martin went around to the back to fetch a flashlight from the toolbox he kept in the cargo compartment. The snow had mostly melted, except for patches here and there in the shadows of juniper trees and manzanita bushes, or next to the occasional large rock. It had made the ground muddy and treacherous, though, and I was glad I was wearing my sturdy hiking boots. Logan had switched out of his lace-ups and into the footwear he'd brought with him from the base, so he was more or less good to go as well.

All right, maybe "good to go" wasn't the best way to describe the situation. His jaw grew tighter and tighter as we approached the hidden entrance to the base, the one we'd come through a few days earlier. I could tell he'd never expected that he would have to return here, and he wasn't liking it one bit.

Not that I could blame him. I didn't want to be here, no matter what secrets the place might still hold. But going along with Kirsten and Martin on this venture seemed infinitely preferable to having them head over to my parents' house to reveal a few home truths about the "IT guy" I'd brought to

Christmas dinner, so I slogged along after them, not speaking until we were almost at our destination.

"Up there," I said, pointing to the metal door that was the side entrance to the base. Because the day was still gray and cloudy, the door was even harder to see than usual.

"Got it," Martin responded, striding up the hill with such ease that I found myself huffing and puffing to keep up, even though ordinarily I would've said I was in very good shape. But then, while I had some alien DNA running through my veins, I wasn't a completely different kind of being the way Martin was. Most of the time I could ignore it, because he was just my Uncle Martin, and he looked pretty much like everyone else. Well, everyone else who'd been a male model in his youth, I supposed.

Logan didn't seem to have any trouble keeping up, either, and because both my aunt and uncle were focused on what lay ahead of them and weren't looking back at us, he reached out and took me by the hand, steadying me as we made the ascent, which seemed worse than it had been only the day before yesterday. Maybe it was. The terrain felt as if it had shifted slightly, as if the melting snow had moved some of the larger rocks around.

Eventually, though, we all made it to the door basically unscathed. Logan let go of my hand, but not before Aunt Kirsten seemed to notice. Again, I saw that flicker in her eyes, but whether it was disapproval or worry or something else entirely, I wasn't sure.

In the meantime, Martin had grasped the round handle in his gloved hands and began to turn it. The door opened into the hillside, and he pulled the flashlight from his coat pocket and switched it on. We followed him into the dark tunnel, Kirsten behind him, with me behind her and Logan taking up the rear. It seemed natural for us to fall into position like that, although I was willing to go out in front to lead the way if necessary.

Oddly, though, Martin seemed to know where he was going, guiding us from the tunnel and into the stairwell. He paused there, asking, "How many levels down?"

"Five," I replied. "But—it seems like you already know where you're going." The sentence ended with the slightest of upward inflections, a question that wasn't entirely a question.

"Not really," he said as we began our descent, our footsteps clanging off the metal stairs. "I've gotten flashes of this base from Lance's thoughts and memories, and Paul's and Persephone's as well. I've never been here in person, though."

I wondered if those "flashes" had been freely shared, or whether he'd gone in and cherry-picked the information he thought was valuable. It seemed kind of rude to me, but then, he'd first met them in an official capacity, in his cover as a Man in Black. No one back then had realized he was something even more exotic than an agent of a government organization that wasn't even supposed to exist.

"And I saw some of it when Grayson...well, when Lance did the remote viewing to watch his mission, and we all linked together to tap into it," Kirsten added. "Not all of it, of course." She glanced around, then shook her head. "I would have expected to see more damage."

"There was a good deal of damage after the reactor was destroyed, but that was on the opposite side of the base," Logan said. His voice was calm, unruffled, as if he was speaking of something that had occurred someplace very far away, rather than the base where he had been created, that would have been his home, if things had gone differently. "Rather than attempt to rebuild it, they closed it off. We have no need to go anywhere near there."

"But we do need to go here," I put in. We'd reached the sixth landing, the place where that inner voice had told me to leave the stairwell. "Through that door."

Martin opened it, and we all filed after him. The red illumination in the hallway hadn't faded, looked exactly the same as it had when I first came down here not quite forty-eight hours earlier. Unlike me, Martin paused from time to time to look at the equipment that lay discarded in the corridor, and even bent down once to lift an angular piece of metal in one hand, then set it back down again.

"What is it?" my Aunt Kirsten asked.

"Nothing," he replied. "The Reptilian version of a wrench. It just looks like they left here in a hurry."

"They *were* in a hurry," she said crisply. "They had to get their scaly asses to Courthouse Butte to tap into the vortex precisely at the moment of the solstice."

"No, it's more than that," he said, expression thoughtful. "The ones we confronted at Courthouse —those were their warriors. They would have left support staff behind at the base. But when their leader and their warriors were defeated, it looks as if they got out of here as quickly as they could. They would not have lasted long, undefended."

Kirsten ground to a halt then, and we all stopped along with her. Hands planted on her hips, she demanded, "You mean we didn't really beat all of them? There were still more left behind? That's not what you told me."

His shoulders lifted. "I didn't see the point. I knew we had won—*you* had won. We had beaten them. They fled this place, knowing they had no future here."

Something in her expression told me she would have liked to argue the point further, but then she shrugged as well. "Are we close?" she asked, shooting me a questioning glance.

"There," I replied, and pointed to the double doors at the end of the hallway.

It couldn't have been easy for Logan to go back into that chamber, to look once again on the pod that had almost become his coffin. But he followed us into the room, although he hung back near the door as Martin looked around, pausing to inspect the control pad on the pod, then moving on to run his hands over the blinking lights on the wall.

"Getting anything?" Kirsten asked. I was glad she'd spoken out loud; after all, she and Martin could have held an entire conversation without either Logan or I knowing what they were saying, if they so wished.

"Life support, mainly." He tapped a bank of lights that seemed dimmer than the others. "It looks like the system that was feeding nutrients into the pod had begun to fail. No big surprise, I suppose. Our enemies are good engineers, but this sort of thing was designed to keep someone alive for months, not years. It compensated as best it could, but...."

The words trailed off, and I could see Logan shift uncomfortably from one foot to the other. He didn't speak though, seemed content to watch as Martin poked around. It made sense for my uncle to be doing that, I supposed, since he was the only one of us who could possibly have had any kind of exposure to Reptilian technology. At last, he shook his head and turned back toward us.

"I'm not seeing much of anything here," he said. "That is, this whole room was designed to support the pod, which is interesting in its own way. From what I've heard and read, hybrids were generally created in batches, which meant a much larger room with banks of these pods, not just one on its own."

"Well, that makes sense," I put in, and both Martin and Kirsten sent me a look, as if to say, *What the heck are you talking about?*

"Logan was…a prototype," I went on. I could see him tense and decided the hell with it—I went over and stood next to him, then took his hand in mine before continuing. "Because of what Grayson had done, the aliens decided his stock was tainted, and so they intended to start over with someone fresh."

"Logan," my aunt said.

"Exactly. Martin, you probably know more about how all that works, but they did whatever it is they do when cooking up a hybrid, and the result was Logan." Even as the words left my mouth, I realized how terrible they sounded. But Logan didn't pull away, although I could feel him tense. Since I'd already put my foot in it, I decided I might as well forge ahead. "He was a…template. He hadn't yet received all his mental conditioning. He was just… left here."

Kirsten shook her head. Even in the dim reddish lighting, I could see the troubled expression in her eyes. "I'm sorry."

"Don't be," Logan said quickly. To my surprise, he managed a ghost of a smile. "It was better that I was left here. I would rather have died than to have that training completed, to be turned into something that only did the masters' bidding. Something that was meant only to destroy."

At his words, I tightened my grip on his fingers. I hadn't even thought of it that way, to realize if the aliens had had their way, he would have been a weapon, something only a few steps up from a machine. How that incomplete training had turned him into the man he'd become, a person I knew I already cared for a great deal more than I should, I didn't know. More of Sedona's magic, working on him even as he slept all those years?

Martin nodded, and Kirsten shifted closer to him. I could tell that Logan's words had moved both of them. Maybe now they would realize that rescuing him had been no mistake at all, that it was the only possible thing I could have done. I needed them on my side, because, no matter how much I knew deep down that Logan was good and not one of the enemy at all, once my parents found out about his true identity, the shit really would hit the fan.

After a long pause, during which none of us seemed to know that to say next, Martin cleared his throat. "I don't see anything much else in here. Let's poke through a few of the other rooms on this level, see if we can find something of interest."

That prospect didn't sound very appealing to me, but I knew better than to argue. We'd come all the way out here, and even though the base and its weird lighting and aura of being abandoned but not completely forgotten creeped me out in ways I really didn't want to analyze, it would be foolish not to look around a bit more.

So we left the pod chamber, as I'd come to think of it, and moved into the room to its immediate left, one full of all sorts of complicated equipment, with tubes and tanks and more banks of computers. Something about it reminded me of one of my college bio labs on steroids, and I raised an inquiring eyebrow at Martin.

"Probably where they synthesized the DNA for the hybrids," he said. "But all this equipment has been shut down for years, so any biologicals they were storing in here would have deteriorated completely."

I tried not to wrinkle my nose. At least that explained why the slightly acrid, slightly musty odor I'd first smelled when I walked into the base seemed so much stronger in here.

Again, Logan hovered near the doorway, clearly reluctant to go into the room where the aliens had mixed up the genetic cocktail that had turned him into...well, him. Although I sort of doubted they'd intended to create a soldier who wanted nothing to do with fighting.

"Martin," my aunt said then, and something in her tone made us all look over at her. She'd been rooting around in the detritus on one of the tabletops, obviously looking for something a little more valuable than rotted tubing or dead autoclaves. It seemed that she'd found it, because she lifted a gleaming, translucent rectangle a little longer than her hand and extended it to him. "Is this…?"

"It is," my uncle cut in, moving quickly so he could take the device from her. I wasn't sure what it was supposed to be. But he seemed to know how to operate it, since he pushed a tab on one end, and at once a heads-up display was projected into the air above him.

"Slick," I commented.

"It's one of their computers, the handheld kind, like one of our tablets, only far more powerful." He frowned as he gazed up at the display. "What we're seeing here is the login screen." A quick glance at Kirsten. "How're your hacking skills these days?"

"A little rusty," she said, but she didn't look dismayed by that admission. Instead, a smile played around the corners of her mouth, and she knotted her fingers together, cracking her knuckles. "But I'm sure I'll get up to speed soon enough, given the right opportunity."

He gave her an answering smile, then pushed the tab again. The display disappeared, and he gave the computer back to my aunt. "We'll take a look at the other rooms, but I think we might have found something valuable here. I doubt whoever owned it meant to leave it behind. That must have been some rush they all were in."

"Well, they *had* just faced the wrath of Kirsten Swenson," she said with a grin.

"True. And even I don't want to be on the

receiving end of that." Martin glanced over at me, then at Logan, who was frowning, clearly not understanding the joke. "This is good news, Logan. If Kirsten can get into that thing, we'll have a better idea of what they were intending, and we can discover if there are any more surprises like you here at the base."

"I was the only one," he said slowly, and Kirsten responded,

"That you know of. This little guy"—she waved the computer she held—"might give us some more insights. In the meantime, though, I'm fine with getting the heck out of here. This place gives me the creeps."

"The other rooms first," Martin said.

She didn't look thrilled by that prospect, but she didn't protest. "If we have to. But I think we're wasting our time."

Her words turned out to be prophetic, because after that first lab, we didn't find much of anything. They were intrigued by the storeroom, once Logan had opened the thumb lock, but there wasn't much out of the ordinary to be discovered in that chamber. Just clothing and boots. Wherever the Reptilians had kept the weapons for their hybrid soldiers, it was someplace else. Another room had rows of the cloning pods, but their displays were dark, and when Martin went to open one of them, it was empty. So probably Logan's "brothers" would have ended up here, if the aliens hadn't run out of time.

Looking at those empty pods, I wondered how close they'd come to achieving their goal. Pretty damn close, if the stories I'd heard were any indication. I flickered a glance in my aunt and uncle's direction, but they were busy inspecting the pods and weren't paying attention to me. Their expressions were serious, their focus on the alien equipment. And yet they looked ordinary enough, two attractive, prosperous people somewhere in their thirties. They were so much more than that, though. Because of my aunt, the Reptilians had been driven away from here, had lost their chance to tap into Sedona's unique energy and twist it to their own purposes. One woman, standing up to an enemy most people didn't even believe existed.

She finally seemed to notice me looking at her, and asked, "Have you found something?"

"No," I replied. "Just thinking."

Only a nod in reply, which could have meant anything. I'd never heard that she was psychic with anyone except Martin—it was something about the way they were bonded as a couple, not an intrinsic gift, the way it was with Persephone and her daughter Taryn—but I got the impression that my aunt had caught a hint of what I was thinking. Something in my expression, possibly.

"Well," Martin said, "it's clear they were planning for a bigger operation but were cut off at the pass. I think that should do it for now. Ready to head home?"

"God, yes," my aunt said. "If you want to come back out here with Lance and poke around, go right ahead."

"I'm not sure that's such a good idea," Martin told her. His gaze slid in my direction and back toward her, and she seemed to get the implication.

"Oh, right. We'll let this be our little secret for now."

I exhaled in relief, then exited the room, Logan right behind me. If I didn't like staring at all those pods, I could only imagine how he must have felt, having to look at them. Every one of those coffin-like contraptions could only serve to remind him that he had never been intended to be unique, that he was only supposed to be one piece in a much bigger army.

This time, I was mentally prepared for the climb back up to the surface, although I couldn't say I enjoyed it any more than I had on the last go-'round. When we emerged, a cold, sleety rain was falling. Too bad it wasn't quite cold enough for snow. That would have been a lot easier to deal with.

We trudged through the mud, not speaking, just wanting to get back to the shelter of the Mercedes. I felt awful about tracking so much red mud into Martin's and Kirsten's car, but there wasn't much I could do about that.

"It's fine," my aunt said, apparently noticing the way I glanced down at the reddish footprints I'd just left on the floor mat. "We'll take it to get cleaned out tomorrow."

"I probably should have checked the weather reports—"

"What good would that have done? Your uncle and I wanted to come out here. A little mud is no big deal...not compared to what we may have found." Her gaze fell to the translucent device she held, and she ran a thumb over its smooth surface. "I can't wait to unlock this thing."

In the back seat, Logan and I exchanged a glance. It didn't appear that either one of us was too eager to discover any secrets his former masters might have left behind.

CHAPTER NINE

THEY DROPPED LOGAN AND ME OFF AT THE COTTAGE, and zoomed away as quickly as the slick streets would allow. It seemed clear enough that Kirsten didn't want to waste any more time before settling down to hack at the alien computer.

Logan watched them disappear around the corner, a frown tugging at his brow. I felt uneasy myself, although I couldn't say why. Maybe it was just that I was cold and damp.

That would be easy enough to remedy, though. I unlocked the door and let us in, then stopped to hang my coat on the rack. It was wool treated to repel water, but there was only so much it could do before it started to get waterlogged. I owned more weather-worthy jackets, but I hadn't thought I'd need something like that on this trip, since they were the sort of thing I wore when I went hiking, and this holiday trip to Sedona had originally been intended as more of an indoor kind of visit.

"Hey," I said to Logan, who was still looking worried, mouth tight. "It'll be all right. We can thaw out a little, change into some dry clothes, and then we'll go to the store and load up on all kinds of fun stuff. How about some fondue and an amusing cabernet?"

He didn't smile. "Fondue?"

"Melted cheese that you eat with bread. The perfect thing for having a picnic in front of the fire-place." I went to him and put my arms around him, and, after a brief hesitation, he responded, holding me in a tight embrace. We stood that way for a moment, and then I said, "I'm sorry you had to go back there."

"It's all right. It's important to have as much data as possible." A second ticked by, and then another. I could feel his hand moving up to brush against the damp ends of my hair. "It is…kind…of your aunt and uncle not to say anything about me."

"My Aunt Kirsten is definitely cool," I said. "That is, I think she understands. She told me once that she felt as if she never really fit in, but she always thought it was because her mother had taken off when she was so little, that she'd been raised by her grandparents. But then when she found out that Gabriel was her father, and what he actually was, she realized she'd felt that way because she really *was* different."

The day my aunt and I had talked was just as vivid to me now as it had been eight years ago, when I'd had a blowout with my mother over my decision to go to school in Tucson rather than stay safely up here in northern Arizona. It hadn't helped that I'd broken up with my boyfriend right before homecoming. I hadn't wanted to, but he'd been putting way too much pressure on me. Not that kind of pressure —I'd lost my virginity to him that summer, while his parents were visiting family in Scottsdale and we had the house to ourselves for the day. Dylan was going to NAU and wanted me to go there, too, so we could stay together. In his mind, he'd already planned out the next five years, had visualized us getting married after we graduated, starting a family. And that thought had terrified me, not just because I didn't want to settle down so soon, but also because I didn't know if I could have normal children, didn't want to even contemplate telling him the truth about my origins.

So it all came to a head, and my mother was giving me a guilt trip about going so far from home, off someplace where Lance and Martin and Kirsten couldn't protect me. "You could attract all kinds of attention!" she'd snapped.

And I'd kind of snapped, too. I didn't even reply, just got my car keys and stormed out of there. At first, I drove into town, not knowing where I was going, and then I found myself heading south before I cut up the road that led to my aunt's house. Why I'd gone there and not to the home of a friend, I didn't know at the time, but after I knocked and Kirsten answered the door, then took one look at me and gave me a hug, I understood why. I could talk to her freely. I wouldn't have to hide anything.

She understood why I felt like such an oddball, and she also understood the need to get away. "It can get a little suffocating here," she'd said. "I think you should go to Tucson, spread your wings a little. We'll all still be here when you're ready to come home."

"And you don't think it will be dangerous?" I asked. "It's been quiet here, but the MUFON groups have never stopped reporting activity in the southern part of the state."

At first, she hadn't answered, but had stared off into the distance, as if she could somehow see across the hundreds of miles that separated her home from the university down in Tucson. "I think it will be fine," she said at last. "If that's where you want to go, then that's where you should go. I'll handle your mother."

Which she had. I didn't know exactly what she said, but my mother backed off, although I knew she still wasn't happy about the situation. That was fine by me; I didn't need her to be happy. I just needed her to be accepting. And she gradually had come to accept the situation as the years went by, but I was pretty sure she still felt rejected in some way, that if she'd been a better mother, I wouldn't have felt the need to leave home and never come back. I knew there was no way I could convince her it was nothing personal, so I'd left it alone, and so had she.

Logan's voice brought me back to the present as he murmured, "I suppose I hadn't thought how difficult it must have been for you. At least where I came from, I would not have had to hide what I was."

"I lived through it." Gently, I pulled away from him, then gazed up into his face. "All the same, I can't tell you how glad I am that I found you, that I have someone I can share all this with, someone who'll believe me."

He bent and kissed the top of my head, lips warm against my damp hair. "I am very glad as well."

We changed into dry clothes after that. Through some unspoken signal, we both seemed to agree that this was not the time for more sex, and after we were dressed and I'd blow-dried the last of the rain out of my hair, we suited back up again and headed out to the store.

By then, the rain had stopped, although the streets were slick and the air very cold. If the clouds stayed around and had some more moisture left in them, then we might get snow again that night. The prospect didn't bother me, as I knew after this outing, we'd cocoon at the cottage for the rest of the day.

So we stocked up on all manner of items that

were tasty rather than nutritious, although I did get some chicken and a few other things so I could make us a real dinner that night. True, I wasn't quite the whiz in the kitchen my mother was, but I did okay, and going over to Gabriel's and watching him cook during the past year had also helped to hone my skills. It would be fine.

At the store, I could see the way Logan looked around in astonishment at the variety of food and other items offered for sale, but he kept his thoughts to himself, seemingly content to nod when I would suggest something to add to the shopping cart. It made sense that he would follow my lead, as I doubted his "training" covered fondue or chicken cacciatore or chocolate cake.

And because it was the day after Christmas, and a lot of people were staying home to work off their respective ham or turkey comas, the store wasn't very busy. Fate must have been smiling on me, because Logan and I didn't bump into one person I knew. Even the check-out girl was someone I hadn't met before, and although she shot an admiring glance in my companion's direction, she didn't say anything except the obligatory "happy holidays" before pushing the button on the register to send the receipt to my phone.

By then, we were both ravenously hungry—it was almost two o'clock, and all we'd had to eat was some croissants that morning—so I got right on the fondue while Logan went out to the living room and started the fire back up again. A little after that, I heard some music come on. Not the holiday standards I'd been playing the other night, but a soft New Age-y piece with native flute accompaniment. It was the sort of thing you might hear in any of the "woo-woo" shops in uptown, but I thought it seemed to fit. Hard-edged guitars or percussive electronica would have been way too disruptive.

"Is it all right?" he asked, coming back into the kitchen.

"Sounds great," I replied as I stirred away at the fondue. It was almost ready to be transferred from the cooktop to the pot I had waiting. Thank goodness my mother kept the kitchen here stocked just as well as she did the bathroom. Fondue pots weren't exactly standard fare in most vacation cottages. "Why did you pick that station?"

"I liked how it sounded," he said simply.

You couldn't really argue with that. I smiled at him, then said, "That tray with the bread and meat is ready to go. Can you go ahead and take it out to the living room?"

"Of course." He picked it up and took it over to the coffee table, where a bottle of wine and two glasses were already waiting. Who cared if it was two o'clock in the afternoon? It was the holidays, after all.

I fetched a spoon and dipped it into the fondue, getting myself a small sample so I'd know it was okay. Actually, it was more than okay, so I nodded in approval and poured the cheese mixture from the saucepan into the fondue pot, then brought it out to the living room before placing it on its little stand. "Lighter?" I asked Logan.

He brought it to me from the spot where it had been resting on the mantel, and I took it and lit the little container of gel fuel under the pot. This procedure clearly puzzled him, since he said, "What is that for?"

"To keep the cheese liquid. Without constant heat being applied, it would go back to a solid form, and that's no fun when you're trying to dip bread into it."

This quasi-scientific explanation appeared to satisfy him, and he sat down on the sofa, then waited for me to join him. It felt good to settle myself down at his side, to be close enough that I could feel the warmth of his body. A thrill went through me, but I told myself there would be plenty of time for that later. Right then, we needed to eat.

So we did, with me showing Logan how to put the cubes of bread on the long-handled little spear-like forks and dunk them in the cheese. He poured wine for me, and we drank and ate and watched the flames dance in the hearth while the day outside grew darker, even though we were hours away from sunset. We didn't talk about the base. Instead, he asked me about why I decided to study meteorology, and I talked about the spectacular weather we had here in Sedona, the monsoon storms in the summer, the light dusting of snow we would sometimes get, the way the sky and the clouds were always doing something different. What I didn't bother to mention was how many people assumed I was majoring in meteorology because I wanted to do weather reports on TV or something—"oh, you're such a pretty girl, that makes sense"—when in reality I just loved weather, in all its various moods and guises.

Maybe some of my passion for the subject got through to him, because he nodded as I spoke, clearly fascinated. And at one point, his gaze flickered toward the window, and he said, "It looks as if your snow has returned."

It was true—light, dry flakes had begun to fall again, their movements slow and delicate, as there wasn't much wind. "This low-pressure system is pretty persistent," I said, then swallowed the last of the wine in my glass and reached out to pour myself some more. "The models could change, but there's a good chance it might hang around for another few days. It's supposed to be clear by New Year's, though." I fell silent then, thinking of how I was due to be back up in Flagstaff on the thirtieth. Would I take Logan with me? I couldn't imagine doing anything else—I certainly didn't want to leave him behind here—but that was sort of a big step, considering I'd only known him for two days.

"This New Year's," he said, watching me carefully. "It is important? Like Christmas?"

"Well, it's a holiday, but it's not really like Christmas. That is, it doesn't have any kind of religious underpinnings. It's just sort of how we celebrate the passage of time. The start of the new year is a time for new beginnings, so we throw a big party on the thirty-first of December to ring in the new."

His eyebrows pulled together as he appeared to mull that over. After spearing a piece of bread, dipping it in the cheese, and eating it thoughtfully, he said, "But surely this is an arbitrary marker? Time is continuous…it doesn't make any distinction between one year and another."

I couldn't help chuckling at his comment. "You sound like Paul Oliver. He's said the same thing on more than one occasion. Of course, Persephone usually tells him to let it go, especially since New Year's is such a great excuse to drink champagne."

"Champagne?"

"Like wine," I explained, lifting my glass. "But fizzy. And much paler than this cabernet we're drinking. It's made from grapes, though, just like wine, and is put through a special fermentation process so it sparkles. We like to drink it for special occasions."

"Like New Year's."

"And birthdays and weddings and…." I let the words trail off, since he was watching me closely, and I could feel my cheeks flush at that foolish mention of weddings. That was a topic I'd prefer to avoid. To cover up my awkwardness, I said quickly, "You know, I thought of something while I was in the kitchen, making the fondue."

"What is that?"

I sipped some more wine, then set my glass back

down on the coffee table. "Well, if the aliens really did…create you…after they discovered it was one of their own hybrids that had attacked their base, then you and I are almost exactly the same age. I was born just a few months afterward."

For a few seconds, he didn't reply, although I could almost see him doing the math in his head. "My information indicates that human females gestate their young for approximately nine months. So how did that happen?"

"Normal human pregnancies last nine months," I replied, wishing we hadn't gotten on this topic, either. Still, if I backpedaled now, it would be painfully obvious what I was doing. "I guess the rules change when the father is a hybrid. My mother only carried me for three months. Luckily, when I came into the world, I looked like any other full-term baby, so that cut down on the explanations." Despite myself, I grinned. "It's probably something she would've kept to herself, even without the whole alien connection, because otherwise, every woman in the world would have wanted to know the secret to delivering a full-term infant after only three months of pregnancy."

"Why?"

"Well, having never been pregnant myself, I can't speak from personal experience. But I suppose pretty much any woman would rather suffer the cravings and the nausea and the bloat and the swollen ankles for only three months rather than nine."

I could tell my answer surprised him. He tilted his head to one side, considering me. "That doesn't sound like a very efficient way to reproduce."

"In a lot of ways, it isn't, but it's kind of what we're stuck with for now, since we don't have teams of cloning experts and nice, neat little pods to grow people in."

As soon as the words left my mouth, I regretted them. Logan's expression clouded, and he glanced away from me. "Perhaps," he said slowly. "But at least you have parents and siblings...family. I have nothing."

My heart ached for him then. Growing up, I'd felt alone, felt isolated, the only one of my kind in the entire world, even if I did look like everyone else. But at least I had my family, annoying as they could be sometimes. Logan had no one.

Well, that wasn't quite true.

"You have me," I said softly, reaching out to him, pulling him toward me so I could kiss him on the mouth.

Almost at once, the darkness I'd seen in his eyes disappeared, and he responded, deepening the kiss so I could taste the richness of his mouth, the traces of the wine he'd just drunk. Warmth flowed through my body, heat curling in my belly. I still wasn't used to the way his touch, his kiss, could make me respond. Before, I'd always been fairly analytical about the whole thing...yes, this feels good, no, I don't like that much. I'd always *thought*.

Now, though, I just wanted to be swept up in him.

And that was what happened next—Logan taking me in his arms, lifting me from the couch as if I weighed nothing. He took me into the bedroom, and soon afterward, the clothes we'd put on just a few hours earlier were discarded on the floor, impediments to the closeness I knew we both craved. His touch awoke fire in every limb, in the very core of my being, and after he made love to me with his fingers and his tongue, he pulled me down on top of him, hands caressing my breasts as I rode him, letting him fill me, bringing me to here and now.

In that moment, the future didn't matter so much. There was only the two of us, finding completion.

The next day was the "spa day" excursion with the gang. I really didn't feel like going, would have much rather stayed at the cottage with Logan, but he assured me he would be all right.

"I have the television, and the internet," he said, gesturing toward my laptop where I'd left it set up on the dining room table for him.

Oddly, I didn't have any problems with leaving my computer for him to use. There wasn't anything incriminating on there, except maybe my master's thesis, an analysis of how global climate change had affected air currents in the northern plateaus of Arizona. Work emails, but even the ones from Nate were all correct and proper. The only intimate thing we'd ever shared was some lingering eye contact from time to time, and of course there was no physical evidence of any of that.

"You'll probably have a better time than I will," I told him, intending my words to be a joke, but he frowned.

"I thought this was supposed to be an enjoyable day for you."

"It is. I mean, I'm sure it will be okay, but...." Shrugging, I let the words die away, since I wasn't sure what I'd intended to say in the first place. "I guess sometimes I get tired of having family togetherness foisted on me."

"They only want to see you. Is that strange?"

I shook my head. "No, it's not strange. I'm the one who's strange."

A smile touched his lips, and I wanted to reach out and pull him to me, kiss him heartily and head straight back to the bedroom. But no—I'd already done my makeup and my hair, and had less than five minutes to get to the spa where we were all meeting. It was silly of me to have done even that much, since I'd opted for a facial, but I was past the point where I was comfortable walking out of the house with absolutely no makeup on. The aesthetician would just have to scrub it off.

"I don't think you're strange," Logan said. "I think...I think you're wonderful."

The breath caught in my throat then. Had anyone I'd been with before ever said anything like that? I didn't think so. Compliments, sure, on the order of "you're looking great tonight" for the occasions when I'd put a little extra effort into my appearance, but that was about it. I couldn't even say whose fault that was. It wasn't as if I'd ever opened up to any of those men. Not really. I'd shared more honest moments with Logan in the few days I'd known him than in the months I'd spent in my longest-running relationship, which had collapsed around the year mark.

"You're pretty amazing yourself," I said lightly, pushing the words past the sudden tightness in my throat. "But I need to get going. There are leftovers in the refrigerator, so you're taken care of for lunch, and I'll be home for dinner. Try not to watch too much porn while I'm gone."

"Porn?" he echoed, with a lift of his eyebrows, and I grinned, kissed him quickly on the cheek, and let myself out without answering.

Luckily, the Sedona Rouge resort wasn't that far from the cottage, so even though I'd left later than I wanted to, I wasn't the last one to show up. No, that honor went to my Aunt Kirsten. She and Callista pulled into the parking lot almost fifteen minutes late, and I could tell from the way my cousin climbed out of the car and stalked toward us that she wasn't exactly thrilled with her mother.

As Callista was greeting the others—my mother and my sisters Kelsey and Melissa, then Persephone and Taryn Oliver—I murmured to Kirsten as she approached, "Everything okay?"

"Oh, sure," she responded, sounding breezy enough, but I could tell something was off. As I shot her a questioning look, she lowered her voice and added, "All right, that computer we found is really kicking my rear end. Apparently, I'm not as up on this stuff as I thought I was. We might have to call in the big guns."

"'Big guns'?" I repeated, but in that moment, my mother approached us, and Kirsten put on what I thought of as her public face, all smiles and cheeriness. Whoever or whatever she was referring to, it would have to wait until we weren't surrounded by a gaggle of other women.

And although I'd been less than thrilled about abandoning Logan for the day, it actually felt good to get that facial, to breathe in the warm, aromatic steam and let myself relax. Although everyone else had opted for massages, Taryn shared my aversion to having strangers touch her, and so she got a facial along with me, as well as a makeup application afterward.

"Now that we're all glam, it's kind of a bummer we're not doing anything special," she said, after inspecting her eye makeup one last time in the mirror, then shaking out her heavy, warm brown curls. She glanced over at me, green eyes glinting. "Or maybe I'm speaking for myself. Do you have any big plans with Logan for tonight?"

Besides getting laid? I thought, but I knew I couldn't respond that way to her. I was just enough older—she'd turned twenty-one this past October—that it would have felt strange to be quite so blunt. Anyway, we were friendly, but not friends, since the separation in our ages had mostly kept us from attending the same school at the same time or hanging out all that much. She and Callista and Kelsey were a lot closer, since my cousin and my sister were both twenty-two.

"I hadn't really thought about it," I said, as casually as I could. "Maybe we'll go out to dinner."

"You should take him out and show him off," Taryn replied. "He's too hot to just sit around the house with."

I tried not to smile too widely. There had been just the slightest touch of jealousy in her tone. She was a very pretty girl, but, just like her mother had back in the day, she didn't have much luck with guys. Being a mind reader could be a turn-off for a lot of men. "I'll keep that in mind."

We all met up for lunch, which was about as chaotic as one would expect of a meal with eight women at the table. Everyone was trying to pry more information from me about Logan, and I found myself having to make up more and more lies—how we'd met, who had asked whom out for the first date, whether I thought it was serious. And all through it, my Aunt Kirsten's blue eyes had danced with amusement, since of course she knew the truth. Thank God she showed no sign of wanting to reveal Logan's secret. But I reflected that she had a vested interest in the subterfuge as well, since I had a feeling my mother would be less than thrilled to discover that her sister had been keeping a secret of such magnitude from her.

After lunch, it was time for our mani/pedis, and although we were a big group, the staff at the resort managed everything fairly well. I did enjoy having my fingers and toes done, even if the man waiting for me back at the house was actually the only person who'd get to see said toes, since late December in northern Arizona wasn't exactly sandal weather.

Because the bad old days of having to wait for a pedicure to dry were long gone, I was able to get back into my boots and socks immediately after we were done. As the others were similarly putting themselves back together, since no one wanted to brave the fifty-degree weather in flip-flops, my mother said, "So, Lance and I were talking about having everyone over on the twenty-eighth to watch the Mars landing. Are you all still interested?"

I really wasn't—that is, I wanted to watch the landing, but I would've much preferred to do it in private with Logan, not at another enormous, exhausting gathering. However, I knew it was best not to fight it. Too much avoiding the family, and my mother would start to pry. My best defense was to act as normal as possible.

"Sure," I said, while my Aunt Kirsten and Persephone voiced their agreement. Their daughters nodded, although Taryn looked more amused than anything...probably because she knew my sister Kelsey was in on the plan mainly since Michael would be there. At least, I assumed he would be.

It was logistics after that, deciding when to convene, working out who would bring what to munch on. Through all of it, I could feel myself getting more and more tense as time ticked on. It was now past four, and Logan had been alone at the house all that time. Anything could have happened.

Nothing has happened, I told myself. *You'll get home, and he'll be sitting on the couch, watching football and drinking a beer.*

Okay, scratch the beer, as there wasn't any at the cottage. Otherwise, I thought I was pretty spot-on in that assessment, except that I had a feeling he'd be watching a nature show or a documentary of some sort. So far, I hadn't seen any evidence of him being interested in sports, for which I was thankful. I'd spent approximately five months being a Sun Devils widow back in college, and that was enough for me.

Eventually, though, we all said our goodbyes, and I slid into the back seat of the car, too tired to deal with driving myself. "Home, James," I said, which the car was smart enough to interpret as "take me back to the house." Even a few years ago, the vehicle's limited AI wouldn't have had the sophistication to understand such differences, and probably would have started driving me back to my apartment in Flagstaff. Now, though, I didn't have to worry.

As we hummed along through traffic, I thought about what Taryn had said, how I should go out someplace with Logan. He'd done well enough at the grocery store; would he be up to a dinner out somewhere? Maybe a quiet meal in one of Sedona's more intimate restaurants. Not that my hometown had much of a bustling nightlife. From time to time, someone had thought to start up a nightclub, at least one place where people could go out dancing, but that just wasn't the vibe here. Even Cottonwood had more to offer when it came to that sort of thing.

However, a nice dinner right in town, not too far from the cottage...that should be fine. I'd bought food to make for tonight, but it could wait until tomorrow.

Humming, I got out of the car and let myself in, expecting to see the flat display mounted above the mantel alive with some kind of documentary or news show. It was quiet and dark, though, as was my laptop, which still sat where I had left it on the dining room table.

"Logan?" I called out. Maybe he was in the bathroom or something.

But the door to the bathroom stood open, as did the doors to the two bedrooms. He wasn't there, and neither was he in the kitchen, raiding the refrigerator. The house was completely empty.

I went back out to the living room, trying to tell myself not to have a panic attack, but I could feel my breathing accelerate even as my pulse ratcheted upward.

Logan was gone.

CHAPTER TEN

I STOOD THERE FOR THE LONGEST MOMENT, FEELING AS IF I was about to pass out at any second. Then my sanity reasserted itself, and asked, *Have you checked outside?*

No, of course not, because I'd been too busy assuming the worst.

Still wearing my coat, I hurried out the back door, then went down the path that led to the creek. Only when I was almost there, could hear it burbling cheerfully away as it flowed over the stones in its bed, did I realize that this was a wasted effort. I'd had to use my key to unlock the deadbolt on the back door to let myself out, so of course Logan couldn't be down here. I hadn't given him a key, since I'd seen no need to. We were together almost all the time anyway.

Even so, even though I knew the effort would be

futile, I walked the last few yards down to the creek. No one was there, of course, except a large raven perched on a log on the other side of the stream. It tilted its head at me, gave what sounded like a very mocking *caw*, and took off into the icy air.

Anxiety sending darting little chills through me, I walked back up to the house. What should I do next? Get in the car and drive all over town looking for him? Call the police? That wouldn't work, obviously. He was a stranger from nowhere, had no identity that could be tracked. Besides, he hadn't been gone long enough for me to file a report.

All right, I couldn't contact the police, but I could call my aunt. At least she knew who—and what—Logan was. She might be able to offer some help. For all I knew, she and Martin could sense where Logan had gone and would be able to track him down right away.

It was a long shot, but it was better than nothing. I let myself back in the house and dug my phone out of my purse, then said, "Kirsten Jones. Home."

I decided to call that number instead of her cell, just because I had a feeling she wouldn't have run any errands on the way home, but would have gone straight back to the house so she could start hacking away at that alien computer again.

The phone rang. "Hello?"

My cousin Callista. "Hey, Cal, can I talk to your mom for a minute?"

"Sure. Just a sec." She set down the phone; I could

hear male voices talking and laughing in the background, although I couldn't make out the individuals involved in the conversation. Clearly, the guys had gotten together while all the "girls" were off at the spa.

I waited, tapping my foot in impatience, although in reality my aunt picked up probably less than thirty seconds later. "Grace?"

"He's gone!" I blurted. "I've looked everywhere, and—"

"Hang on a sec," she said, sounding too calm for my taste. "Who's gone?"

"Logan! I got back to the house, and—"

She broke in again. "He's not gone, Grace...he's right here."

That one took a few seconds to sink in. "He's *what?*"

"He's here. Apparently, the guys decided it would be fun to go out shooting while we were at the spa, and they went by and collected Logan not too long after you left. Martin said he sent you a text."

I hadn't looked at my phone after I got to the spa, mostly because I was busy, and I'd figured that anyone who would be calling me was probably right there at the spa with me. "Well, I didn't get it."

A pause. "Oh, sweetie, sorry about that. I'm sure he didn't mean to worry you." Her voice lowered, and she added, "It wasn't really his idea. Lance and Paul started talking about bringing Logan along, getting to know him better, and Martin went along with it because he figured it would be safer if he was there to do any necessary damage control."

"And was there any?" I asked, trying to control the fury boiling inside me.

"Any what?"

"Damage control."

"No," she said. "It was fine. *He's* fine. They hadn't meant to stay out this long, but they ended up back here, having a beer. But they're wrapping it up. I'll have Martin drop Logan back at your place as soon as they're done."

It was on my lips to say forget it, that I'd be right over to get Logan myself, but I knew that suggestion wouldn't go over very well. The last thing I wanted was to look as if I was overly concerned about the situation. If it had been Lance offering to bring Logan over, I might have still forced the issue, but Martin seemed safe enough.

"Okay," I said at last. "Tell him he shouldn't be too late, since we have dinner reservations."

"All right," my aunt replied, sounding surprised. But she didn't challenge me, and merely added, "I'll let him know." Then she hung up, and I tossed my phone in my purse, making a sound just a little too close to a growl.

Obviously, I couldn't leave the man alone for even a few hours.

To be fair, he did come home not too long after I'd spoken to Kirsten—twenty minutes at the most. I'd decided that standing at the door and waiting with my arms crossed was a little too 1950s housewife, so I settled for sitting down at the dining room table and checking my neglected email. Nothing much of note there, except one email from, of all people, Nate Williams.

I hope you had a good holiday. We're all looking forward to seeing you back here on Mars Hill. There'll be a landing viewing party here on the 28th, just in case you were thinking about coming back early.

Was that the world's most oblique invitation for a date, or was I reading way more into Nate's email than I should? Anyway, that ship had sailed…or rather, it hadn't figured out how to get itself untied from the dock.

Before I could lose my nerve, I quickly replied, *That sounds like fun, Nate, but my family is having their own viewing party here in Sedona. I'll see you on the 30th. Take care!*

Then I hit "send," and right after that, I heard a knock at the door. I closed the laptop and went to answer the knock. Logan was standing there, wearing his overcoat, combat boots spattered with red Sedona mud, a sheepish expression on his face.

"I—" he began, and I shook my head.

"It's fine. Just get inside."

He obeyed with some alacrity, and I shut the door. For a few seconds, neither of us spoke. Then, probably just so he would be doing something, he began to unbutton his coat. I waited, not sure what to say. I was angry, but not really with him. What else could he have done but go along? If he'd protested too loudly, it would have just raised their suspicions... Lance's particularly. Now, Lance I could have cheerfully smacked upside the head. Not that I would ever have the *cojones* to do something like that.

At last, Logan hung up his coat and turned to look at me, gaze intent on my face. "I'm sorry," he said.

"No need," I replied crisply. "It's not your fault." I paused, trying to think of the best way to get into this without Logan thinking my anger was directed at him instead of Lance. "Can you tell me what happened?"

"They came by," Logan said. "Your father... Lance, that is...and your brother, then Paul Oliver and his son, and Martin Jones. Martin said they would have called, but they didn't know if I would have picked up. So they drove over, asked me if I wanted to go shooting with them...although it didn't feel quite like a request."

"That's because it wasn't." I'd lived with Lance for way too long not to know how he would've handled it. He'd be all casual, not-quite smiling, giving the distinct impression that if you didn't go along with him, you'd be in a world of trouble. Guess you could take the man out of Special Forces, but you couldn't take the Special Forces out of the man.

Logan appeared to digest my reply for a few seconds, then went on, "But Martin nodded at me when the others weren't looking. I assumed that was his way of saying it was all right. So I told them it sounded like fun, and I went along."

"And was it?"

"What?"

"Fun."

Another hesitation. "It is—I'm not sure, to be frank. I find it a little difficult to understand a pastime that includes using weapons meant for killing people, simply to shoot at targets or empty cans and bottles."

Despite myself, I couldn't help smiling at that observation, since I'd thought the same thing more than once over the years. Yes, I could shoot, because Lance wouldn't have it any other way, but that didn't mean I particularly enjoyed it. "I hope you kept those thoughts to yourself."

"Of course. In fact, Lance was surprised by how well I could shoot. He asked me if I'd ever been in the military."

Oh, boy. "What did you tell him?"

"That no, I hadn't, but I played a lot of your video games."

I would have loved to have seen Lance's expression following that reply, especially since he thought video games were a waste of time and would give Kevin holy hell if he wasted more than a half hour or so on them at any one time. That wasn't as much of a hardship as it might have been for other people, since Kevin took after Lance and was naturally outdoorsy, would prefer to be out hiking around or trailblazing in the Jeep or whatever. That was probably why he didn't have a problem working basically full-time hours in Lance's tour business.

"So what did Lance say to that?"

A shrug. "Not much."

All right, so it sounded as if Logan had handled himself far better than I might have, had our situations been reversed. "And that was it?"

"Mainly. We went shooting for a few hours, had a late lunch at a restaurant where I had something called a cheeseburger." An expression that was dangerously close to pure bliss passed over his face. "It was very good."

"I'm sure it was."

He seemed to understand from my tone that I wanted him to tell me more, so he added, "After lunch, we went shooting again, at a different spot where Lance had to take the Jeep off the road for a while, and then we went to Martin's house and drank what you call a beer."

"Did you like it?" I inquired, wondering if the guys had managed to turn my hybrid soldier into an American good ol' boy in one afternoon.

"Not particularly. I would have preferred to have a glass of wine."

I couldn't help it. I burst out laughing, then went over and wrapped my arms around him, holding him close. He smelled of pine and juniper and clean male sweat, and I just wanted to bury my face in his chest and breathe him in.

"Well, I think we can manage that," I said, after pulling away slightly. "I was thinking we could go out for a nice dinner tonight. If, that is, you're not too full of cheeseburger to enjoy it."

Being Logan, he considered my comment carefully before he replied. "I think it should be all right. I was fairly active today."

"Yes, I suppose you were," I said. "In fact, you were active enough that I think you should have another shower."

Something silvery glinted in those clear gray eyes of his. "Would you like to join me?"

I would have…if I hadn't just had someone make sure my face was looking just about as good as it possibly could. "Not this time. I don't want to wash off this makeup."

He regarded me for a few seconds. "You do look…different."

"Different how?"

"Like you…but not."

I wasn't going to try to figure out if that was a compliment or not. "Get in the shower, Logan. You and I can play rubber duckie later."

And while he was puzzling that out, I chuckled and went to retrieve my phone. It was late in the day, but I figured I'd still be able to get us a reservation someplace decent.

Sure enough, about an hour and a half later, we were sitting in Mariposa, a restaurant that during the day had a spectacular view of some of Sedona's more distinctive formations—Coffeepot Rock, Big Thunder Mountain. Now it was full dark, and so you couldn't see much of anything except the faint flickers from the lights of houses built across the gully, and even those were mostly obscured by the junipers that grew so thickly in the area.

Even so, the place was beautiful, with its soaring ceilings and use of natural wood and stone. Logan and I were given a secluded table near one of the windows, and he stared out into the blackness as if he could actually see what was out there. For all I knew, maybe he could. I had very good night vision —better than anyone else I knew—and it was entirely possible that Logan's would be even better, since he didn't have nearly as much human blood mixed in as I did.

But I really didn't want to think about that right then. I just wanted to gaze across the table at him, think how handsome he looked in his dark button-down shirt, remember what it was like to kiss those firm, beautifully shaped lips, to run my hands over the muscles that the shirt really couldn't hide.

I'd been lucky avoiding contact with casual friends and acquaintances so far, but I should have known my luck wouldn't last forever. The young woman who headed over to our table to take our order looked familiar even from far away, and as she approached, I realized she was someone I'd gone to high school with…and someone I hadn't been exactly good friends with, either. She'd dated my ex-boyfriend Dylan before he and I got together, and although I certainly wasn't the reason for their breakup, she always believed it was my fault somehow.

You'd think the passage of time might have healed that wound, but apparently not. She stopped at our table, gave Logan a not very professional once-over, and then tracked toward me, the fake smile on her face disappearing once she recognized who I was.

"Hi, Alex," I said, figuring I might as well get it over with.

"Oh, hi, Grace. I didn't recognize you at first." She pulled the waiter's notepad out of her pocket. "Welcome to Mariposa. Your first time here?" Her tone seemed to indicate that I wasn't classy enough to frequent an establishment like this, but the joke was on her. She couldn't have been working here all that long, or she would have known it was a family favorite for special occasions.

But since the last thing I wanted was a confrontation, I decided to compromise. "No, it's not my first time, but it's been a while. I'm up in Flagstaff now."

"Oh," she said, sounding singularly unimpressed. "And this is…?"

I really didn't want to make the introduction, but there wasn't much I could do about it now. "Alex, this is Logan Myles. He came down to Sedona to spend the holidays with me." I let her stew on that for a few seconds; in general, you just didn't bring a significant other around for the holidays unless whatever relationship you had was fairly serious. "Logan, this is Alex Jacoby. We went to high school together."

"It's very nice to meet you," he said in that charming, grave way he had.

It had an effect on her, I could tell. Her cheeks grew a little pink, and she replied, "Very nice to meet you, too." She paused, then said, "Anyway...our specials tonight are a chile tamale with bison, wild boar, and venison, seared swordfish, or prime rib. Have you looked at the wine list?"

"Not yet," I replied. "We'll take a look and let you know."

"Take your time," she said. Her tone seemed to indicate she'd let us stew in our own juices for far longer than it would actually take to choose our entrees and the wine to accompany them.

After she had gone, Logan set down his menu and gave me a considering look. "It could be that I'm imagining things, but I get the impression that you two aren't actually friends."

"That's an understatement." I really didn't want to go into the whole thing, especially since it was all high school stuff and therefore shouldn't even be relevant anymore, but I could tell he wanted to hear what I had to say on the subject. "It's silly—she used to date a boy in high school, and he broke up with her and started dating me, and it just…upset her."

"But why would it still be bothering her? You would have attended your secondary school some years ago, correct?"

"That's right." I lifted my glass of water and drank, aware of Logan's eyes on me the whole time. "Some people have a hard time letting go, I guess. Also, she was pretty popular in high school, and I really wasn't, so I think she was annoyed that Dylan apparently preferred being with me."

Logan glanced away from me in the direction Alex had gone, but she was nowhere in sight. "I'm not sure I understand this popularity concept. You're certainly much lovelier than she is."

My cheeks heated, but I hoped he wouldn't be able to tell. The lighting in the restaurant was dim, intimate, designed to work with the muted colors of the natural materials used in its interior. I drank some more water before saying, "Well, thank you… but people can change a lot over the years. I always thought she was very pretty. Anyway, I think what upset her even more was how serious Dylan was about me, and that I eventually ended up being the one to break up with him. Sort of like…she wanted him, but I didn't."

"Why not?"

I laughed. "Besides thinking that seventeen was

kind of young to be making a lifetime commitment to anybody?"

"Yes, besides that."

Obviously, he didn't see anything particularly odd about it, but then, Logan, despite the familiarity with human life and customs he often displayed, clearly had large gaps in that knowledge. I glanced around, but no one seemed to be paying any attention to us, and of course Alex was nowhere in sight. "Because of who I was. Who I am. I couldn't tell him the truth about my father. I didn't want to think about a future with anyone, not just because I was too young, but because I was worried I'd never have a future."

Logan's expression shifted to one of concern, and he reached across the table to take my hand. "Are you thinking about a future now?"

Oh, God, why had he asked that? It was too soon to even think about that subject, especially as it related to him. He'd come into my life only a few days earlier, and though I knew in my heart and my gut that I'd never imagined being with someone could feel this way, how could I possibly make any kind of decision, even think more than a day or so ahead, with everything so new and fragile? "I—"

A female voice, vaguely hostile. "Have you made a decision?"

Well, if nothing else, Alex had definitely perfected the quintessential waiter's art of popping up at precisely the wrong time. Thinking fast, I said, "We'll both have the prime rib, medium rare, and a bottle of the Diseno Malbec."

Her mouth tightened, although I wasn't sure whether that was because I actually had been ready when she reappeared, or whether she didn't care for me ordering for Logan. Not that it mattered; I knew he wouldn't mind, was probably grateful that I'd navigated the unfamiliar offerings for him.

"Got it," she replied, then snatched up our menus and headed off toward the kitchen.

"What is a prime rib?" Logan asked.

"It's…meat. From the same animal as the cheese-burger you ate earlier today. I figured if you were macking down on burgers, you weren't exactly avoiding red meat."

"No. Such proteins were incorporated in our diets, although in different forms." He stopped then, thought for a moment, and corrected himself. "That is, I never had it, as I received all my nutrients intra-venously, but from what I can tell, that is what I would have been fed, if…."

He let the words die away, and I just nodded. It must have been strange, to have knowledge of these things fed to him as part of the training his wired-up brain was receiving as he lay there in suspended animation, and yet never to have experienced them for himself.

"Well, I doubt those other soldiers were getting prime rib, so you're in for a treat. I think you'll like it very much."

Our eyes met, and I felt another one of those warm little thrills run down my back. I thought of the way his hands had wrapped around my waist, how we had moved together as one, of how I'd had sex before Logan, but I didn't think I'd ever made love. Not truly.

And how big a step was it from making love to the actual thing itself? Maybe not as big as I had once thought it was.

Oh, shit.

Hand shaking, I reached out for my water and took another large swallow. At the rate I was going, they might as well just leave the pitcher at our table.

"Are you all right?" Logan asked, eyes narrowing with concern.

"I'm fine," I said at once, and made myself breathe deeply through my nose. All the angst would have to wait until we were safely back home. I couldn't lose it here, not in front of all these people, and especially not in front of Alex Jacoby.

Who showed up then, bottle of wine clutched in one hand. "The Diseno," she announced, producing a corkscrew from her pocket and inserting it in the cork. Whatever I might think of her personally, she had that part of the job down, and extracted the cork with one smooth motion. She then tipped a small amount of wine into Logan's glass. He stared at it blankly, then at me.

"Go ahead—see if you like it," I told him.

"And if I don't?"

Good question. I supposed we would send it back, although I'd certainly never done such a thing, or ever been around anyone who had. "Just try it."

So he lifted the glass and drank—not the cautious sip one would usually take in that situation, but a healthy swallow. I could see Alex smile slightly, as if amused by his *faux pas*.

"It's very good," he said.

"Great," she responded, still smiling, although in a tight-lipped sort of way. She poured more wine into his glass, filled mine precisely to the halfway point, and added, "Your salads will be out shortly."

To my relief, she didn't loiter but took off immediately afterward. I reflected on the awkwardness of living in a small town, of the way you could bump into people you really didn't want to see. A lot of Sedona's visitors probably thought the place was bigger than it actually was, only because its ranks were swollen on a daily basis by all the tourists coming and going. In reality, the permanent year-round population numbered about ten thousand, give or take, which wasn't all that big. I still remembered how shocked I was the first time I'd gone to Phoenix, seeing all that city sprawl in every direction. It was hard to wrap my brain around, when even the smallest suburb there was many times larger than my hometown.

"Are you all right, Grace?"

I blinked, bringing myself back to the here and now, to the man who sat across the table from me.

From the way he looked at me, I could tell he was worried. And even that small sign of his concern sent a little stab through my heart. I wasn't used to the man I was with being so...solicitous. It wasn't that any of my ex-boyfriends had been abusive or anything, just sort of absorbed in their own stuff. What was going on with me, with my feelings, had never been that big a concern. At the time, their indifference had irritated me to no end, but now I wondered if I'd deliberately chosen men like that just so it would be easy to break up with them when the time came. No real connection, no loose ends.

No love.

Swallowing, I said, "I'm fine, Logan. I shouldn't let her get to me." I managed a smile, then lifted my glass. "Here's to getting out of the house."

His answering smile was somewhat uncertain, but he raised his glass as well, and drank with me. And when Alex came back with our salads, I thanked her in the most neutral of tones, barely paying her any attention, keeping my gaze fixed on Logan. I could tell that annoyed her, although that wasn't my intention. No, I just thought if I stayed focused on him, on the conversation we'd been having about the sights he'd seen while out with the guys, on the way Sedona's beauty had impressed him, then I wouldn't let my thoughts stray to dangerous places, to subjects I really didn't want to address yet.

Well, that was my intention, anyway.

The rest of dinner was uneventful, and we let the

car drive us back to the cottage as we sat in the back seat, my head on Logan's shoulder. It bothered me, how good that felt, how comfortable it was to be with him.

Easy now, I thought. *You've created your own little idyll here, and you've got Martin and Kirsten running interference for you, helping you keep Logan's identity hidden. But it's really going to hit the fan when that gets out.*

All right, so what if the worst happened? My parents would freak out, but I was a grown woman. And how much shit could my mother even give me over being with Logan, when she'd done almost the same thing so many years before?

Yes, but she gave Grayson up when she found out who...what...he really was. You know the truth about Logan and don't care.

Actually, I wasn't sure if that was the best way of describing the situation. It wasn't that I didn't care, more that I wouldn't allow his origins to interfere with what I felt for him...was beginning to feel for him. I didn't know what to do about those feelings, as I'd never experienced anything like this before. Attraction, yes, although I'd never acted on physical attraction so quickly with anyone else. But being quiet with him like this, knowing that was enough?

It was new, and it was scary.

He remained silent as well as we got out of the car and went into the house. The scent of wood smoke still lingered in the air, even though we'd put out the fire hours ago. I wasn't sure if he meant to start another one when he walked into the living room, but he paused by the sofa, watching me as I unwound the scarf from my throat and draped it over the coat I'd already removed.

"It seems as if you have something on your mind," he said.

"I do, I suppose."

"What is it?"

"You."

"Me?" He stuck his hands in the pockets of his jeans and shifted his weight, clearly uncertain about how he should react to my reply.

The gesture was so human that a little shiver went over me. Had he picked that up by watching television, or observing the men he'd spent the afternoon with? Or was it something he knew because it had been programmed into him?

"Yes, you." I smiled then, hoping that would reassure him, but he just continued to watch me, waiting. "It's just—I've brought you into my life, and I'm glad of it, but at some point we have to think about what comes next."

"Next?"

"This here" —I gestured at the cottage around us — "this isn't my life. Not really. It's a part of it, sure, but the real part, where I live and where I work and all that, that's up in Flagstaff. And I have to be there three days from now. So where does that leave you, or us?"

Something about his jaw seemed to harden. "I would suppose that is up to you."

"No," I said, "it's up to *us*. Sometime over the past few days, we've become an us, or at least it feels that way to me. Maybe I'm wrong."

"No," he said at once. "You're not wrong." He reached up and ran a hand through his hair, clearly unsettled. His eyes sought mine. I'd been standing some distance from him, but I went to Logan then, stopping a foot or so away and threading my fingers through his. As I did so, he seemed to visibly relax, some of the stiffness leaving his shoulders. "I'm not sure what I should be saying to you, Grace. I have no knowledge of what a relationship should be like. Before I spent time with you, I couldn't have begun to describe what a relationship even was. Not this kind, at least. All I know is that I want to be with you...if you'll let me. Although I'll admit I don't know what that even means."

The worry was clear in his eyes, so I let go of his hands and put my arms around him, holding him, letting him know that I did want him, whatever that meant. "We'll figure it out," I told him. "You can come up to Flagstaff with me, and we'll work it out somehow. My apartment is tiny, but I'm on a month-to-month lease, so I can find something better. And we'll get an identity for you. I'm not sure how, but with all my parents' contacts, I know someone will be able to help us. And—"

I didn't have a chance to say anything more after

that, because Logan had brought his mouth to mine, was kissing me, tasting me, and then his arms were tightening around me, lifting me. He took me to the bedroom, his fingers busy with finding the zipper of my dress, unclasping the bra underneath. We sank onto the bed, bare flesh against bare flesh, his fingers stroking my breast, my hand wrapping around his shaft, feeling how aroused he already was. And then we were one again, moving together in a rhythm I'd never found with anyone else, until at last the climax swept over us at the same time and we collapsed in one another's arms.

Before sleep claimed me, I finally allowed myself to think the words I'd been avoiding all night.

I love you.

CHAPTER ELEVEN

THE NEXT MORNING, WE DID ALLOW OURSELVES THAT shared shower, and then I made breakfast—a *real* breakfast, with eggs and bacon and English muffins. Logan sat at the table with me and devoured it all, which, after our exertions of the evening before, didn't seem all that odd.

A peek outside told me that the storm had finally moved on, leaving in its wake skies of a pure, deep blue untainted by any pollution, and soft, drifting clouds, not organized enough to threaten further precipitation. Although all signs of the previous snowfall seemed to have disappeared down here in Sedona, the ridge lines, more than a thousand feet above us, still glinted with fresh snow.

All in all, it was a gorgeous day, not the kind where you would want to stay indoors. Although my own car wasn't suited for off-roading—and I didn't dare ask to borrow Lance's Jeep, which was his pride and joy—I thought maybe Logan and I could go to one of the Jeep rental places in town and get a vehicle that would take us pretty much wherever we wanted to go. Maybe a picnic lunch and a drive out to the Palatki ruins, about a half hour outside Sedona. The family had gone there once when I was in junior high, but I'd never been back. The site was beautiful, though, and the storm hadn't been severe enough that it should have affected the roads too badly.

I'd just pulled up the website for the ruins so I could show them to Logan when my cell phone rang inside my purse. For a second, I contemplated ignoring it, but I decided that probably wasn't the best course of action. The call could have been from work; it could have been my mother. Either way, under normal circumstances, I would have picked up, so I didn't have much choice now.

After I grabbed my purse from where it had been sitting on one of the empty dining room chairs, though, I saw that the call was from my Aunt Kirsten. Could she have cracked the encryption on the alien computer already?

I swiped the screen to accept the call but kept the video function turned off. Logan and I were dressed, but I hadn't done my hair or makeup yet...and that makeup would be necessary today, to hide some of the marks he'd left on my neck the night before.

"Hi, Kirsten," I said cheerily. "What's up?"

Her video was on, so I could see she looked tense, wasn't smiling. "Are you busy?"

I glanced over at Logan. He lifted the last piece of bacon and gave me an inquiring look. I nodded, and he began happily munching away at it. A vegetarian he most definitely was not. "Um…define 'busy.'"

"Well, as soon as I got back from the spa, I started hacking at that computer again, but I could tell it was going to be a wasted effort. I wasn't exaggerating when I told your uncle that I was rusty." She shook her head, as if annoyed with herself. "So you know how I told you I might have to call in the big guns?"

"Yes," I replied, recalling that I had wondered exactly who she'd meant by that.

"Last night I called Jeff Makowski. You might have heard us mention him a time or two."

"Uh-huh." A mention was all he'd gotten, but I knew he'd been part of the group who'd gone up against the aliens on the first go-'round. "He's some kind of hacker, right?"

"That's putting it mildly. We've kept in touch on and off, although I haven't seen him in years. Anyway, when I saw what I was working with, I knew Jeff was the logical person to help me out. He did a lot of work hacking the aliens' code back in the day, even though he wasn't entirely successful. So I called him and explained the situation, and he came right out."

"He did?" My mind was working away, trying to

figure out exactly what was going on. "He lives in L.A., right?"

"Yes, and he got in around three o'clock this morning. But he's been working on it since then... and now he wants to talk to you."

"Me?" I couldn't figure that one out. I certainly didn't have any skills that would be of any use to a computer hacker. "Why?"

"He wasn't entirely clear as to why. But with Jeff, it's best to humor him. Can I come by and gather you up in, say, half an hour? Martin already said he'd be happy to have Logan come over here to the house, so you won't have to leave him at the cottage by himself."

That sounded suspiciously like Martin offering to babysit Logan, but I couldn't argue. Logan seemed to have enjoyed his time with the guys, beer notwithstanding, and at least that way, he might get another chance to go out in the Jeep and see some more of Sedona.

"Sure," I told my aunt, since I knew I couldn't really say no. "We'll be ready."

They came in separate cars, Martin in the all-terrain Mercedes, Kirsten also in a Mercedes, but the sedan that was the family car. It had been a little difficult to explain to Logan exactly what was going on, since I didn't know for sure myself. "But you should have fun with the guys," I told him, "and I'll call Martin when I get home, so he can drop you back off."

"Of course," Logan replied, questions in his eyes. But he didn't ask any of them, only waved as he got into the passenger seat of Martin's SUV, right before they pulled away from the curb.

I locked the front door to the cottage and got into Kirsten's car. There was so much instrumentation on the dashboard that it looked as if we were about to launch into orbit instead of merely drive down the street. But as much as I wanted to ask how the heck she and Martin could afford vehicles like this, I knew that would be horribly rude. So I sat in silence as she backed out of the driveway, then headed over to 89A. I noticed she had engaged the manual drive, wasn't letting the car drive us. That seemed to be common behavior when it came to people of her and my parents' generation—they liked to be in control.

Once we were out in traffic and heading west, I said, "So…anything else you'd like to tell me about before I meet this Jeff guy?"

She didn't look over at me, but kept her gaze fixed on the road in front of her. As usual, she looked effortlessly chic, dark sweater and slim jeans, leather jacket and leather boots laced up to her knees. I wondered if my alien DNA would allow me to age that well. Hard to know for sure; I'd gotten the impression that the Reptilians hadn't worried too much about the longevity of their hybrid soldiers. What was the point? They could always make more.

Then she said, "Jeff is...brilliant. Difficult. I never had the guts to ask, but my guess is he's somewhere along the autism continuum. He never met a computer system he couldn't hack."

"Okay," I replied. That was valuable intel, but I sort of got the impression my aunt was still holding something back. "Anything else?"

Her knuckles tightened on the steering wheel, and she slowed as she pulled into the suicide lane, clearly preparing us for a left turn into the condo complex on that side of the street. It was the sort of place used by people with timeshares. I'd never heard that my aunt and uncle owned a timeshare, but they were the sort of people who seemed able to pull all kinds of strings...even if that involved setting up a condo for a mad computer genius at three o'clock in the morning.

Then she let out a sigh and said, "Well, he sort of had a thing for me back in the day. I'd never looked on him as anything but a friend, and then Martin came along...." She didn't bother to add anything to that, but she'd told me enough. True, that had all been years and years ago, but if this Jeff Makowski had the kind of temperament she'd hinted at, he might not have let it go, not even after a quarter-century had passed.

She found an empty parking space in the visitors' area and pulled into it, then reached back and retrieved her purse from the back seat. "Anyway, I'm sure it's no big deal, but I haven't seen Jeff since a month or so after you were born, so…it could be a little strange. I just wanted to give you a heads-up."

"I appreciate it," I said, and I did. Nothing worse than walking into a situation littered with emotional land mines without knowing what you might be getting yourself into.

I followed her along a winding path tastefully xeriscaped with several varieties of cacti and low-growing juniper ground cover. The complex was an attractive one, and, from what I could tell, each unit had its own fireplace.

"How did you get Jeff a place here?" I asked, only half expecting my aunt to answer.

"Called a friend who called a friend."

And that was clearly all she intended to say on the subject. We came to a unit at the end of a row, a place that was obviously two stories high, since it didn't have an exterior staircase going to a landing the way the single-level condos did. Kirsten went to the front door, but instead of knocking, she pulled out her phone and sent a text. I raised an eyebrow and she said, "I have to let him know it's me. He won't answer just because someone is knocking."

My other eyebrow went up. "Paranoid much?"

She chuckled, although she didn't sound all that amused. "You have no idea."

The door opened, and a tall, thin man in his middle or late fifties scowled down at us. His hair was a medium brown liberally streaked with gray and needed cutting. Hazel eyes glared at us from behind rimless glasses. That was sort of odd, since almost everyone these days got surgery instead of wearing corrective lenses. Maybe Mr. Makowski's paranoia prevented him from allowing anyone to poke at his eyes.

"Come in," he said with absolutely no ceremony, then stepped aside just enough to let us squeeze past.

The interior of the condo was just as tastefully Southwestern as the exterior—red tile floors, a kiva-style fireplace in one corner, plain, sturdy furniture in dark wood with deep tan upholstery. The effect was somewhat lessened by the takeout cartons and empty soda bottles that littered the dining room table, however.

Without looking at us, Jeff strode over to that table and picked up a half-drunk bottle of Coke. I couldn't help blinking at that. No one in my family drank soda, and in fact, it wasn't even offered at a lot of the local restaurants anymore. Maybe he'd gone to the grocery store and stocked up on his favorite poison before coming here.

Finally, he turned back toward us. I could see him stare at Kirsten for a long moment, and she didn't flinch, only looked back at him without blinking. Was this really the first time that they'd met since he'd come to Sedona? I could see that happening, possibly, if she'd made arrangements to leave the key for him but hadn't come here to let him in herself.

"You look good," he said at last.

"Thanks," she replied, although I noticed she

didn't return the compliment. I sort of doubted that Jeff was a stunner even at twenty-five, and the intervening years didn't seem to have been particularly kind.

But then he glanced over at me, and I had to force myself not to look away, to stare back at him the way Kirsten had, expression completely neutral. Something about his inspection made me want to flinch, as if he was looking at an exhibit in a zoo and not at an actual person.

"So you're the alien baby," he said at last.

Ah, so that was it. I planted my hands on my hips and replied, "Well, I was once, but that was a while ago. And technically, I was the 'half human/half hybrid' baby."

He seemed to consider that response, then nodded. His gaze shifted back to Kirsten. "So she's been entirely stable this whole time?"

"Stable"? What the hell?

As if she could sense my rapidly growing ire, my aunt made a quick waving gesture with one hand, down low by her hip where probably only I would notice. Her meaning was clear: *Don't let him get to you.*

Easier said than done. Somehow, I managed to remain where I was, hands on my hips, doing my best to stay out of it, although what I really wanted to do was pull that Coke bottle out of Jeff Makowski's hand and dump its contents over his head.

Then Kirsten smiled and said, "Well, I don't think

Grace was any more stable during her high school years than any other teenager, but otherwise, yes, I'd say she's been stable. Why would you ask that?"

Behind the glasses, his murky hazel eyes glinted. "Because she wasn't created in a controlled way. The hybrid's genes mixed with your sister's genetic material without any technological intervention. I doubt the aliens ever planned for that. Some recessives could have emerged as she matured. Scales, for example."

What he was saying was a little too close to some of the same fears I'd harbored over the years, but that didn't mean I enjoyed hearing my own worries coming out of someone else's mouth. "No scales," I said, my tone too deliberately sweet, and Kirsten shot me warning look. "No claws, no red eyes, no…whatever else you might've been expecting. Sorry to disappoint you."

"Oh, I'm not disappointed," Jeff replied, apparently not offended at all. "It's actually fascinating. She looks completely normal."

"'She' is standing right in front of you, you know," I remarked, hands still on my hips.

"Did you have something you wanted to say to us?" Kirsten cut in. I could tell she wanted to get the conversation back on track.

Jeff blinked, then went over to his laptop and began typing so quickly that his long, pale fingers were practically a blur. "Not particularly. That is, I did keep all my files from the last time I had to take a crack at the alien encoding, but this is somewhat different, so things may not go as quickly as I'd hoped."

"Different how?"

The alien computer was sitting next to his laptop, and he flicked the tab to activate the heads-up display. The image projected into the air in front of him didn't appear to be the same as what I'd seen when Martin activated it back at the base, had instead columns of strange, angular symbols filling it.

"Well, I was able to get past the login," Jeff explained. "Silly, really. It was basically the Reptilian equivalent of having 'ABCDE123' as your password. I doubted whoever left it behind ever thought it would fall into enemy hands."

"Probably not," my aunt agreed. "But if it was that easy to get past the login...."

"That was a simple code. What we're looking at here is their actual language. Have you ever had to break an unknown language apart, decipher both its orthography and its vocabulary?"

"Well, no."

"Precisely." He left the heads-up display in place and began tapping away on his laptop again. Since the screen was angled away from me, I couldn't really tell what he was doing. "The enemy never cracked the Navajo language back during World War II, you know. And they had entire teams working on it."

"Are you saying you can't do it?"

"No," he snapped. "I'm only saying that this isn't a simple in-and-out operation. If I'm lucky, the algorithms I've been working on may be able to find the aliens' Rosetta Stone, as it were, buried in the data. But I can't make any promises."

"Well, we're not going anywhere," I said. "But it's important that we find out what's on that computer if at all possible."

"I *know* that." His gaze sharpened as he stared at me. "So you really did find another one?"

"Another one what?"

"A hybrid. Like your father."

There was something almost insinuating about the way he said it, as if Logan was exactly the same as my father, as if something vaguely incestuous was going on. I scowled. "Yes, Logan is a hybrid, but he is *not* like my father. That is, he's from a completely different genetic stock. They don't look at all alike."

"How would you know?"

"Photographic evidence," I replied, resisting the urge to dig the photo of my father out of my wallet, where I always carried it tucked into the "secret" slot behind my driver's license. "But you'll just have to take my word for that."

His gaze slipped toward Kirsten, as if seeking confirmation as to whether pushing the subject any further was a good idea. She shook her head, just slightly, and he shrugged.

"If you say so. But was this 'Logan' the only one?"

"As far as we could tell, yes," she said. "We only explored the level where Grace found him, so I suppose there could be more."

"There aren't," I cut in. "Logan says he was the only one of the new 'batch,' if you want to put it that way. They didn't have time to start full production before Kirsten wiped out their soldiers and the rest of them fled the base."

"'Logan says,'" Jeff repeated. "How can you trust what he says? You should've been thoroughly exploring the base." He sent a cutting stare in my aunt's direction. "In fact, you all should have done that years ago. I tried to tell you—"

"We wanted to let it go, Jeff." Kirsten crossed her arms, and I could tell she was annoyed by the direction he was trying to take the conversation. "We'd won. The aliens were gone. We all agreed— Martin and Paul and Persephone and Kara and Lance and I—that it was better to let sleeping dogs lie. There was no trace of the alien presence remaining. We didn't see the point in going into the base and rooting around. Besides, parts of it were heavily damaged...still are, as far as we know. Logan's pod was on the southwest side, opposite from the location where Grayson blew up the reactor."

"Martin, huh," Jeff said, seeming to have ignored most of what she'd just said. "How *is* Martin?"

She sent the hacker a sharp look. "He's fine. Now, I know it's a difficult project, but do you have any kind of an ETA on when you think you might make some progress?"

"No." His face had gone blank, and he turned back to his computer and began typing some more. "If I find something, I'll let you know. I assume you won't mind a ping, even if it's in the middle of the night?"

"No," she said wearily, as if she knew he'd text her at o'dark-thirty, just to be a jackass. "Getting the information off that computer is more important than a little sleep."

"Okay, then." And he went into another of those staccato bursts of typing, fingers flying across the keyboard.

Although nothing felt all that settled to me, Kirsten seemed to realize that was his way of dismissing us. She murmured, "Come on, Grace," and we left the condo, my aunt shutting the door quietly behind us, as if she didn't want to disturb Jeff now that he was back at work.

Once we were halfway to the car and safely out of ear- or eyeshot, I said, "What an asshole."

"I know. But he's very good at what he does."

I glanced over at her. "And he really had a thing for you? I could've sworn he had absolutely no feelings of any kind."

She let out a little gust of breath, kissing cousin to a sigh. "And you would be wrong." Her gaze was fixed someplace ahead of her, as if she wasn't looking at the path we were currently walking down, with its borders of desert plants, but something much farther away. "The human heart is a very complicated thing."

Didn't I know it. And it was even more complicated when it wasn't completely human....

On the way back to the house, I texted Martin to let him know I'd be home soon. He replied a short time later, saying the guys were currently on top of Schnebly Hill, enjoying the view, but that they'd start the trek back down into Sedona in a bit.

I tossed my phone back into my purse. "Sounds like they're having a much better time than we are."

She smiled. "I have no doubt about that." Tapping her fingers on the steering wheel, she went on, "I'd apologize for some of things Jeff said to you, but I suppose you could tell that he doesn't have much of a filter."

I had to ask. "And did you—did *you* all worry about me? Wonder whether I'd suddenly start popping out some alien physical traits?"

A long pause. "There were some concerns. Not because you didn't look completely normal, develop in a completely ordinary way after you were born, but because we were in totally unfamiliar territory. We had no way of knowing what would happen. And Martin and Gabriel couldn't really provide much insight, because although they knew that cross-breeding with their own race didn't result in any issues, they had no idea what would happen when a hybrid bred with a human woman."

I must have winced, because she went on quickly, "I know that sounds terrible. I mean, I'm talking about my own sister. But the Reptilians guard their breeding programs with the utmost secrecy. We still don't know exactly how they create the hybrids. There were just a lot of factors we couldn't account for." At last, she looked over at me, just a quick glance before she returned her attention to the road. Even in profile, though, she looked worried. Not about me, though...rather, more *for* me, for what she seemed to guess I might be thinking. "You're fine, Grace. You know that. We all know that. So don't let anything Jeff said get to you."

Intellectually, I knew she was right. If anything in my system had intended to start breaking down, it would have done so long before this. The hormonal upheavals of puberty should have been enough to set things off, but I had matured just like any other normal human girl.

Since the condo complex wasn't that far from the cottage, my aunt had already turned off the main road and was only a block away from our destination. I knew it would take some time for the guys to negotiate the rough road that wound down from Schnebly Hill, so I said, somewhat impulsively, "Could you come in for a cup of coffee or something?

I doubt Martin and Logan will be back for another half-hour or so."

My aunt flickered another one of those sidelong glances at me before nodding. "Sure. That sounds good."

We parked and got out of the car, and I led her inside. At least I'd cleared the dining room table, but the breakfast dishes were still stacked next to the sink, as I hadn't had time to take care of them before rushing out to that "meeting" with Jeff Makowski, which I now guessed was more so he could see me in person and determine whether I'd sprouted scales or a tail than because he had anything to say that couldn't have been said in a text or email.

"Sorry about the mess," I said to Kirsten as I went to get some mugs.

"It's fine." She leaned against the counter, watching while I poured a measure of beans in the coffeemaker and got it started.

Once that was going, there wasn't much to do except wait. My aunt was silent, seeming content to wait until I spoke again. Fair enough; I'd invited her in because I needed someone to talk to, and my mother was really out of the question at the moment.

"How do you manage it?" I asked at last, and she smiled, as if she knew exactly what I was talking about.

"It's easier when you have someone to go through it with," she said. "If I'd learned about my origins when I was alone, when I didn't have Martin to help me adjust to who and what I was, then it would have been very difficult. But you've always had all of us to support you."

"That's not the same, though." At least, I didn't think it was. Family was important, I couldn't deny that, and yet making a connection with someone who knew the worst, scariest thing about you and didn't care…that was so much more.

The heavy aroma of brewing coffee began to fill the kitchen, and I saw Kirsten take in a deep breath, not quite shutting her eyes. "No, it's not," she said frankly. "I can't blame you for wanting to latch on to Logan. We all seek out our own kind, even if we're not aware that we're doing it at the time. I mean, the first time I saw Martin—"

"Did you just *know?*" This was something I'd wanted to ask for years but never really had the opportunity. Maybe it was something she'd shared with her own daughter. But I wasn't her daughter. Even so, most of the time, I felt as if I was far more closely connected to my Aunt Kirsten than I was to my own mother. Yes, my mother had had her own share of struggles, but not the kind I was attempting to deal with now.

"I did. That is, I felt a pull toward him that was unlike anything else I'd ever experienced." Her mouth quirked just a little, and she added, "I tried to tell myself that it was only because he was the best-looking man I'd ever seen, but I knew it was more than that. It was as if we were two halves just waiting to be whole."

Her explanation was so close to what I'd thought about Logan and myself that I couldn't help shivering a bit, although the kitchen was quite warm. "So you don't think—that is, you don't see anything horribly strange about feeling as if you were meant to be with someone, even if you've only known them a short while."

"No." Her eyes met mine, and I could see such empathy and understanding in them that my throat tightened. Had I ever seen those same emotions in my mother? I wasn't sure. Love, yes, of course, and pride in who I'd become, but she had no way of truly comprehending what it felt like to be so outside the human race sometimes.

The coffeemaker beeped, and with some relief, I went over to it and poured us both some. Kirsten took it with lots of milk but no sugar, and so I busied myself with preparing our drinks, my mind working away the whole time. I'd already basically told Logan that I wanted us to stay together, for him to come up to Flagstaff with me, and so I knew I couldn't keep the truth of his identity from my family forever. That was not a confrontation I looked forward to, but at the same time, I didn't want to keep lying.

After handing my aunt her coffee, I said, "I think I'm going to have to come clean about Logan. I have no idea where all this is going, but…"

"…but you don't want to build whatever you might have with him on a lie." She wrapped her hands around her mug, the big diamond on her ring finger blinking as she did so. "I'm glad to hear you say that. Martin and I were keeping silent, since it was your place to tell your parents the truth, but even so, we were wondering how long you were going to keep it up."

"Not long," I said. "Just long enough for me to figure out what was really going on." I gave her a rueful smile before taking a sip of my coffee. "Not that I'm actually sure of that yet."

"But you're sure of him."

"I am." Oddly, I knew that was the simple truth. However he had come into this world, for whatever reason the aliens had made him—none of that seemed to matter when I considered how I felt when I was with him. Logic would say that attitude was crazy, but I could feel his goodness, for lack of a better term. The easy way we could be together, whether sitting quietly or going out somewhere or making love. It didn't seem to matter what we did, as long as it was something we did together. I never felt on edge with him, constantly wondering what his reaction would be if I ever did tell him the truth. Logan knew the truth, and because it was partly his truth as well, he didn't care, but accepted me for who I was. *What* I was.

"Good." She drank some of her own coffee as well, seeming to ponder her next words. "He feels— well, he feels like good people to me. I know that sounds strange, considering his origins, but it's the truth. It was the same with your father. In his case, one might have argued that his temperament had far more to do with the power of Sedona working through him, rather than what his creators might have intended, but now I'm not so sure. It's almost as if their humanness is fighting to come through, no matter what. When they were being directly controlled by their masters, they were very different, but in this case…."

She let the words die away, but I thought I knew what she meant. Logan's alien masters were long gone. No one was making him their puppet. He was free to make his own choices, be his own person. And by some miracle, he'd made the choice to be with me.

"In this case, he can be himself," I said, and she gave me a nod.

"Exactly." For a few seconds, she was quiet, sipping at her coffee. I almost suggested that we should go into the living room and sit down, but something about being here in the kitchen, leaning against the counters, felt cozier, not so formal. Then she said, "We'll be there to support you, if you want."

I hadn't expected her to make the offer, and the rush of gratitude that went over me in response to her words was very real. At the same time, though, I knew this was something I should do on my own. "Thanks, Kirsten. I appreciate that. But I think it might be better if it's just Logan and me talking to them. I'm a grown-up, and my parents need to respect my decisions."

She didn't seem all that surprised that I had declined her offer. Her head tilted slightly, and I could see her shrug. "True, you are a grown woman. Just remember that parents don't always see it that way."

I couldn't argue with that observation. But now that I'd made up my mind, I knew nothing was going to change it.

CHAPTER TWELVE

MARTIN DROPPED LOGAN OFF SHORTLY AFTER THAT, AND he and my Aunt Kirsten said their goodbyes and headed for home in their separate vehicles. Logan looked windblown and happy, his skin a bit more tanned than it had been when he'd left that morning.

"Good time?" I asked him, and he nodded and came over to give me a kiss on the cheek. Even that slight contact was enough to get my blood racing, but I knew I needed to stay focused.

"Very. You can see for miles atop that hill. The landscape around here really is extraordinary. Paul said he has some good books on the geology of the area that he'll loan me, but I'll need something to read them on."

Right. Logan didn't have a phone or a tablet or a computer, so books were pretty much inaccessible to him at the moment. "I'll have Paul send them to my laptop, and you can read them on there."

"That sounds like an excellent idea."

Even though I'd made up my mind that we needed to go talk to my parents...*really* talk...now that the time had come to broach the subject to Logan, I wasn't sure where to start. But I didn't want to put it off any longer. The afternoon was wearing away, and although I knew both Kevin and Kelsey were working, they'd probably still be home for dinner. There wasn't much time left where Logan and I could talk to my parents in private.

"Um, Logan...."

He'd gone to the fridge to get some water, but turned around at the sound of his name. "What is it?"

"You know how we talked last night about going to Flagstaff together after this, of...being with each other?"

"Yes?" Now his expression was uncertain, as if he halfway expected me to say that I'd changed my mind, that I'd been half-drunk on Malbec and didn't know what I was saying.

"I still want that...more than ever...but I also don't want to keep lying about you to my family. Would you mind—that is, I want to go talk to them. Do you think you could do that?"

In answer, he set the glass he'd been holding down on the counter and came over to me, wrapping me in his arms and pulling me close. His lips touched the top of my head, so gently I could barely feel them. Even so, a delicious shiver went through me. How was he able to make me feel so cherished with the simplest of gestures?

"I know I can do that," he replied, his breath warm against my hair. "I'll admit that I didn't feel comfortable being around your father and continuing to pretend I was someone I was not. But...how do you think he will react?"

Not well, I thought, but I only said, "I suppose that's what we're about to find out."

———

My mother had sounded somewhat mystified at my request to come over, especially since Logan had just spent a few hours in Lance's company, but she didn't say no. "That sounds wonderful," she said. "I'll make your favorite artichoke dip. It'll be nice to have a chance to chat."

I wasn't so sure she'd feel the same way once she heard what we had to say, but I kept my thoughts to myself, instead telling her that we'd be over in a half-hour or so.

Now, Logan and I were cruising up into the canyon, me behind the wheel and him in the passenger seat. I'd wanted to drive myself this time, mostly because I needed to do something with all the nervous energy I could feel crackling through me. Logan didn't seem nearly as worked up as I was, but watched the landscape pass by outside, looming red rocks and bare oaks and the dark shapes of juniper and pine and fir, the trees in shadow still with the faintest traces of snow glimmering along their branches.

When I pulled in the driveway, I saw Lance's Jeep but no other vehicles, which meant all the siblings were out and about. Thank God for that. I knew I couldn't have even attempted this conversation if either Kelsey or Melissa were hanging around, trying to catch a hint of anything juicy. Kevin would never have indulged in such behavior, not out of any moral high ground, but because he really didn't give a crap about what he tended to refer to as "girl stuff."

Lance answered the door, and surprised me by offering the two of us a smile. Had he ever smiled at any of the other guys I'd dated? I didn't think so. Maybe he and Logan had begun to hit it off. Of course, it probably didn't hurt that Logan had opened relations by referring to Lance as "sir." As a former member of the armed services, Lance appreciated it when people showed the proper respect. How Logan had known to do that, I wasn't sure, unless he had gathered enough from my stepfather's bearing and manner to realize he had a military background.

We exchanged greetings, Logan and I pausing to leave our coats on the rack in the foyer. Then, because this was supposed to be a casual call and nothing formal, we headed back to the family room, where my mother was just putting out the dip, along with some homemade pita chips.

"Hi, you two," she said, beaming so broadly that I felt a pang of guilt go through me at what I was about to reveal. In that moment, I wished I really could be a normal daughter, the sort who did manage to meet men who were presentable and worthy of taking home to the family. Well, not that I didn't think Logan was worthy on every level that mattered, but there was no question that he'd be much more acceptable if he was just a regular guy who worked with computers and liked to go hiking on the weekend.

"Hi," Logan and I replied, more or less in unison. I went and sat down on the sofa, and Logan seated himself next to me a few seconds later.

"Beer?" Lance inquired. From a certain glint in his eyes, I could almost tell he knew Logan didn't particularly care for it and that he was just messing with us.

"Um, no," I said hastily. "Water is fine."

"Water for me as well, thank you," Logan added.

Lance headed off toward the kitchen, and my mother sat down on the sofa across from ours. She already had a glass of water sitting on the coaster directly in front of her, so somehow she must have guessed this wasn't a "wine and cheese" sort of visit.

"So…what's this all about?" she inquired, clearly trying to act casual. But since she looked all bright and shiny, I had a feeling she was hoping we had the traditional "big news" that so many couples liked to spring on their parents around the holidays.

Well, our news was big…it just wasn't the kind she was probably hoping for.

Lance returned and set down two glasses of water on the coffee table, making sure to use coasters. We'd all learned the hard way that my mother was fanatical about coasters. "Yes," he said, "Kara made it sound as if it was pretty important."

I swallowed. Even though I hadn't made any sort of movement, Logan reached over and took my hand in his. The touch of his warm fingers against mine gave me some courage.

"It's…." I gulped in a breath. "It's about Logan."

My parents looked at each other and then both swiveled their heads to stare at the man sitting beside me. He didn't flinch but only regarded them calmly, his back straight, even though the couch was one of those overly soft kinds that felt as if it was going to swallow you up at any moment.

Lance spoke first. "What about Logan?" His tone was even, but I heard an edge to it that I didn't like. Had he picked up on something? Hard to say, because Lance generally only let you know what he wanted you to know. Unlike Persephone, he wasn't what you could call a true psychic, but I knew he'd been part of the government's remote-viewing program back in the day, which meant he had abilities that most regular people didn't.

"He's…." God, this was hard. I was beginning to

kick myself mentally for even coming here in the first place.

"She concealed this because she didn't want to upset you," Logan said, taking over when he could tell I seemed to have momentarily lost my powers of speech. "But we didn't want to hide the truth any longer."

"And what exactly have you been hiding?" Lance asked. His voice was still cool—neutral, even—but I knew better than to take that as a positive sign. Next to him, my mother sat quiet, tense, although I noticed the way her gaze darted to my midsection.

No, Mom, I'm not pregnant. That would have been so much easier than this.

"We did not meet at work," Logan replied. His chin was up, but not in a confrontational way…more like he wanted to show that he was not ashamed of what he was going to say next. "She found me out at the abandoned base in Secret Canyon."

Dead silence, so deathly still, I could hear my heart hammering away in my chest.

To my surprise, my mother spoke first. "You… what?" Her eyes met mine, and I could see her flinch when I didn't blink, didn't try to deny it.

At last, I found my voice. "I went out there the day I came back to Sedona, after I dropped my stuff at the cottage. I don't know why. Something…drew me there."

"'Something,'" Lance echoed. His gaze had gone flat and cold, and even the faint amiability he'd shown toward Logan earlier had disappeared as if it had never existed. His hands tightened on the knees of his jeans. "Do you mind being a bit more specific, Grace?"

"I can't be more specific because I don't know what it was. Not really." I could hear my voice ratcheting higher, and I gulped in some air, trying to calm myself. "I just felt like I needed to go out there. I went in the same entrance you used with Persephone and Michael Lightfoot all those years ago, and I went down six levels and found Logan in a...a pod sort of thing. It looked as if his vitals were failing. So I opened it up and let him out."

"Just like that," Lance said, his tone as scary and flat as the look he kept giving Logan.

"'Just like that,'" I repeated, since I didn't know what else to say.

"I was dying," Logan said bluntly. "Or rather, the systems that had been sustaining me were going offline. If Grace hadn't come to me then, I would not have survived for much longer."

My mother was staring at me as if she'd never seen me before. Maybe she hadn't, not really...she'd seen the daughter she wanted me to be, the daughter she thought I was. But this? This was something completely outside her expectations, even if it wasn't outside her personal experience.

"Why didn't you say something?" she asked, her voice barely above a whisper.

"Because I knew you would flip out!" I snapped,

then wished I hadn't. Logan gave my fingers a squeeze, although whether that was in warning or reassurance, I didn't know.

"Do we look like we're flipping out?" Lance's fists were now white-knuckled on his knees, but his voice was still deadly calm.

"On the surface, no, but…." I shook my head. "Look, at first, I didn't even know what I was doing. I saw him and knew I couldn't leave him there to die. The rest just sort of…happened afterward."

From the looks on their faces, I could tell I didn't have to go into what the "rest" actually entailed. My mother especially. She knew, having been in a similar position about twenty-five years ago.

"I know this must be difficult for you," Logan began, and my mother whipped her head around in his direction, mouth tight with anger.

"Difficult? Yes, I'd say it's difficult, watching my daughter make the same mistake I made twenty-five years ago!"

Even though I knew she really hadn't meant it that way, hurt and anger knotted together in my belly at her words. I let go of Logan's head and propelled myself to my feet. "Oh, so I was a mistake?"

At once, she shook her head, horror spreading over her features as she realized what she'd just said. "No, Grace, that's not what I meant—"

"Oh, I think it was," I said coldly. "Maybe not intentionally, but it's probably something you've thought a time or two over the years. Anyway, I wanted you to know the truth. You can make your own judgments about me, or Logan, or us being together. I can't do anything to stop that. But you also can't stop me from having him come home to Flagstaff with me, which is what I intend to do—probably sooner rather than later." I glanced down at Logan, and he seemed to understand that I was done here, that I just wanted to get out as soon as possible, because he rose to his feet and stood beside me.

Lance realized that, too, because he got up as well, glaring at us all the while. "Don't think this is all we have to say on the subject—"

"I doubt it is," I retorted, too angry to care about the way I'd cut him off, something I would normally never dare to do. "But we're not going to stick around to listen to it."

Since I knew I couldn't come up with a better exit line than that, I took Logan by the hand and stalked out of the family room. I didn't even want to waste the time to put on my coat, but instead slung it over my arm as he did the same.

I could hear Lance's and my mother's footsteps following us, and I knew I wouldn't be able to avoid one last confrontation. My hand was on the door-knob as I heard my mother say,

"Grace, please. Stay and talk about this."

Reluctantly, I let go of the knob and turned back toward her. She and Lance stood on the opposite side of the foyer. Her expression was a study in anguish, while he was stony-faced as usual.

"I don't think we have anything to talk about," I said coolly. "You liked Logan when you thought he was just a co-worker of mine that I'd started dating. He's still the same person."

"It's not that simple," Lance began, and I shook my head.

"Actually, it is. Come on, Logan."

And I opened the door and let myself out, Logan just a pace behind me. I noticed that this time, neither my mother nor Lance tried to stop us.

At first, Logan didn't say anything. Then, as we entered the town limits and slowed to deal with the inevitable traffic in Uptown Sedona, he ventured, "That could have gone better."

"In a perfect world, maybe. Here?" I lifted my shoulders, then scowled when I had to hit the brake as an over-zealous tourist darted right in front of the car, obviously too lazy to walk the half a block to get to a crosswalk. "I guess I should have known better. To Lance, you're the enemy. Period. Full stop. And my mother can't get beyond her own past to see that what you and I have is very different from what she shared with my father."

"Is it?"

I glanced over at him. His expression was openly curious. It didn't look as if he had any hidden agenda in asking that question. "Well, for one thing, I'm not in love with someone else."

"And she was…with Lance."

"Yes. She'd had the hots for him forever, I guess, but since he didn't seem to feel the same way, she convinced herself that it was time to move on, and how better to do that than with my father?" I knew it really wasn't her fault, that she'd been confused and sort of swept off her feet by a handsome stranger who had shown up out of nowhere, but in the back of my mind, I couldn't help thinking that it still felt like cheating. Yes, she hadn't been with Lance at all, but if she knew she loved him, why hadn't she fought harder for him? Not that I minded, because if she had, I wouldn't have existed at all, but still….

"I suppose our situation is different, then, even if your father and I have similar backgrounds." Logan hesitated.

"Very different," I said firmly. "I mean, I know she cared for Grayson, but…."

"But?"

Maybe the inside of a car as we maneuvered through Uptown Sedona wasn't the best place to say it, but the words slipped out anyway. "But I love you. That's the one thing I do know."

His face lit up, and he reached over to stroke the side of my cheek. Softly, though, and he pulled his hand away at once, as if he knew he shouldn't be distracting me while I was driving. "Is that what this is? This warmth I feel when I look at you, this need to be with you?"

My heart gave a funny little thump in my chest. "Yes, that sounds like love to me."

The phone at the cottage was ringing when we entered the house, but I ignored it. Only family members had that number, and I figured they'd given up on my cell phone, which I'd turned off right before climbing in the car to come back here. Obviously, my mother and Lance weren't quite willing to let all this go just yet.

"Maybe we should head up to Flagstaff now," I said after pushing the button to turn off the ringer on the landline phone. "I doubt that will stop them from calling, but at least it will put some distance between us."

"If you want," Logan replied, but something in his expression told me he wasn't all that enthused by the prospect.

"You'll like Flagstaff," I said. "It's beautiful. Sorry we're going to miss the Mars party tomorrow, but I have a feeling we're sort of *persona non grata* around the old homestead right now."

"*Persona*...what?"

"It means unwelcome."

He didn't say anything, only gazed around the living room, at the firewood we'd left stacked in the hearth so we could get things going quickly tonight, at the take-out menus on the coffee table. In that moment, I thought I understood the reason for his reluctance. This little house was the only place he knew. Flagstaff would be foreign territory for him. Of course, he'd adjust to it, but he'd had enough shocks in the few days he'd been out in the world.

And my dinky little apartment didn't have a fireplace....

"All right," I said. "We'll stay here tonight. The phone's turned off, and I doubt they'll try to break down the door."

A smile spread across his face, not quite as beatific as the one he'd worn in the car when I told him I loved him...but not far off, either. "Thank you, Grace."

So we settled in that night, ordering in Chinese food, propping our feet up on the coffee table and eating in companionable silence, like two people who'd been together far longer than a few days. I didn't have much of a preference as to what to watch, as long as I could sit there on the couch and not think about anything much, but Logan flipped to a news station. It was the top of the hour, and they were leading with an update on the Mars mission. Apparently, the crew had encountered a technical setback as they were testing the landing module, and so touchdown had been delayed while they attempted to address the problem. Now the landing had been rescheduled for the thirty-first, although that was dependent on the issue being sorted out by then.

There goes the Mars party, I thought. Not that Logan and I would have been attending, anyway.

"Does this happen often?" he asked.

"Well, I don't know about 'often,' since this is the first time we've attempted a manned landing on Mars, but yes, sometimes there are little hiccups that need to be worked out," I told him. "But it's just a delay, not a cancellation."

He nodded, looking thoughtful, and then started surfing through the channels again. In that intuitive way of his, he seemed to have realized that I didn't want to talk about what had happened at my parents' house, that I just wanted to let things go for now. I knew I couldn't allow the current state of affairs to continue indefinitely, but it could certainly wait a night. Maybe the next day I'd talk to my Aunt Kirsten, see if she could help smooth things over.

We ended up watching an action film from a few years back, something mindless enough that I could let myself halfway doze on Logan's shoulder, only rousing myself from time to time if he asked a question, usually about some nuance in the dialogue or plot that he didn't understand. When it was over, we went into the bedroom and got out of our clothes and into our sleeping things. That is, I did; Logan didn't own anything that could be labeled as sleepwear, although he did keep his T-shirt on. We took turns in the bathroom, and then fell asleep holding one another. It was okay that we didn't have sex. It was enough to be there in his arms, feeling warm and safe and contented.

Feeling loved.

Since we'd gone to bed fairly early, we were also up relatively early, and showered and dressed by around nine o'clock. Just as well, as I figured it would be good to get up to Flag early in the day so I'd have time to show Logan around. Was that a coward's maneuver, sneaking out of Sedona with everything so up in the air with my parents? Possibly, but a cooling-off period might be what we all needed. If I could let a little time pass, allow them to see that the world wasn't going to end just because I was with Logan, then maybe at some point, they'd reconcile themselves to the situation. At least, that was what I hoped in the back of my mind, although I didn't voice aloud anything about what I was thinking.

No, we ate, cleaned up the kitchen, then did some more general tidying in preparation for our departure. I had a new text from Noelle, complaining about not being able to find a babysitter—her parents had gone to visit her sister in Colorado for the holidays—and that maybe we could get together sometime after New Year's. I texted her back and let her know I understood, while inwardly I was relieved. The situation was complicated enough without trying to shoehorn a visit with Noelle into the midst of everything.

I could tell Logan still wasn't happy to be leaving, although it seemed he'd reconciled himself to the situation. He folded the clothes I'd bought him and somehow got them to fit in my weekender bag, and stuffed the dirty items in one of the bags from Penney's, which apparently he'd held on to for some reason.

To be honest, I shared some of his reticence. It was going to be cramped quarters until I could find some-place better for the two of us to live, and although my salary was certainly adequate to cover the cost of a bigger apartment or even a condo, it would still probably take a while to locate something suitable. Housing was at a premium in Flagstaff because of the university, even though Logan and I would have something of a leg up since we weren't students. There were some landlords, especially those who were renting houses or condos, who wouldn't even lease a place to students, and although I thought that was a bit discriminatory, I couldn't really blame them. I wouldn't want my own property trashed by someone having keggers every weekend.

But since there weren't any keggers in Logan's and my future, and because I had a good job, I knew we'd find something. The only question was when.

"Ready?" I asked Logan, who was still messing around in the bathroom

"Yes." He came out into the living room, where I

was waiting by the sofa, our baggage sitting on the floor near my feet. As he reached down to pick up the weekender bag, someone knocked on the front door.

Great. It could have been a couple of Jehovah's Witnesses out canvassing the neighborhood...but I kind of doubted it. No, I had a feeling it was either my mother or Lance or maybe the both of them, tired of getting voicemail so they came to force the issue in person.

Some part of me wanted to ignore the knocking, to have Logan and me sneak out the back door to avoid whoever it was, but I realized that wouldn't work. If nothing else, I'd still have to come back around to the front of the house to retrieve my car. Besides, I knew I would never do anything so cowardly. I'd told my mother I was a grown-up, so I needed to act like one.

Instead, I made myself take a deep breath, and after doing so, I went to the door and opened it. Waiting outside was neither my mother nor Lance, but my Aunt Kirsten. She didn't smile when she saw me, but only sent a quick glance past me to where Logan stood.

"Um...Kirsten?" I ventured.

She still didn't smile. "I need you to come with me," she said. "Jeff's cracked the code."

CHAPTER THIRTEEN

She insisted on driving, so I got in on the passenger side of her Mercedes, while Logan somehow managed to fold himself into the back seat.

"What did Jeff find?" I asked, and she shook her head.

"He wouldn't tell me. Just said I needed to go and get you and Logan, stat. So here I am."

That could have been ominous...or just more of Jeff Makowski's neuroses manifesting themselves. I'd gotten the impression from my aunt that he didn't much care for relaying any kind of important information on networks he wasn't sure were secure. So, fine, we'd play along. All this would delay our departure for Flagstaff, but it was far more important to know what exactly had been on that alien computer.

Traffic was heavy, even for a Saturday. Probably,

all the people who'd waited for Christmas to be over were now coming into town for a weekend resort getaway. The snow was still sticking to the ridge lines, which meant we'd probably get more than our share of day-trippers from Phoenix in addition to the travelers staying for the weekend or even through New Year's.

I tried not to fidget with the strap of my purse as we lurched our way along 89A until we got to the condo complex. The lot was packed, and I wondered if my aunt would even be able to find someplace to park. Luckily, though, someone was backing out of a space not too far from the building where Jeff was staying, and Kirsten pulled into it almost the second it was safe to do so.

"Here we are," she said, quite unnecessarily, but maybe she just wanted to fill the awkward silence that seemed to have filled the car.

Almost at the same time, Logan and I opened our doors and got out. Once he was outside, I could see him gazing up at the condo building with some curiosity. It did look very different from the cottage, or the similarly modest one-story houses in that neighborhood, or even my parents' big two-story home. True, he probably would've seen a variety of different types of housing when watching TV, but he wouldn't have experienced any of them in person until now.

"This way," Kirsten told us, although I thought her words were directed more at Logan. Once I'd been someplace, I could always find my way back. Another aspect of the enhanced faculties my alien DNA appeared to have given me, I supposed.

We followed her along the path until we came to the condo's door. Once again, she pulled out her phone to text Jeff that we'd arrived, and not quite a minute later, he was opening the door and letting us enter. I could see the way his eyes narrowed as he took in Logan. They were of a height, but of course Logan was much broader and looked like he could put Jeff through a wall without breaking a sweat.

And since it was Jeff, there was no "thank you for coming" or "can I get you something to drink?" He merely stalked back over to the dining room table, which had obviously become his current work station, and pushed the tab on the alien computer. The heads-up display once again projected itself into the air, showing columns of those strange, angular alien characters.

"Once my algorithms detected its underlying structure, the language itself wasn't too difficult to decipher. In fact, it isn't that different from English in terms of its basic subject-predicate makeup. The notation was slightly more challenging, as it is neither precisely a pictogram-based language, nor an alphabet-based one, but—"

"While that's fascinating, Jeff, I think we're all curious to know what it said," Kirsten broke in, but so gently that it didn't sound like an interruption.

Her attempt to soft pedal apparently didn't work,

since Jeff scowled, then jerked his chin toward Logan. "Why don't you ask him?"

Logan's eyes widened. "I don't know anything about what might be contained in that computer's files."

"Is that a fact?" Jeff did something so the display rotated, the columns of alien writing now facing directly at us. "Are you able to read that?"

Something in Logan's demeanor changed. I couldn't even quite put my finger on what it was, except for possibly the smallest tensing of the muscles along his jaw, a narrowing of his eyes so infinitesimal that one blink, and you would've missed it. He said slowly, "Yes, I can read it."

I couldn't help wondering then why Jeff hadn't asked Logan to translate in the first place. But then I realized that cracking the language on his own was something he'd been emotionally invested in. Well, that, and Jeff being so paranoid that he probably wouldn't have trusted anything Logan said without being able to verify it independently.

"Then go ahead and read it, why don't you? Enlighten us, Logan. I can read your language, but I'm not so sure of my pronunciation. But then, you can probably translate on the fly, can't you?"

His tone was so hostile that I began to open my mouth to protest, to tell him he had no right to be speaking to Logan that way. I must have telegraphed my intent to my aunt, however, because I could see her shake her head slightly. All I could do was cross my arms and wait to see what Logan would do.

"Yes, I can translate," he said, reluctance clear in his tone. "But—"

"No buts. I want them to hear this from you."

A long pause. Logan looked over at me, his mouth tight.

"It's all right, Logan," I said. "Nothing you read on there is going to change how I feel about you."

Jeff didn't seem shocked by that statement, although his lip curled slightly. I supposed even an Aspergers-affected recluse like him would have been able to figure out that Logan's and my relationship wasn't exactly platonic.

"Very well," Logan said at last. "If you truly want me to read it."

"Oh, we do," Jeff remarked, and Kirsten frowned. Was that some kind of satisfaction underlying his tone? But why would he be so invested in this?

Well, except for spending the last thirty-six hours hacking away at it. Judging by the bags under his eyes, somehow magnified by the glasses he wore, I had a feeling he hadn't slept in any of those thirty-six hours, either. That would make anyone cranky, especially if they'd already started out that way.

Logan buried his hands in his jeans pockets and stared up at the display. The seconds ticked by, and I wondered if he really was going to read what those symbols said, or whether the delay was simply because he was familiarizing himself with the content first so it would be easier to translate on the fly.

Then he said, tone flatter than I'd ever heard it before, "This is an entry dated to what corresponds on your calendar as September thirtieth. 'The new specimen has passed its preliminary checks and will be placed in cryo-storage pending further testing. The project is on track for a complete replacement of the current troop complement, with final roll-out commencing in ninety days.'"

"And the 'new specimen' was you, correct?" Jeff inquired, although it seemed clear enough that he already knew the answer, from the slightly arch inflection in his tone.

"Yes, I believe so." Logan wouldn't look at me as he made that reply, his gaze still fixed on the display that shimmered in the air before him.

Right then, I wanted nothing more than to go to him and put my arms around him, to tell him that I didn't care if some alien scientist had once referred to him as a "specimen." Logan was a man to me, a wonderful man. Who cared if he'd begun his existence in the alien equivalent of a test tube?

"Just wanted to clarify. Skip ahead to the entry that correlates to December twentieth. I think Grace will find that to be *very* educational." Jeff waved a hand toward the display.

It was sort of amazing how much I could dislike someone whose presence I'd only been in for about a half hour, tops. I could feel my hands curl into fists at my sides, and although of course I would never actually go over and punch Jeff in the head, I sure *wanted* to.

Kirsten didn't say anything, but I could see her watching me, knew she could tell how upset I was on Logan's behalf. Maybe if Jeff got really out of hand, she'd do something to rein him in. The question was…could she?

Logan said, still in that monotone which didn't sound anything like his usual self, "Because of the resistance we've encountered, and because the hybrid's infant is so closely guarded, the decision has been made to leave a fail-safe in the unlikely event that we are not successful tomorrow. Specimen L-110's cryo-pod has been enhanced to sustain him for approximately 12.78 times longer than would normally be deemed necessary. We are confident that, based on the human female's reaction to D-7957, her child will react similarly to L-110 when they meet in the future."

It took me a few seconds to process all that. Then I realized the "human female" was my mother…and presumably "D-7957" was my father. So the aliens had been planning a hook-up for me when I was just a baby? Creepy, but certainly not enough to set off any alarm bells.

"Modifications have been made to the training L-110 is receiving to ensure he understands what is required of him and that he will do what is necessary when the time comes."

All right, that sounded a lot worse. "'Do what is necessary'?" I demanded. "What the hell is that supposed to mean?"

He faltered then, steel-gray eyes avoiding mine. "I don't know."

"Still going to keep playing the innocent?" Jeff asked.

Logan stared at him in bewilderment, even as he said, "I truly don't know what the aliens' intentions were. I would say they are now immaterial, since they were defeated and driven from their base."

"You don't know?" Jeff did something to the computer, and the display appeared to jump forward a page. "Well, I can't give a word-for-word translation, but this should be close enough—the aliens knew, based on Logan's genome and the hybrid blood Grace carries, that there would be a strong attraction between them if they were to meet. It appears there was some kind of link between all hybrids, some sort of psychic connection that allowed them to work more effectively together. The aliens were counting on that link to draw Grace to L-110—sorry, *Logan*. Then the training they'd given him would kick in, with the result being her eventual impregnation. They were very curious to see what the children of such a mating would be like." A shrug. "Those Reptilians and their breeding programs. They do seem a little obsessed."

"Breeding programs—" It felt as if all the blood in my veins had turned to ice. Lord knows what I must have looked like, because my aunt took a step toward me, one hand reaching out, as if she intended to either console me or tell me to calm down. I wasn't planning on doing that, however.

Jeff went on, his tone almost conversational, "I suppose it's not really Logan's fault—I mean, he was just doing what he had been trained to do. Following orders, I suppose."

"No!" Logan burst out. In the first real flash of anger I'd ever seen from him, he went to the table and knocked the alien computer to the tiled floor. The heads-up display abruptly shut off, but otherwise, the device didn't seem to have been damaged. "Grace, what he's saying—this isn't true. It can't be."

My aunt hadn't moved, was looking from Jeff to Logan to me, as if she wasn't sure which of us she should be addressing first. "I'm sure there must be some kind of explanation—"

"There is an explanation," Logan said, staring at Jeff with narrowed eyes. The muscles in his biceps bulged as he clenched his fists, and in that moment, he did look very dangerous, exactly like someone who had been bred for combat. Bred to kill.

Jeff took a step backward, and I could see my Aunt Kirsten tense. Although I knew she'd somehow managed to defeat the aliens before, drawing on the very power hidden within Sedona's red rocks to assist her, I didn't know if she was capable, on her own, of subduing a genetically enhanced super-soldier.

No, she wouldn't have to. As angry as Logan appeared, I knew he wouldn't do anything that might hurt my aunt. Jeff, on the other hand....

Actually, the hacker surprised me. Although he'd retreated slightly, he did stop when he was more or less out of arm's reach. "We want to hear that explanation, Logan. So what is it?"

A second passed, then another. And another. Logan's brow was knotted, his gaze turned inward, as if he was wrestling with some part of himself. Worry began to churn away in me, roiling my stomach. "Logan...." I began, then stopped myself. As awful as what Jeff had discovered might be, I had to believe that Logan knew nothing of any of it. He might be a pawn, but an innocent one. As to the idea that the aliens had somehow engineered him to be a match for me...well, I'd think about that later. Right then, I only wanted to reassure him that my feelings for him hadn't changed, no matter what a report by some alien scientist or engineer might say.

"Doesn't look like he has much to say for himself, does he? Maybe this will jog his memory." Jeff went to retrieve the computer from the floor, tapped away at it. Once again, the heads-up display activated, but instead of showing the columns of alien writing it had displayed before, it showed a man's face.

Logan's face.

From somewhere off-camera, I heard a voice speaking a language I had never heard before, but the sound of it made shivers run down my spine and goosebumps prickle my skin. That voice was harsh, yet sibilant, the words it spoke seeming to be hissed more than spoken. Surely that must have been one of Logan's Reptilian masters.

One of my Aunt Kirsten's hands went to her throat, and the color left her face. "My God," she whispered. "I'd almost forgotten what they sounded like. I wanted to forget."

Hearing that cold, inimical voice, I found myself agreeing with her. Still, frightening as it might be, it didn't prove anything about Logan's guilt or innocence, since none of us could understand what the alien was saying.

But then someone—whether the speaker or another alien in the room—gave Logan another of the small hand-held computers they seemed to favor. I didn't get much of a glimpse of whoever it was, just a dark-sleeved arm with a greenish-brown scaled hand emerging from it, but that was enough to send a whole other set of shivers tingling across my skin. Yes, I'd known they were sentient reptiles, more or less, but my brain hadn't really grasped that concept. Not until now, knowing that what I looked at was the real thing, not some CG in a movie or an artist's rendering on a UFO conspiracy website.

The harsh voice spoke again, and Logan activated the display on the computer. In front of his face materialized an image of my mother, much younger. Of course she was younger; all this had to have been happening some twenty-five years in the past.

That image disappeared, replaced by one of the hybrid who was my father—only he looked different from the photo my mother had given me. In this image, he was blank-faced and stared straight ahead, and his eyes were dark, although in the photo I kept hidden in my wallet, those same eyes blazed a brilliant green. Well, I knew something had altered him —the combination of Persephone's psychic blast and the energy flowing up from Secret Canyon was the latest hypothesis—so that didn't surprise me too much.

What did shock me, enough so I let out a startled gasp before I got control of myself, was the next image projected in the heads-up display. That image was of me.

All right, not exactly, not once I recovered myself enough to take a closer look. The young woman in the image was dark-haired and had blue eyes like me, and her mouth and chin were almost exactly right, since they were so similar to my mother's. My cheekbones were maybe a bit wider and higher, the brows more arched, but still, considering the aliens must have extrapolated my appearance based on the most likely combination of my parents' genetic material, they'd gotten it darn close.

"Good God," Kirsten murmured.

Unfortunately, I didn't think God had very much to do with any of this.

The alien spoke again, and I saw the Logan in the recording survey the image carefully, then nod, as if he had committed it to memory. He spoke, his tone flat, the words of the Reptilian language sounding strange coming from his mouth, as if his tongue and palate weren't quite up to the task. Maybe they weren't; maybe the aliens' tongues were just as lizard-like as the rest of them.

Then he turned off the computer and handed it back to his master, and the image we were watching also went dark, Jeff deactivating it now that the damage had been done. "You see?" he asked. "It's clear that Logan was given very specific orders by his handlers. Why else would they create a simulation of the woman they wanted him to seek out?"

My mouth was dry and my brain darted this way and that, desperately trying to find some sort of logical explanation but coming up desperately short. At last I said, the words forcing their way out of my parched throat, "Logan, please tell me that what we just saw isn't what we thought it was."

Still, his eyes wouldn't meet mine, which was a more damning reaction than anything else he could have done. But he did reply, saying, "I know that looked terrible. And I can't really explain it—I just know I don't recall anything of that, don't have any memory of being given any sort of agenda. Truly, I don't. I haven't been following orders. I've—I've been following my heart."

"How very sweet. And also convenient," Jeff said. He set the computer down amongst the clutter on the dining room table. "However, claiming to have forgotten isn't exactly a valid excuse, is it?"

Logan didn't answer, but instead finally looked over in my direction. His expression was pleading. Clearly, he thought it was excuse enough.

And I—I didn't know what to think. I wanted to believe him, but something in me just couldn't. Maybe on some level, he had forgotten about the orders he'd been given, but the more I reflected on the time we'd spent together, the way he'd interacted with me, the more I began to feel how wrong it had all been. How strongly he'd come on, that Christmas Eve when I'd gotten home from my parents' house. At the time, I'd thought it was simply the wine talking, that his system couldn't handle the alcohol...but what if it was something else entirely? What if it had been his programming activating itself, knowing that if he reached out to me, he had a very good chance of success?

"I feel sick," I whispered. The room suddenly was too hot, the air stifling me. I realized I'd never taken off or even unbuttoned my coat, and Jeff had the thermostat jacked way up. Although I hadn't eaten all that recently, I still tasted the sourness of nausea in my throat. I had to get out of there.

"Grace—" Logan began, taking a step forward.

I couldn't speak then, couldn't do anything but shake my head at him, hold up a hand...as if that would be enough to ward him off.

"It's all right," my aunt said then. "I'll take care of

this." Her gaze flickered toward the front door, as if she knew the only thing I wanted to do in that moment was flee.

In that moment, I was happy for having quasi-telepathic family members. I shot one last despairing glance over my shoulder at Logan, then lunged for the door, slipping outside so I could draw in huge gasps of the cold air. Although I'd hoped that might clear my head, it didn't seem to be working. The world continued to spin around me, blue sky and reddish stucco buildings and dark evergreens whirling in a kaleidoscope of disjointed colors and patterns. Nothing looked the way it should.

I put out a hand against a support column, hoping to steady myself. A couple in their thirties passed by along the walk, gave me a curious look, and sped up their pace slightly. I must have looked like a madwoman, with my flushed face and agonized breathing.

It had all been a lie. I could deny the evidence if I wanted to, but that would have made me even more self-deluding than I'd already been. The one time I'd let my heart overrule my head, and now my head was having the last laugh. I should have known better. Falling in love wasn't that easy. I'd avoided it my whole life, and the only reason I'd thought it had finally happened to me was that I'd been manipulated to have it look that way.

I heard quiet footsteps and looked up to see Kirsten approaching. Her eyes as they met mine were the saddest I'd ever seen them. However, she sounded calm enough as she said, "Sweetie, what do you want me to do?"

"Logan?" I asked.

"I told him you needed some time alone, so he's staying inside. But we have to figure out what we're going to do next."

"I can't—I can't look at him right now." Even as I said the words, they hurt. Some part of me still wanted to go to him, to take refuge in his arms, although I knew those arms offered only a false impression of security. I had to be stronger than that.

"Okay." Hesitating, she glanced over at the door to the condo and back at me. "Do you want me to call Kara?"

No, I really didn't. I wanted to run away and pretend none of this had ever happened. But that was the reaction of a coward, and I'd already screwed this up badly enough. "I suppose you'd better. I can—I can go crash there for a while, I suppose. But what about Logan?"

It seemed she'd already been thinking this over, because she responded immediately. "He can stay at the cottage. We'll have the guys take turns watching him, I think. That is, he doesn't seem dangerous, but we don't know what other programming the aliens might have implanted in him. It's probably better to keep him isolated for now. Lance and Martin will have to take turns at it."

"What about Paul, or Michael?" I thought it

sounded kind of rough to have my stepfather and my uncle bear the brunt of babysitting duties.

She shook her head. "Because, capable as they are in other ways, they're not really equipped to handle this sort of thing. Maybe I'll call my father to come down as well, so he can spell the other two as necessary."

That did make some sort of sense—of course Martin and Gabriel were also aliens, and Lance, well, he wasn't, but he was still one of the most capable people I knew. At the same time, I hated to inconvenience anyone, and prying Gabriel out of his beautiful house in Flagstaff so he could come down here and play nursemaid to a possible hybrid spy rubbed me the wrong way. I was the one who'd screwed things up, and yet it seemed everyone else had to be on clean-up duty.

"I'm sorry," I whispered. "I didn't mean for any of this to happen."

"Of course you didn't," she said. "And we'll—we'll fix it."

How, I had no idea. Right then, all I could do was watch as she pulled out her phone and made two quick calls—one to my mother, and one to Martin. She pitched her voice low on purpose, so I couldn't hear precisely what she was saying. Maybe that was for the better. At least I wouldn't have to know which words she was using to explain how her niece was an utter screw-up, and could her mommy come get her, please?

After she was done, Kirsten came over and laid a hand on my arm. "I need to go back inside. Lord knows what Jeff and Logan are saying to each other. But Kara will be here in about fifteen minutes. Will you be okay until then?"

I nodded and gave her a dreary smile. "Sure."

We both knew I was lying, but there wasn't much else I could say or do right then. Only wait, and hope that I might wake up to discover this had all been a bad dream.

CHAPTER FOURTEEN

No such luck. I was all too awake and aware when my mother hurried down the pathway toward me about fifteen minutes later. I could only stand there and stare at her, whereupon she came to me and folded me into her arms. Up until then, I'd been calm and cold, my thoughts feeling somehow detached from my body, as if they were little birds fluttering high above my head, not touching me. But once I felt my mother holding me, I broke into noisy tears. She didn't say anything, just continued to hug me, until I more or less got enough control of myself to respond with a nod when she asked if I was ready to go.

She made a quick detour inside, murmuring that she needed to give Kirsten the spare key to the cottage, then guided me down the path through the condo complex and into the parking lot, where we had to walk some distance to get to her SUV. Once we were inside and I was buckling my seatbelt, she asked, "Do you want to stop by the cottage to get your things?"

About all I could manage was a nod. That seemed to be enough, though, because she pointed the car in that direction after we left the parking lot. A few minutes later, she was pulling into the short driveway at the cottage. She hesitated, then said, "I can go in and get your bags, if you don't want to get out of the car."

That was tempting, but I thought of how Logan had packed all his clothing in with mine in preparation for going up to Flagstaff. I'd have to take his things out of my weekender bag, and I couldn't exactly ask my mother to do that.

"No, it's okay," I said quietly before I let myself out of the car and headed up the walk to the front door. I got out my key and let myself in.

It was harder than I'd thought it would be to look at the place where I fooled myself into thinking I'd fallen in love with Logan. But I forced myself to pick up my bags and take them back into the bedroom, then carefully extract all Logan's belongings and stow them in the dresser. At least he and I had already tidied the place up, and so there wasn't anything much else I needed to do.

I came back to the living room, the bags I carried much lighter now. "Ready," I told her.

She didn't say anything, only gave the main

living room a quick once-over, as if to satisfy herself that everything was as it should be. As if it mattered. But that was just her way.

We left after that, and I locked the door and handed her the key. For a second or two, she only looked at it where it lay in the palm of her hand. Then she gave the smallest of sighs, tucking it away in a pocket of her purse.

Traffic was thick as we wended our way back through town and then into the less congested and more serene canyon. It was hard to remember that it was still Saturday, that all these people here to have a good time had no knowledge of the drama playing out within my family. I pressed my face against the window and wished for another snowstorm, a thick, heavy one that would shut down the roads and keep anyone from coming to bother me at my parents' house. It wouldn't happen; we hardly ever got that kind of snow in Sedona, and besides, a heavy snow-fall was the last thing we needed if it turned out that Gabriel really did have to make the drive down from Flagstaff to help watch over Logan.

I did make one request, though. Since I knew it was coming up on our right, I said, "Can we stop at the drugstore? There's something I need to get."

She shot me a curious look, but only replied, "Sure," then pulled into the parking lot at Walgreens.

"This'll just be a minute," I told her. "I'll be right back."

Seeming to get the hint, she nodded and made no

move to get out of the car. I went into the store, dodging the throngs of tourists who were in there to buy aspirin and lip balm and sunscreen and anything else they might have forgotten when they packed for their trips, and headed to the family planning section of the store. Without even stopping to really scan the labels, I reached out and grabbed a home pregnancy test.

If the worst really had happened, I wanted to know. What I'd do about it, I had no idea, but the phrase "breeding program" was still rattling around in my brain, and I had a feeling I'd go crazy if I didn't at least get some resolution on that one issue.

I didn't know if it was luck or my mother's maneuvering that had caused the house to be empty when we got there. Since it was a busy Saturday, Lance and Kevin were most likely out running a Jeep tour, and maybe Kelsey and Melissa were also at work. Melissa didn't get a ton of hours at the boutique where she was a part-time clerk, but it made sense that she wouldn't be home on such a busy holiday weekend, either.

Whatever the reason for their absence, I couldn't help letting out a relieved breath as I followed my mother inside and was only greeted with silence. We went upstairs to the room that had once been mine and was now the guest room; it felt strangely dissonant to walk in there and recognize the bones of the space, the height of the ceiling and the spacing of the windows and even the angle of the light coming in through those windows, and at the same time see it as something strange, with its new furniture and new paint and blinds.

My mother hovered at the doorway as I set down my bags and looked around. I could tell she desperately wanted to talk, but in that moment, I knew I couldn't discuss Logan with her. Not yet. I needed time, needed peace and quiet. Maybe then I could get my brain functioning again.

Well, after I made sure he hadn't knocked me up. Yes, I'd gotten my shots, but my mother had been on the pill when she was with my father, and that hadn't worked out so well for her, had it?

"I think I just want to cocoon a bit," I said, once the silence had begun to strain and stretch a little too much. "And—and whenever Lance gets home, I really don't want to talk to him."

Her brows creased. "You can't hide up here forever, Grace."

"I'm not talking about forever. I'm just talking about tonight. Please."

I could tell she still didn't like it, but she didn't protest. A nod, and then she said, "I love you, Grace."

Despite everything that had happened, warmth flooded through me. I'd been prepared for recriminations, scolding…not such a simple declaration of support. "Love you, too, Mom." It was all I said, but she seemed to understand, because she smiled and headed off down the hallway toward the staircase.

I shut the door, leaning my head against it as I let the quiet of the house envelop me. It wouldn't always be like this, but for now I could let myself float in that peace and hope some of it would penetrate to soothe the ache in my heart.

First things first, though. I'd unpack later. For now, all I could think of was the box resting in my purse, and what its results would mean for me.

There were two bathrooms upstairs, although neither of them had been built *en suite*. Probably smart planning on my parents' part, since otherwise there would have been far too much arguing over who got the favored suite with the private bath. Now, though, I knew I wanted to hurry, since I had no idea when any—or all—of my siblings might get home.

I went into the nearest bathroom and shut the door. Because I'd been careful my entire adult life, I'd never needed to use a pregnancy test before this. Still, I knew the basics. They were very accurate these days, even within twenty-four hours of fertilization. The test should tell me what I needed to know. The thing was, was I brave enough to face it?

Hesitation would only cost me my nerve, so I unwrapped the thing, then squatted over the toilet. Hideously awkward position. You'd think they would've come up with a home blood test by now. But this was the only route available to me at the moment, so I finished up and held the stick, waiting to see what the LED readout would say.

The seconds ticked by. Maybe I remembered to breathe. I wasn't sure.

No silly lines, no plus or minus sign. Just a single word.

No.

Air suddenly filled my lungs again, and once again, I had that sensation of the world tilting around me. I held on to the counter with one hand and blinked, trying to center myself, to not let the relief overwhelm me. There, cool tile of the counter beneath my fingers, and above, a soft glow from the alabaster glass fixture over the mirror. My own reflection in the mirror, so pale, blue eyes wide and worried. No need to be worried, though. Well, at least not as worried as I had been a few seconds ago.

I wrapped the stick in some toilet paper and deposited it in the trash, then dropped more toilet paper on top to conceal its shape. The box I'd take back with me to my room, since there was no easy way to disguise that.

Downstairs, I could hear the front door shut, followed by a murmur of voices. It sounded as if Kevin and Lance had just gotten home, so I'd finished up not a moment too soon. I tiptoed back to the guest room—my room again, it seemed—and closed the door as quietly as I could. It wasn't quiet enough to muffle the sound of Lance's voice, raised, as if my mother had just told him about my being here…and why.

Footsteps coming up the stairs. Goddamn it. Once

upon a time, I'd put a lock on this door, wanting my privacy, but they'd clearly removed the lock when they remodeled the room.

My mother's voice, following him down the hallway. "Lance, leave her alone."

No answer. The footsteps stopped in front of my door. "Grace."

If I remained silent, made no reply, would he leave? Knowing Lance, probably not. I cleared my throat. "I don't want to talk right now."

"Do you think you can stay in there forever?"

Part of me wanted to answer "yes," just to be snotty. That was probably the worst thing I could have said, though, and besides, I had to try to act like an adult about all this. Bad enough that I'd jumped into bed with Logan without hardly a second thought. No, scratch that. What was even worse was that I'd gotten him out of that pod without thinking of the possible consequences.

I placed my hand on the knob, then gritted my teeth and turned it. Lance stood right outside the door. His expression, however, was not one of anger or annoyance—what I'd been expecting—but rather worry.

"I'm not going to turn into a hermit," I told him. "I just—it's like I told Mom. I want to be alone for a little while. I promise I'll come out and rejoin the human race tomorrow. But right now, I just want to wallow."

He didn't reply immediately, but remained quiet,

seeming to weigh what I had just said. When he spoke, his words surprised me. "Is there anything you need?"

I shook my head. "I'm okay. That is—maybe a sandwich or something in a few hours. But that's it."

A brief pat on my shoulder, surprising me even further, since Lance was not the type to offer physical expressions of affection, especially toward me. "I think your mother can manage that."

And because he was Lance, he left it at that, turning away from me and going back downstairs. I had a feeling it might have escalated into more of a confrontation if I'd refused to open the door, but since we'd met each other halfway, he was willing to let it go for now.

I closed the door, but softly, then began pulling my clothes out of my bags and putting them away. Even as I did so, I wondered why I was going to the effort. Surely the next day I'd be on my way back to Flagstaff. No, that wasn't right. I'd made this mess, and it wouldn't be fair for me to leave it for everyone else to clean up while I went back to my life…such as it was…and pretended the whole Logan incident had never happened.

Probably I was occupying myself with unpacking because there was something oddly soothing about it, something mindless and at the same time ritualistic. Skirt and sweaters and jacket in the closet. Jeans and T-shirts and underwear in the highboy. And so on.

Underneath it all, though, was a dull, nagging ache. I knew what I'd seen on that footage, and yet I still missed Logan. I wanted to hear his voice. I wanted to turn around and see him sitting on the window seat and smiling at me. Was this all merely the result of our compatible genomes? Were these my hormones talking, or did I really care for him?

You'd better hope it's just hormones, I told myself. *Because he was, as they say, just following orders, or at least following what some implanted conditioning told him to do.*

When that dreary thought crossed my mind, I could feel the tears begin to well up. This time, I didn't bother to stop them. I was alone, and no one would even see me crying my eyes out. Who knows —I might even feel better when it was all over.

So I crawled up onto the window seat, stared out at the bare, wintry oaks that ringed the property, the patches of snow still huddling at the base of the pine trees, and let it go.

I didn't know how much time had passed. The sun slipped down behind the ridges to the west, and the property fell into shadow. Kelsey's bright yellow compact SUV pulled up into the empty area we'd designated as the overflow parking area, and both my sisters got out. From downstairs, I could hear doors slamming and a hubbub of voices now that everyone was home, but it all sounded so very far away, almost otherworldly, drifting up from a place to which I had no real connection.

Something told me that was wrong, that of course I had a connection to those voices, those people, but I still couldn't shake that feeling of detachment, of looking and listening to them from very far away. And maybe that had been my problem my whole life. I'd never felt completely at ease, simply because I knew I was different. Some part of me wasn't human.

One could argue that my cousin Callista had been forced to wrestle with the same problems, but it was different for her. For one thing, her father…her biological father…was around. Also, while Martin and Gabriel might be Nords, and my aunt half that race, the Nords looked completely human. Gorgeous nearly perfect humans, but still. They didn't have DNA mixed in there from something that looked like that—that thing I'd seen on the recording. Just getting a glimpse of its hand had been enough to send cold nausea through me. And yet I had some of those same Reptilian genes buried within my genetic code.

I got up from the window seat, retrieved a tissue from the box on top of the highboy, and blotted my eyes and blew my nose. Lord knows I probably looked a complete wreck, but it wasn't as if I had to impress anyone at the moment. My mother could handle some puffy eyes and a red nose.

Right then, I heard a soft knock at the door,

followed by her voice saying, "Grace? I've brought up some chili."

Infinitely better than a sandwich. My stomach growled, telling me that it cared about being fed regularly even if I didn't. When was the last time I'd eaten? Around nine-thirty that morning, which had to be at least nine hours ago.

I dropped the used tissue I held in the trash, then went to open the door. My mother came in holding a tray with a bowl of chili, the way I liked it with lots of shredded cheddar cheese on top, along with a square of fresh cornbread, and some butter and honey. There was also a tall glass of some pale gold liquid that bubbled gently, and I raised an eyebrow at her.

"It's just hard cider," she said. "I thought it might help you relax a little."

That wasn't such a bad idea. I'd learned the hard way that drowning my sorrows in anything stronger than a glass of wine was not a good solution, but cider was even milder than wine. Maybe it would give me just the slightest of buzzes, just enough to smooth down some of reality's harder edges.

"Thank you," I said, taking the tray from her and setting it down on the window seat, which was the handiest level surface. "It smells great." Her chili was one of my favorites, and I'd been hoping she might make up a batch while I was visiting. I just hadn't thought I'd be eating it in quite these circumstances.

"Oh, you're welcome. I'm glad I'd decided to

make it today." A pause, during which she regarded me quietly, no doubt taking in my blotched cheeks and red eyes. Then she asked, tone so diffident that it hardly sounded like her, "Do you want to talk now?"

I really didn't. What was there to say? I'd screwed up royally, and now we all would have to figure out what to do about it. But I knew continually putting her off wouldn't solve anything, either.

To stall, I broke off a piece of cornbread and spread a little honey and butter on it, then popped it in my mouth. Well, there was some comfort in the form of a square inch of heaven. I washed down the cornbread with a swallow of cider before telling her, "I'm not sure what there is to talk about."

Her eyebrow went up, a signal I recognized all too well as her version of saying "bullshit."

"Okay," I amended, "maybe it's not so much that there's nothing to talk about, and more that I'm not sure how talking about it is going to change anything."

"I don't know about 'changing' things," she said. "But it might make you feel better."

I sighed and broke off another piece of cornbread. "Aren't you missing dinner?"

"It's chili. I'll get myself a bowl at some point. In the meantime, everyone else in this house is an adult, so I assume they can manage to dish up some chili on their own without my being there."

True. I ate the piece of cornbread I held, then spooned up some chili to go along with it. Mmm. It had been way too long since I'd had my mother's chili. Not sure how to start, I blurted out the first thing that came to my mind. "What did it feel like when you first found out about my father?"

Frowning, she ran her fingers through her hair, then pushed it back over her shoulder. "It felt like... complete disbelief at first. Although I knew consciously that it was nothing Persephone and Paul would joke about it, still I thought they had to be pulling some sort of prank on me. And then when it sank in that they were telling the truth, that he really was one of the hybrids from the base...well, I ran to the bathroom and threw up, actually."

I stared at her. She'd never told me about that before. "Seriously?"

"Seriously. Of course, I was pregnant at the time, although I didn't know it, so that could have had something to do with my reaction, but...." Her shoulders lifted. "I was shocked, and scared. I didn't know what to do. And I felt like an idiot for letting him into my life so easily."

"That sounds familiar," I remarked, my tone bitter. "Well, except for the throwing-up part."

"But you're not an idiot, sweetheart," my mother said. "And neither was I. Opening yourself up to care about someone...it's a very brave act. Especially for you."

"Me?" I asked, glass of cider lifted halfway to my lips. I took a sip, glad of its cool sweetness. Somewhere in the back of my throat, disappointment still burned.

Her expression softened, and a faint smile touched her mouth, still full and pretty. "Oh, Grace. Do you think I haven't noticed the way you've held yourself apart from everyone you've ever dated? Even the relationships that looked as if they might have had a chance. Somehow you always found a way to end them, and yet you never seemed all that upset by it."

"And here I thought I was acting all cool and mysterious."

"You're my daughter, Grace." She crossed her arms, and I noticed a new ring glittering next to her wedding band, a circle of diamonds I'd never seen before. Well, their twenty-fifth wedding anniversary was coming up. It looked as if Lance had given her a special present this Christmas. Head tilting slightly as she regarded me, she said, "You know, you're not his blood, but of all my children, you're the most like Lance."

That wasn't something I really wanted to hear. I raised an eyebrow, then said, "How so?"

"Because you're both stubborn and determined, and you won't give up on something once you have your mind set on it. Sometimes, it's been like living with a couple of mules."

Despite myself, I couldn't help smiling. "I suppose it wasn't easy, being caught between the two of us."

"You could say that." She offered me a smile in return, one that faded as she went on, "But I always knew that once you had fixed on something, you'd see it through. That was why I knew none of your other boyfriends would work out...I could tell you weren't set on them. When you came here the first time with Logan, though, I could see that he was different. *You* were different around him. And when you came back to tell us the truth about him, I saw that look in your eyes. I used to call it the 'digging in your heels' look, and I knew you were going to do what you wanted, regardless of what we might have to say on the subject."

"Well, in that case, being stubborn didn't pay off so well, did it?"

"I don't know." A hesitation, as if she was trying to decide how to word what she wanted to say next. "I still feel as if we're not getting the whole picture. Maybe Martin has been able to talk to Logan, get some more information."

How had she known that I'd been secretly harboring the same hope, a hope I hadn't wanted to admit even to myself? Everything I'd seen in that recording and heard from the alien scientist's account of Martin's training had been damning enough, but maybe there was something we were missing....

Because I didn't want my mother to see how much I wanted her to be right, I shrugged, then took another sip of my cider. "I don't know what else Logan could possibly say. It looked pretty clear to me that he'd been more or less set up as a guided missile intent on getting in my pants."

That remark earned me a reproving look. "Grace—"

"Well, it's true." And, given the Reptilians' emphasis on breeding hybrids and making genetics their personal bitch, I could see why they would have been itching to find out what would happen if they made a cocktail of Logan's and my DNA. Abruptly, I added, "But I'm not pregnant."

She didn't exactly sigh in relief, but I could tell from the way her shoulders relaxed that she'd been worrying about the box I'd bought at Walgreens, and whether my fate would have ended up looking not very different from hers. "I—well, that's good news, isn't it?"

"Yes," I said automatically. And it was. Never mind that I couldn't help wondering what it would have been like to have Logan's child. No, that was ridiculous. It could have come out looking like a refugee from the cantina scene in *Star Wars*. "I'm not sure why, when you were on the pill and still got pregnant, but...."

"I've thought about that," my mother said. "I was on the mini pill, which normally would have worked perfectly well. But it worked more by preventing implantation than preventing ovulation, so it probably would have been easier to disrupt." Her fingers played with the edge of her sweater, and I could tell she wasn't exactly comfortable with the subject at hand. "Anyway, that's my theory. I suppose we'll never know for sure."

No, we wouldn't. In fact, there were a disturbing number of things we'd probably never know. I'd taken that as a fact of existence for most of my life, considering that my extended family had been surrounded by paranormal happenings ever since I was born. Now, though, that state of affairs seemed particularly frustrating.

My mother laid a gentle hand on my arm. "I'd better let you finish eating that before it gets completely cold. And afterward, if you want to come downstairs—"

I shook my head.

"All right," she said, sounding resigned. "Then try to rest. The password for the wireless is the same, so if you want to get online, you can do that, too."

"Thanks." I was surprised they hadn't changed the password, considering how militant Lance generally was about security, but the property did stand on its own, far away from any other houses. The closest neighbor was way outside the range of our wireless network, and any hacker trying to skim into it would have been very conspicuous. It wasn't like the tracts of houses I'd seen down in Phoenix and Tucson, where it appeared to me as if people were practically living in each other's laps. "Right now I feel as if I could sleep for a hundred years."

"Well, maybe not quite that long." Her blue eyes twinkled. "Just set the tray outside the door when you're done, and I'll have one of your sisters bring it down later."

Out of impulse, I went over and threw my arms around her neck. "Thank you, Mom," I whispered.

She hugged me back, briefly but fiercely, and then let herself out.

I went back and picked up the discarded spoon for my chili. It wasn't piping hot anymore, but it still tasted good. I'd eat it all, and the cornbread, then finish the cider. After that, I'd get out my computer, check my email, make sure the world was still out there somewhere.

And after that...well, I'd worry about that tomorrow.

CHAPTER FIFTEEN

I<small>T WAS LATE MORNING BEFORE</small> I <small>CREPT OUT OF MY ROOM</small> and down the stairs, more because I was going stir-crazy than because I really felt like dealing with anyone right then. But the only person I saw was my brother Kevin, who had his feet up on the coffee table in the family room—a total no-no—and was watching some kind of extreme sports program on the TV.

He kind of grunted at me when I went into the kitchen to start a fresh pot of coffee brewing, but it was clear that, if he knew anything at all about my extraterrestrial amatory woes, he didn't much care.

"Where is everyone?" I asked.

Without looking away from the TV, he said, "Dad went out late last night—to the cottage, I think. Kelsey and Melissa had to work. And Mom's out in the greenhouse."

So at least I wouldn't have to face the horde. At the same time, though, a pang of guilt went through me. I knew exactly why Lance was at the cottage—he was taking his shift at babysitting Logan. It wasn't fair that he'd had to sacrifice a night's sleep just because of my mistake. At the same time, I knew he would never have allowed anyone else to do it.

The coffee was just wrapping up the perk cycle when my mother came back in through the kitchen door, a gust of cold, pine-scented air blowing in with her as she did so. She had on a pair of faded jeans and an oversized anorak that must have belonged to Lance, and her hair was piled up on her head.

"Grace," she said, spotting me. "How are you?"

"Okay," I replied. I didn't think I was, but I really didn't want to say anything more revealing than that in front of Kevin. But at least I'd taken a long, hot shower, letting myself breathe in the warm steam and think about nothing, and I did feel better after that. A good shower always improved my outlook on life, and getting some of the coffee I'd just made inside me would help even more.

She nodded but looked abstracted, as if she could tell I wasn't exactly giving her the whole truth. I never wore a lot of makeup; however, this morning I'd spent more time than usual applying cosmetics, trying to hide the evidence of my mostly sleepless and teary night. Since my mother had eagle eyes, I was sure she'd be able to spot the telltales. There wasn't much I could do about that, though.

After sipping some coffee, I asked in a murmur, "Any reports from the cottage?"

A quick glance in Kevin's direction, although it was clear he was engrossed in the TV and not paying us any attention. "Your father texted me early this morning. Logan did finally go to sleep around midnight. Up until then, he just kept asking to see you."

Pain lanced through me, and I looked away from her, pretending to be involved in blowing on my coffee to cool it down more. When I thought I could speak in a normal voice, I asked, "What did Lance tell him?"

"That he didn't think that was such a good idea right now."

No, it probably wasn't. The need I still felt coursing through me told me I wasn't exactly thinking clearly when it came to the hybrid soldier. How long would it take for the desire to go away completely? What if it didn't? Could I move on with my life, knowing that I still wanted him?

I didn't know what to say, so I drank some more coffee. Although usually I welcomed that morning cup, right then, it seemed to burn in my stomach, sour as bile. Maybe I should have eaten something, although I didn't have much of an appetite right then.

The doorbell rang, and my mother slanted a look over at the time display on the refrigerator door. Almost eleven-thirty, which wasn't a strange hour for someone to be dropping by, even on a Sunday morning. But I could tell she was puzzled.

"Kevin, were you expecting anyone?" she called out, and he shook his head.

"Nope."

She shrugged and headed out to the front door. We'd never gotten much in the way of canvassers, mostly because the house was isolated from the road by such a long drive. It wasn't really worth the effort.

I stayed in the kitchen, sipping my coffee and contemplating whether I should toast a bagel or an English muffin to soak up the stomach acid.

Then I heard my mother say, "Taryn! Well...this is a surprise."

Taryn Oliver. I set down my coffee mug and frowned, wondering what in the world she was doing here. Yes, she and Kelsey were friendly enough, but with Kelsey at work, there didn't seem to be much reason for Taryn to be dropping by.

"Sorry to just come by like this, but...." Her voice got louder as they came down the hall, and then she and my mother paused at the entrance to the great room that encompassed the kitchen and family room. Her gaze flicked over toward me and then back to my mother. "Do you think I could talk to you and Grace?"

Curioser and curioser. Taryn and I had never had a lot of interaction, mostly because the four-year difference in our ages was large enough that we didn't have a lot in common. I had a feeling she knew all about my current difficulties with Logan, because even though her father hadn't been tapped for babysitting duties, he still would have been informed of the situation. But what that had to do with Taryn, I had no idea.

"Of course," my mother said, after a perceptible hesitation. She glanced over at Kevin, but it was clear it would take at least a grenade to dislodge him from his current spot on the couch. Not quite sighing, she went on, "Let's go into the living room."

So we all trooped into that much more formal space, although it was cheerier now because of the enormous Christmas tree in one corner. Taryn sat down in one of the wing chairs, and my mother and I settled ourselves on the couch. It said something about how flummoxed my mother must have been that she didn't offer Taryn something to drink, not even a glass of water.

Not that Taryn seemed to notice. She looked almost nervous, which was unusual for her. Normally, she seemed fairly in command of herself. I supposed she had to be, since she worked off and on as a psychic at one of the shops in Uptown. No one wanted a nervous psychic.

At last, she clasped her hands in her lap and gazed at us with earnest green eyes, rimmed in lashes so heavy and dark that I didn't think she ever had to wear mascara. I got the distinct impression that she'd come here on her own volition, that her parents didn't know what she was doing. It was a pretty good guess that they thought she'd gone in to work or something.

"What is it, Taryn?" my mother asked gently.

"I—I heard what happened," she said, looking more at my mother than at me. "With Logan, I mean."

About what I had expected, but it didn't make me feel any less foolish. However, I didn't see any judgment in Taryn's expression. Whatever her reason for coming here, it obviously wasn't to rub salt in that particular wound.

"I'm…getting a feeling," she went on, and I sat up a little straighter. As with her mother, Taryn's "feelings" were something we all tended to take seriously.

"About Logan?" I said.

A nod, and this time her eyes did meet mine. I could tell she was uncomfortable, but I wondered if that was more because she was putting herself out there right now. Her gifts, from what I'd seen, were pretty prodigious, as she shared her mother's abilities of clairvoyance and clairsentience, but also possessed a talent beyond that—the power to see into people's thoughts, to actually read their minds. It wasn't anything she would ever do without being invited, and she didn't, from what I'd heard, use that gift on the tourists who came to the shops to learn about their futures. For that, she used the Tarot, just as Persephone always had. Taryn didn't need to read people's minds to get a glimpse of where they might be headed.

And now I thought I knew exactly why she'd come here. "You want to look into his mind?"

"Yes," she said, obviously relieved that I'd brought it up first. "If he'll let me, that is. It just seems that if I could see what he has buried there, then we'd be able to know for sure whether he really doesn't remember anything of why he'd been left behind in that pod."

My mother looked doubtful. "I don't know, Taryn—"

"Kara, I think it's the best chance," she said. "I can do this. I want to, or I wouldn't have offered. I just thought it would help to settle things, one way or another."

One way or another. And would I be okay with having concrete evidence of Logan's duplicity, beyond what I'd already seen? I supposed I would have to be.

And if he hadn't been lying, if his masters' programming never really had taken hold….

Well, in some ways that was even more frightening, because then there wouldn't be much of an impediment to our being together. But I would have to deal with that eventuality when the time came. If it ever came.

"It's very generous of you," I said. "And I appreciate it." I turned toward my mother. "I want to have her do this…if Logan will let her."

Since she seemed to understand that any further protests would only make it look as if she didn't want me to know the truth, she said, "All right. I'll call Lance." She paused. "Would you rather go to the cottage, Taryn, or would you rather have Logan come here?"

Taryn shut her eyes for a few seconds, seeming to consider. Or maybe she was reaching out with that strange sense of hers, attempting to see which alternative felt best. "The cottage," she said at last. "That seems the right place to do it."

I couldn't really argue with that. Here at the house, you ran the danger of someone barging in at any moment. Since I hadn't lived at home for a long time, I had no clear idea of my sisters' schedules, only that their jobs were part-time and therefore not the sort of thing that would keep them out of the house all day.

"All right," my mother said, sounding resigned. "Let me give Lance a call." She got up from the couch and went into the first-floor study that she and Lance shared for work-related tasks. It would have been closer to go back to the kitchen and use the phone there, but Kevin would have overheard everything she said. And even though it seemed they upgraded the cell towers in the area every few years, the signal was still not all that strong down here in the canyon, so my family was still pretty much stuck with land lines when at home.

Left to ourselves, Taryn and I sat in a somewhat awkward silence. After what felt like the world's longest pause, she ventured, "I hope you don't mind me coming here like this. I just—I wanted to see if I could do something to help."

"No, I don't mind. I'm glad." Would I have had the guts to come forth like this, if our situations had been reversed? I wasn't sure. "It will help to have some kind of resolution. I mean, I don't know what Lance and Martin were even planning to do in the long run. It's not as if they can keep taking babysitting shifts at the cottage indefinitely."

"No, I suppose not," she replied, looking a little taken aback by my somewhat breezy tone. Maybe I should have been a little more serious, but the situation was so crazy that the only way I found I could really deal with it was to retreat to sarcasm. "And I'm glad, too. I wanted to give him a chance to clear his name."

I reflected then that Taryn might have a bit of a romantic streak. Well, who could blame her? The way her parents had met was sort of romantic. Well, except for the whole getting chased all over Arizona and Southern California by alien-infected humans thing.

"Yes, he should have that chance," I agreed. "Let's hope he takes it."

My mother came back to the living room then. Her expression was still troubled, but she said, "Logan wants to do it. He's very eager, in fact. Do you have time now?"

"Absolutely," Taryn replied, getting up from the chair where she sat. "I don't have to work today, so my afternoon is open. I told my mom I was going shopping and maybe meeting some friends at the movies, so she won't suspect anything." A certain rueful light gleamed in her eyes, and she added, "Well, unless she has one of her 'flashes,' in which case I'll have some explaining to do. But that's okay. It's all in a good cause."

"Thank you," I said, and I meant it.

She grinned. "Why don't you wait to thank me until after we see how this all works out?"

I rode with my mother, Taryn following in the little crossover vehicle that she'd inherited from her mother when Persephone upgraded to something bigger a few years ago. Although I knew the Olivers were doing just fine financially, they seemed to be fairly circumspect when it came to those sorts of things. Taryn definitely didn't get the brand-new BMW when she graduated from high school the way my cousin Callista had.

In all the hubbub yesterday, I hadn't even though about getting my own car, which was still sitting in the driveway at the cottage. If nothing else, this would give me the chance to retrieve it, bring it back to my parents' house. I still couldn't quite believe that I'd forgotten all about it.

Because my car was already taking up valuable space in the driveway, and Lance's Jeep was parked next to it, both my mother and Taryn had to leave their vehicles on the street. We met on the pathway that led to the entry, then trailed along, single file, as we made our way to the front door. My heart was beginning to hammer in my chest at the thought of seeing Logan again. Would he be calm, or would he be angry with me for disappearing on him like that without even saying goodbye?

I couldn't begin to guess. I could only hope that he'd realized this interview with Taryn meant I hadn't given up completely. The only way that would happen was if she saw something in his mind to prove he had been lying to me all along, that his apparent affection was born only from an implanted directive to make sure he had sex with me.

Well, let's call a spade a spade. *Mated* with me. I was pretty sure the aliens didn't bother with friendlier terms such as "making love" or "having sex."

Lance opened the door almost as soon as my mother knocked, so he must have been keeping an eye out for us. Although he couldn't have gotten much sleep last night—if any—he didn't look that much the worse for wear. Maybe a few more shadows under his eyes, but that was about it.

I couldn't say the same for Logan. He rose from the couch as the three of us entered the house, and even though his innocence hadn't been proven yet, I couldn't help feeling a pang of remorse for my abandonment as I looked at him. His own eyes were deeply shadowed, and it almost seemed as if there were new furrows in his brow. His cheeks and chin were dusted with stubble.

My mother, bless her, stepped right in so things couldn't get any more awkward than they already were. "Logan, this is Taryn, Paul and Persephone's daughter. She's the one who will be...speaking... with you."

His gaze slid toward Taryn, then moved back toward me, as if he didn't have the energy to focus on anyone else. But he did sound almost normal when he said, "Hello, Taryn."

"Hi, Logan," she responded. "I'm glad you were willing to let me help."

"If it means even a chance—" He swallowed. "That is, I'm glad of the offer."

"Good," she said, and something in her voice altered subtly. It sounded crisper, more in charge, and I wondered if I was looking at the face her clients saw. "Let's take two of the dining room chairs. I find this seems to work better when the format is a little more structured."

"Of course," he replied, although he sounded somewhat uncertain. Again, those gray eyes flickered in my direction, but he did as Taryn had instructed and pulled out one of the dining room chairs, then sat down on it.

She did the same, setting up her seat so she was facing him directly, so close that their knees almost touched. Her gaze was focused on Logan, but her next words were directed at Lance and my mother and me. "You go ahead and sit down in the living room, but please, no talking."

As if I would have uttered a word while she was working. I certainly didn't want to miss anything of what she might say to Logan…or what he would tell her in response to her questions.

The three of us sat down in the living room, Lance on a chair, my mother and I on the sofa. The way it was oriented, I was facing the fireplace, and Logan and Taryn off to my right. Not caring what it might look like, I swiveled in that direction, my right leg tucked under me so I was in a position to better see what was going on.

"All right, Logan," Taryn said. "I want you to close your eyes. I'm not hypnotizing you or anything, but I need you to sit as quietly and as calmly as you can. Do I have your permission to enter your thoughts?"

The question sounded formal, as if it was a ritual she needed to follow every time she did this. Maybe it was. It couldn't be easy, to go tromping through someone else's mind, someone else's memories. By formalizing the procedure, maybe she was giving herself permission to do something that must be very difficult. And if it was hard with a regular person, what would it be like with Logan, whose mind had been constructed and then programmed more like that of a machine rather than a living, breathing man?

"Yes, you have my permission," he said quietly but firmly.

"Thank you, Logan." She paused, and I could see her closing her eyes as well. Almost by their own volition, her hands crept forward until they found Logan's. He started but kept his eyes shut, holding himself still as her fingers laced through his.

It was stupid, but a small dart of jealousy stabbed through me. I wanted to be the one holding his hands like that. Or rather, if I couldn't be doing it, I wasn't sure if I wanted anyone else to, either.

She's not making a move, I scolded myself. *She's just trying to help.*

Feeling chastened, I took the accent pillow I was leaning against and held it to me, wrapping my arms around it. Strange as it might sound, I did feel a little more relaxed afterward. Beside me, my mother shifted her weight, and although I wasn't looking in that direction, I could tell she'd shot a worried look at Lance.

"I'm going into your thoughts now," Taryn went on. Her voice had grown softer, almost dreamy, and although she had said she wasn't really hypnotizing Logan, there was something almost hypnotic about the way she spoke. Maybe it was a sort of relaxation technique.

A pause, and then Logan said, "I can feel you."

"Is it intrusive?"

"No. I can tell your intentions are benign."

"Good." She went quiet for a moment, appearing

to consider her next step. "Think back to your training. What did your masters tell you about Grace?"

"Nothing."

Taryn nodded, mahogany curls slipping over her
shoulders. Even though she was wearing a plain
dark jacket over what looked like a man's white T-
shirt, there was something exotic about her looks.
The Greek blood from her mother's side, I supposed.
She didn't quite turn her head toward the living
room, but her next words were clearly directed at us.
"He's not lying about that. I can't see anything in his
memories to show he even knew you existed, Grace."

"That's what I tried to tell her—" he began.

"I know," Taryn said, the soothing note back in
her voice. "That's why we're doing this. Let me probe
a little more deeply."

Something about the way his shoulders tensed at
that comment told me he wasn't very happy about
having her delve even further into his mind, but he
didn't protest, just gave a slight nod.

She shut her eyes, her fingers tightening on his.
"Okay, I'm seeing something…hearing it, I suppose.
If I try to listen to it consciously, I can't understand it
because of the language barrier, but if I listen as
Logan listened, then I can just barely grab on to it."
Taking in a breath, she cocked her head to one side,
as if listening to voices only she could hear. "All
right…yes, they are saying something about Grace,
and he's looking at an image of her…or rather, the
way they imagined she would look as an adult. It's

happening, and the memory is there, but there's another layer over that. He says he doesn't remember because he really doesn't. Something must have blocked those memories."

Despite her earlier admonition that I remain silent during this whole process, I asked, "What blocked them?"

"I don't know." She glanced up at Logan, who'd been sitting rigid and silent through all this. "Do you have any idea, Logan?"

"No." He shifted, almost looking as if he was about to pull his fingers from her grasp, but then he subsided. "I don't understand how you can see those memories and I can't."

Her mouth curved in a half-smile. "The mind is a very complicated thing, even when it hasn't been messed with the way yours has. Maybe it was all those years in suspended animation, or some other trauma blocked all that out. In fact, I'm going to try something else."

"What?" His tone was guarded, to say the least.

"I'm going to go forward a little. I want to see what you remember of the day you were left at the base."

Frowning, he asked, "What will that prove?"

"It might show something of why selected memories have been blocked. It's pretty common in people who've suffered certain traumas. But there's only one way for me to find out."

"All right." But he shifted in his seat, and once

again I got the impression that he almost yanked his hands away from hers, only to stop when he realized this went more easily for her if she had some kind of physical contact with her subject.

I couldn't tell what Taryn was seeing, but it couldn't have been good, because I saw her brows draw together, and she bit her lip. Logan was dead silent, and I wondered if he could see anything of what was troubling her, or whether all he could tell was that she was currently tromping around in his brain.

"Oh, God," she murmured at last.

"What is it?" I asked.

Instead of replying, she let go of Logan's hands and stood up abruptly. "I need some water," she said, then hurried into the kitchen.

Left behind, Logan opened his eyes and glanced around in bewilderment. "I don't understand."

That makes two of us, I thought, but I only gave him a helpless shrug.

Still looking shaken, Taryn came back out to the dining room—or rather, she paused in the entrance to the kitchen, leaning against the doorframe. "Just before they began to evacuate the base, Logan wasn't in his pod. He was in another room, one that had a lot of pods—"

"I know that room," I broke in. "It's down the hallway from where I found him."

"Right. Well, the pods were occupied. It looks like they'd made their first batch of—well, clones who looked like Logan." She shot an apologetic look at him, and he lifted his shoulders, as if resigned to his status as someone who'd originally come out of a test tube.

Her words puzzled me, because those pods had clearly been empty when Kirsten and Martin and I stumbled on them.

"And then the order came down, and the—the alien in charge basically told Logan that the clones had to be disposed of, that their pods weren't modified like his and wouldn't be able to sustain them long enough to survive. So he—well, he shot them all in the head, one by one, and then picked up the bodies and dropped them down some sort of chute in the wall."

No wonder Taryn had appeared so upset when she dug up that particular memory. Yes, one could argue that the clones weren't really people, hadn't even been given the basic behavioral conditioning that would allow them to function as analogues of people. Even so, having to kill ten men who looked just like you and dispose of their bodies couldn't have been exactly fun. No wonder Logan had blocked those memories.

He was staring at Taryn, eyes wide and startled, and then he put a hand up to his temple, wincing as if he'd suddenly seen what she'd just described, and it pained him.

"They're back, aren't they?" she asked, and he nodded.

"But...how?"

"Sometimes the mere mention of the buried memory is enough to get it to surface. I'm sorry," she added, then left the doorway and approached him. She set down her glass of water and put her hands on his shoulders. "It's not something you should feel responsible for. You'd been conditioned to accept the aliens' orders without question."

He lifted his head to stare at her. "And if that's true, then...so is the rest of it. I went to Grace because I was told to."

"But you didn't *know* that." The briefest of hesitations as she looked back at me, then returned her attention to the man who sat before her. "And I don't think it changes how you feel now."

"How do I feel?"

She smiled. "Well, I think that's between you and Grace." Moving away from him, she came into the living room and stopped in front of the fireplace so she could face my mother and Lance and me. "He really had blocked all those memories, so he wasn't lying when he said he thought he was acting on his own motivations. Maybe there was a plot here, but it wasn't his."

Some of my own turbulent emotions must have shown in my face, because she went on, "And I guess you'll need to figure out what you're going to do with that information, Grace. All I can say is that he never intended to deceive you." Shifting slightly, she said to my mother and Lance, "Maybe we should leave them alone to talk it over."

"I'm not sure—" Lance began, but my mother laid a hand on his arm and gave me a very direct look.

"Are you all right with that?" she asked.

Was I? I couldn't begin to figure out what I was thinking in that moment, but it did seem as if some time alone with Logan might be for the best. He looked so stricken, I couldn't imagine he would do me any kind of harm.

"Yes, I am," I said. "I think that's actually a very good idea."

Lance's expression told me he thought the exact opposite. He didn't protest, though, but pushed himself up from the couch and gave Logan one very dark glare before returning his attention to me. "You call if you need to. You hear me?"

Funny how my stepfather could make me feel like I was thirteen again and sneaking into the house after curfew, rather than a grown woman who'd been on her own for years. "I will. Don't worry."

"Of course we worry. That's what parents do." After glaring daggers at Logan once again, he nodded at my mother, and they headed out, Taryn right behind them.

At the doorway, she paused, then said, "It'll be all right. Just trust yourself—and him."

Easy for her to say. But I knew any further discussion had to be between Logan and me, not me and Taryn. So I nodded and murmured goodbye, shutting the door behind her after she stepped out onto the porch.

Even though I closed the door softly, the sound of the lock clicking into place seemed to echo in the little house. I turned and faced Logan, who had gotten up out of his chair and come into the living room, and now stood there, watching me.

What to say? What to say? My mind couldn't seem to come up with anything coherent, so I blurted, "I'm sorry."

"*You're* sorry?" He seemed genuinely puzzled. "You were working from the evidence you had at the time."

"Maybe, but…." The distance between us seemed huge, even though the living room in actuality was quite small. I moved away from the door, pausing a few feet from him.

"I'm the one who should be apologizing," he said.

"Why? You weren't lying to me."

"But I wasn't telling the whole truth."

"You didn't know the whole truth to be able to tell it."

During this entire exchange, we had inched closer and closer to one another, as if we were two magnetized objects being inexorably drawn together. Now we stood barely a foot apart, close enough that I could see the faint sheen of sweat on his brow, as if digging up those painful memories had been just as much effort as living through them the first time.

His hands curled into fists as they hung by his

sides. "I was programmed to be with you. How is that not a lie?"

A question I wasn't sure I wanted to answer—doubly so, because standing this close to him, I could feel a surge of need wash over me. Never mind that he was stubbled and shadowed and sleep-deprived. In a way, that made him even more desirable, as if this rumpled Logan was even better than his usual perfection.

"I'm not sure," I said slowly. "I suppose if you could look at me, knowing that, and tell me that everything you felt after we were first together was a lie, too. Because that programming—conditioning, whatever you want to call it—might have brought us together, but it doesn't seem like the sort of thing that would *keep* us together. Once you'd carried out what you were programmed to do, you should have lost interest...rebooted or shut down and left me, right?"

A frown pulled at his brows as he seemed to consider what I had just asked. "I'm not sure—possibly. That is, it is true that once we'd achieved a mission objective, that objective was no longer worthy of our attention."

A-ha. I thought I might have him there. I smiled, asking, "So do you think I'm still worthy of your attention?"

His eyes were steely gray, but they burned with a veritable flame then. "Oh, yes. I think you're very worthy."

My hands went to my hips. "Prove it."

He moved so fast, I barely had time to react. Within the space of a second, it seemed, I was in his arms and being carried into the bedroom. The bed was rumpled and unmade, but that was even better, because then we didn't have to waste valuable time pulling back the covers. Hands and fingers were tugging at buttons and zippers and clasps, and in less than a minute, all our clothing was in a messy heap on the floor, and we were falling onto the bed, mouths open to one another, limbs entwined, as we did our best to make our two separate bodies one perfect whole.

Afterward, I cradled my head on his chest and listened to his heart beating, steady, strong. I hadn't realized how much I missed it until now, thinking that restless night back at my parents' house had come solely from my unsettled state of mind and not my unconscious telling me what it already knew— that this was where I was meant to be. Yes, the aliens might have plotted and planned for this, but they'd forgotten to take into consideration one very impor- tant thing: Logan might have their DNA buried within his genetic code, but he was also human. And for all our faults and foibles, we humans had some- thing that made us stronger than the aliens would ever acknowledge.

We had love.

CHAPTER SIXTEEN

I DID CALL MY MOTHER AN HOUR OR SO AFTER THAT, just to let her know that Logan and I had worked things out.

"That's wonderful, Grace," she told me. "So should I pack up your things and bring them to you?"

Oh, that was right. Everything I'd brought with me from Flagstaff was still at my parents' house. "Would you? I can come get them, but—"

"It's fine, sweetie," she said. "I understand your not wanting to leave. I need to go into town for some things at the store anyway, so I'll just drop your bags on the porch when I come through."

"Thank you," I told her, and I meant it.

I hung up, then sat there for a moment, staring at the date and time on my phone. December twenty-ninth. I was due back in Flagstaff the next day, and

God, I didn't want to go. Yes, Logan and I had already discussed heading up there, but now, after everything we'd been through, I only wanted to stay in this little cottage and enjoy each other's company. I didn't want to have to go back to the daily grind. Not yet. I knew I couldn't avoid reality forever, but surely there must be a way to stretch this out a few more days?

Logan came in the living room and sat next to me on the couch. "Would you like a fire? The sun is almost down."

"That would be nice," I said absently.

"Is something wrong? You look worried."

"Oh, not wrong, per se, just—" I broke off, shaking my head. "I'm supposed to be back at work tomorrow, and I'm desperately trying to think of a way to avoid it. But it's not really fair to Dave, who's been working this past week, to ask him have to keep on through New Year's. He deserves a bit of a break."

"Does he?" Logan inquired. "I seem to recall you intimating in an earlier conversation that he was happy to be working over the holidays because his marriage had broken up, and he needed something to distract himself."

True. I'd forgotten discussing that in front of Logan, but he was right. Well, a simple text couldn't hurt. All Dave had to do was say no, and I'd dutifully schlep back up to Flagstaff tonight, even though my heart wouldn't be in it.

So I dictated the text, saying, *Hi, Dave. I've had some personal business come up and was wondering if you could keep taking care of things for a few more days. If you can't, that's fine. Just let me know.*

I sent the text and set my phone down on the coffee table. While I was busy with the text, Logan had gotten up from the couch and was messing with the logs in the hearth.

"Are you sure you should bother?" I asked. "I just realized that if Dave says no, we'll have to head out in a few hours. A fire might be kind of a waste of effort."

"We can enjoy it while we're here, even if we do have to go up to Flagstaff afterward."

That sounded like a good plan to me. Maybe that was one of the things I loved about Logan, that he was willing to do something even if the immediate benefit wasn't all that obvious. Then my phone buzzed, and I picked it up.

Not a problem. Thank you for rescuing me from having New Year's open. Have a good time in Sedona.~Dave

I made a mental note to get Dave a bottle of champagne when I got back to Flagstaff. Or his favorite six-pack. Just something to say thank you.

"We're safe," I told Logan, who smiled as he placed the lighter against the kindling and got the fire going. "Dave's happy to play relief for me for as long as it takes."

"Perfect." Logan came back to the couch and sat down next to me.

I scooted over so we could be even closer, sitting thigh to thigh. That felt good. He seemed to be thinking the same thing, because he moved even closer to me, his warmth not just touching that one side but seeming to envelop me somehow. How could I have thought I could live without him, without the way he made me feel? Some part of me had known I couldn't. Oh, if Taryn had revealed that Logan was truly the aliens' puppet, didn't care for me at all, then I would have some found some way to go on without him, as much as it would have hurt. But it was so clear that, even if some implanted suggestion had first brought us together, it was the spark we'd found afterward that was the real truth.

"Takeout?" he asked.

"What?"

"We'll need to eat soon, I would think. But I guessed that you wouldn't want to go back out."

"You're right, of course," I said, my stomach rumbling its agreement. After we'd made love, I went to the kitchen and ate half a bagel, but it was now getting on toward six o'clock, and otherwise I hadn't eaten anything else since the chili of the night before. "Pizza?"

"This Thai sounded interesting," he replied, leaning away from me briefly so he could pick up the take-out menu from the coffee table. I realized that he'd set the stack of them there, clearly preparing for a cozy night in.

"Sure." I shot him an amused sideways look. "What about the Thai attracted you?"

"Just that it sounded…different."

"And different is good?"

"It can be," he said. He shifted on the couch, hands reaching out to grasp me by the waist and set me down on his lap so I was straddling him. In that position, it was very easy to tell he felt primed and ready for a second go-'round.

I bent forward and kissed him, rocking against him. A soft moan escaped his lips. "Yes," I said, reaching down to pull his shirt over his head. "I think I might like different."

———

Eventually, we did order the Thai, and we ate in the living room, the TV on and the fire stoked up with a fresh batch of logs. According to the news, the Mars landing looked like it was back on track—the engineers had figured out the problem with the faulty module, and so the landing had been rescheduled for the next day, around approximately eight-thirty our time.

New Year's Eve. I supposed that was a good time to be landing on a whole new world, and also hoped someone on board that spaceship had been prescient enough to bring along a bottle or two of champagne. They would have earned it.

My phone, which I'd left sitting on the coffee

table, buzzed. I picked it up, seeing that I had a new text from my mother. *Landing party's back on. Tomorrow night at 7:30. Can you and Logan make it?*

I glanced over at him. He was sitting with his elbows on his knees, chin in his hands as he watched the computer simulations of the Mars landing and the commentators' discussion of the logistics involved. "Want to go to a party tomorrow night?"

"A party?" His brows drew together slightly as he seemed to consider the word. "Oh—it's this New Year's of yours, isn't it?"

"New Year's Eve. And yes, we all tend to party harder than we should on that night, but since it looks like the landing is definitely going to happen, my parents are going ahead with the get-together they were supposed to have on Saturday night. Want to go?"

"And I—I'm invited? That won't be a problem?"

I scooted over closer to him so I could show him the text. "See? She asked for you specifically."

"Oh." He didn't exactly smile, but something about his expression brightened at that concrete evidence of inclusion. "Well, then, yes—I think I would like to go to a party."

"Smart decision. My mother makes the world's most awesome chili cheese dip."

He frowned again, confused, and I laughed.

"Trust me on this one." I quickly typed in, *We'll be there,* along with the obligatory, *You need me to bring anything?* She never did, but the exchange was part of our ritual.

I sent the text, reflecting that this would be a good way to sort of ease Logan into the family. Everyone would most likely be there, and if I showed up with him as if it was nothing out of the ordinary, just the new normal, then maybe it would help to ease some of the tension. I was sure the Olivers knew pretty much the whole story, and I guessed my mother had to have told Kirsten what had been revealed when Taryn went into Logan's thoughts to discover the real truth of the situation.

The only wild card was Jeff Makowski. I had a feeling he'd be less than thrilled that Logan and I had kissed and made up. Why he'd seemed so pleased to dig up that dirt on Logan in the first place, I wasn't sure. If I had the opportunity, I'd try to pick my aunt's brain on the subject. In the meantime, I had a feeling that Jeff wasn't much of a party animal. For all I knew, he'd already left Sedona and gone back to Southern California, his work done.

Well, if we were lucky, anyway.

———

New Year's Eve was clear and bright, not a cloud in the sky. The stars shimmered overhead as we drove through town and up into the canyon, undimmed by any moon. As I looked up through my car's moon-roof, I wondered which of those stars the aliens who'd created Logan had come from. UFO lore claimed their origins were in the Alpha Draconis system, but that theory was still hotly debated. Maybe it didn't really matter where they had come from, as long as they'd returned there and had truly given up on their dreams of world domination.

"Are you looking for Mars?" Logan asked, his hand resting on top of my mine. We were letting the car drive, and had snuggled up against each other in the back seat.

"No point. It won't rise until around four in the morning."

He accepted this statement without question, although most people would have wondered how I had that particular tidbit so easily at hand. I didn't bother to add that I'd read up on the various planetary positions for the year some six months ago, and all those numbers were still firmly stuck in my brain. From what I could tell, Logan had a similar mental capacity. At least, once he read a take-out menu, he never had to look at it again, since he had it memorized.

After the car pulled in next to my aunt and uncle's Mercedes and stopped, Logan and I unbuckled our seatbelts and got out. Naturally, my mother had texted back that we didn't need to bring anything, but I'd still stopped at the grocery store and splurged on some good champagne. With Logan and me reconciled, and it being New Year's Eve and the first time in history man had set foot on Mars—

well, I thought the situation called for something good, even though this was supposed to be a more or less non-drinking party, since we had no idea how late we might actually be up.

Holding the champagne in one hand and Logan's hand in the other, I went up the front walk to the door. Our breath puffed out in the icy air as we walked, but I could smell wood smoke coming from the chimney and knew that it would be cozy and warm inside.

I didn't bother to knock, as I knew my mother never locked the door when she was expecting this much company, even though it was now dark outside. We simply walked in, heading back to the family room, as that was where the big TV was located. The chatter of voices grew louder as we approached, and when Logan and I entered, I saw that everyone was there—the Olivers with Michael and Taryn, who smiled at us, Uncle Martin and Aunt Kirsten and Callista, my brother and sisters, Kelsey trying not to appear as if she was watching Michael Oliver and failing miserably, and Kevin looking cranky that the television was tuned, of course, to the live feed straight from NASA. No one in my family had much patience for the talking heads on cable news channels, although Logan did seem to find them fascinating.

"Hi!" I called out, and received a chorus of "hi"s in return. Maybe Callista and my sisters sent Logan a curious look, but everyone else seemed almost studiously casual about his presence. Good. At least they weren't going to make a big deal out of it.

My mother was, of course, bustling around in the kitchen, and I went over to her and gave her a quick kiss on the cheek. "Any room in the fridge?" I asked, lifting the bottle of champagne in question.

"It'll be tight, but I think I can manage it." She looked at the flowery Perrier-Jouët bottle and raised an eyebrow. "I wasn't aware you were this invested in the Mars landing."

"Well, maybe not the landing, but...other things." My gaze strayed to Logan, who had approached Lance and seemed to be asking something about the images currently being shown on the broadcast. I tensed, wondering how Lance was going to react, but he only shook his head and pointed at Paul, as if indicating that the astronomer was really the best person to answer those sorts of questions.

A faint sigh of relief escaped my lips. "So he's okay with it?" I asked in an undertone, although really, with all the chatter in the other room, I could have spoken in a normal voice and not been overheard.

My mother didn't bother to ask who I meant by "he." "I think he's...learning to accept it. I told him how happy you sounded, and he was glad about that. That's all he ever wanted, Grace. For you to be happy."

Something warm and contented seemed to rise up in me then. Lance and I had been at odds for so many years that I'd never stopped to think a good part of it might have been exactly what she'd pointed out only a day earlier—that he and I were too much alike, and so of course we'd always been at loggerheads. Through it all, though, he had loved me like a daughter...at least, he would have if I'd let him.

"I am happy," I said, smiling and looking over at Logan. Someone had handed him a bottle of water, and he was talking with Paul and Martin and Lance as if he'd always been a part of that group. Michael had joined in, too, which told me the conversation was probably getting technical. Persephone and Kirsten were laughing about something, and the younger generation—my sisters and Callista and Taryn—were taking advantage of the opportunity to make some serious inroads on the chili cheese dip. "This is great. I'm glad you were able to pull it together so quickly."

"This?" My mother gave an off-hand wave. "This is nothing. A few appetizers, some chicken skewers for later so it's not all junk food...not a big deal. Actually, I was glad of a chance to have everyone here, and so was Kirsten. Callista got wind of some party a group of college students were having at one of the condos over in Los Abrigados, and Kelsey and Melissa were thinking about going with her. But Kelsey wouldn't budge once she knew Michael would be here, and so that plan sort of collapsed. I'm not sure how thrilled Callista is about the whole thing, but at least they're all here and not off at a party with a bunch of drunk frat guys."

It was funny how my mother seemed to include me with the older set when she made these confidences, even though of course I was only a few years older than my cousin and my sisters. But they were still in what my mother thought of as their college years, whereas I had a job and was properly out on my own. But at the grand old age of twenty-five, I at least had enough hindsight to appreciate that it was probably better if the girls were here and not around a group of college guys they didn't even know.

I glanced over at my cousin. She was perched at the edge of the couch, munching on a chip, and didn't look overly disappointed at being stuck at home with her family. One might have wondered how she'd even heard about something like the condo party in the first place, but Callista always had those sorts of things more or less falling in her lap. She was the kind of person who literally would turn heads as she walked down the street—that fall of pale blonde hair, almost to her waist, was eye-catching enough, but she had a face to match. Not that surprising, considering her parents' genetic contribution, but still.

"Good call," I told my mother, then offered her another grin before I went to join Logan and the rest of the crew. I paused at his side, laced my fingers in his, and said, "I hope you all aren't totally filling his head with facts and figures. It kind of takes some of the fun out of it, don't you think?"

"Just the opposite, actually," Michael protested after glancing quickly at Logan's and my intertwined hands and then away again. "I think it really adds to the whole experience when you know more about the scope of the mission."

And that right there was why the whole thing with Michael would never have worked out. We always seemed to end up on opposite sides of a discussion. At the moment, though, I really didn't care. Instead, I smiled sweetly and replied, "Well, that's an interesting perspective. I'll have to bear that in mind."

Martin chuckled but knew better than to say anything, and Paul and Lance also remained wisely silent. From across the room, I saw my aunt Kirsten catch my eye and give me the smallest of nods, seeming to indicate she had something she wanted to say to me. I murmured to Logan, "Will you be okay on your own for a couple of minutes?"

He glanced at me, then at my aunt. "Of course," he replied, his tone equally subdued.

I let go of his hand and drifted from the room, then stopped partway down the hall. A few seconds later, Kirsten joined me there.

"What's up?" I asked.

"I just wanted to see how you were doing."

"Great," I replied. Something in my face should have told her that was the truth, or maybe she sensed the happiness emanating from me, because she seemed to relax.

"Good." A pause as she glanced down the hallway before looking back at me. "I just wanted to apologize about Jeff."

"No need," I assured her. Yes, he'd made a hash of things for a while there, but everything had worked out in the end.

"I feel like there's a need." She hesitated again, then said, "Jeff's never been what you'd call tactful, but I think he was pushing hard for Logan's guilt partly because of me."

I blinked. "Come again?"

"Well, he wasn't all that thrilled when Martin came on the scene. I got the distinct impression that he wanted things to fall apart for you and Logan because he didn't want to see another Swenson woman end up with an alien."

Considering their history, I supposed I could just wrap my brain around such twisted logic. Even so, I couldn't help saying, "That's nuts."

"I agree. But…you can see why I think it was partly my fault. I'm glad it all worked out, and Jeff is probably back in L.A. by now, but…."

"It's fine." Since she still looked troubled, I added, "In a way, it's good that Jeff was such an asshole about the whole thing. I'd rather know the truth about Logan than have this mystery hanging over us. And, as you said, it all worked out in the end. No harm, no foul."

She smiled then. "Thank you, Grace."

Since that seemed to be all we needed to say on the subject, we headed back into the family room. Martin quirked an eyebrow at Kirsten, and she just gave him the smallest shake of the head. I came back up to Logan after grabbing a bite of chili cheese dip on the way over, and then we were all quiet for a while, watching the television as the last checks on the landing module were performed.

"Go for separation," came the tinny-sounding voice from the NASA feed, and I shivered slightly as I thought of how many millions of miles of empty space those words had to cross, and how much time had passed since they'd been spoken. With the current relative positions of the Earth and Mars, that would be just a hair over nine minutes.

The feed switched over to the cameras mounted on the lander. Although they recorded in 360 degrees, at the moment all that was being sent out for public viewing was the shots from the forward-focused cameras. It made sense, because what everyone really wanted to see was the image of Mars growing larger and larger, morphing from a sandy-red disk to suddenly looking like a real planet, with geographical features easily distinguishable even at this distance. Unlike Earth, there were no clouds, nothing to block the view of the barren, arid landscape.

"It is beautiful, isn't it?" Logan murmured to me.

I hadn't really thought about it, but as I gazed at the steadily increasing surface of the planet, I thought he might be right. There was something in those craggy, reddish formations that reminded me of Sedona, although of course there could be no dark junipers on Mars, no elegantly bare cottonwoods and sycamores and oaks.

He was the only one who spoke. Everyone else was transfixed, watching as the lander sailed through Mars' thin atmosphere, banking down to the designated landing site on Utopia Planitia. I wasn't sure any of us even breathed until we saw the image from the cameras jolt slightly, and we realized that jolt was the shock of the lander setting itself down, using thrusters to lower itself the final few meters to the surface of the alien planet.

Silence. We all watched, waiting, until we heard the voice of the lander's captain, Gonzalo Cruz, say, "*Venture* has landed. I repeat, *Venture* has landed." A pause, and then he added, in a much less matter-of-fact tone, "'It is good to renew one's wonder, said the philosopher. Space travel has again made children of us all.'"

I recognized the quote—Ray Bradbury's *Martian Chronicles*. There would be no Martians, but there would certainly be wonders.

Paul was the first to let out a whoop of triumph. I supposed that made sense, since he was one of those dreamers who had stared at the stars and had hoped and prayed for years that a mission like this would finally be made a reality. Martin was next, and then we were all laughing and cheering, even Logan, who looked a little confused by the commotion—after all, space travel was a commonplace to the ones who had created him—but who gamely joined in.

"I think this calls for a celebration," Paul said, then went to the refrigerator and pulled out two bottles of Cristal. Wow, he really had been confident the landing would be a success. That Cristal would make my Perrier-Jouët taste like bad grape juice in comparison.

And my mother was fetching down champagne flutes and regular old wine glasses, since she didn't have enough flutes to go around in such a throng, and Paul was filling them up and handing them around until all of us had some champagne to drink.

"To the next chapter in the history of the human race," he said, holding up his glass.

"To Mars!" Martin added.

"To getting to drink champagne!" my sister Melissa burbled, since of course she was underage.

Everyone laughed and then drank. I clinked glasses with Logan, who smiled down at me.

"This is very important for all of you, isn't it?"

"Well, yes. We've gone to the moon, but Mars is so much farther away, and it's a real planet, not just our world's satellite. This is the first step to setting up a colony there." That would be some years off, of course, but first it had to be proven that manned travel to the red planet was both viable and safe.

After that, we all settled back down to watch as the ritual testing of the rover vehicle was carried out.

This was the next step—two of the astronauts would drive the rover out a distance of approximately five kilometers, to a crater of some geological significance. They would gather samples and take them back to the lander, and that would be the beginning of a month-long expedition that would include trips to various points of interest, all in the name of using boots on the ground to determine the most feasible locations for a future colony.

The tests took some time, but no one seemed to mind too much; we all drank champagne and nibbled on appetizers, until at last the ramp lowered itself from the rear of the landing module, and the rover took off across the Martian landscape, kicking up red dust. Even though we couldn't see through the reflective film on their spacesuits' visors, I had to think that the two explorers—a man and a woman— had to be grinning like idiots behind there. I knew I would be.

After they'd gone a hundred yards or so, the feed switched to one from the camera mounted on the dashboard of the rover. More red dust swirled around, but you could still see that they were moving with decent speed across an open plain with rocks of various sizes scattered across it. They dipped slightly, moving into a deeper depression and then flattening out again. Off in the distance I could see a dark line, which I guessed must be the edge of the crater.

As they approached, they slowed, then slowed further, until they came to a stop, red dust drifting up into the air. The view switched again, this time to cameras mounted on the two astronauts' helmets, as they moved toward the edge of the crater.

A woman's voice came over the feed. "*Venture, this is Cheng. We are about to start our descent.*"

"Copy that, Cheng."

The astronaut moved to the edge of the crater and began to inch her way down its side. In reality, it didn't look that steep, or that deep, which was probably why they'd chosen this particular geographic feature as a destination. Once she reached the bottom, her companion only a pace or two behind her, she turned to look around her, the camera moving with her.

What the—

I don't even know what it was, but there was *something* down in the crater. Dark, looming, square —obviously, something that couldn't have been formed by nature.

Persephone gave voice to my confusion. "Paul, what the heck is that?"

He shook his head. "I don't know. We've never landed anything here, though. I know that."

Beside me, Logan shifted, then said, "Oh, no—"

It happened so fast, I couldn't tell what was going on, only that there was a sudden blur of movement, the impression of several large shapes surrounding the astronauts. A sickening crunch, followed by another, and then the feed went completely black. We all sat there in horror, watching the blank television.

A second or two later, the words *please stand by—we are experiencing a temporary interruption of the feed* scrolled across the screen.

Paul set down his champagne glass, and got to his feet, frowning. "What the hell?"

"Was someone there?" Melissa chimed in, looking scared.

"Of course not. That's stupid," Kelsey said scornfully, but I could tell from the look in her eyes that her remark was false bravado, and behind it, she was just as frightened as our sister.

I noticed that Martin and Kirsten didn't say anything, but only glanced at each other and then, more subtly over at Logan, who was sitting frozen beside me, champagne glass still in one hand, the other on mine, although I noticed his fingers had gone limp and were merely lying on top of mine, rather than holding them.

And then the room was filled with a searing white light, and from the center of that light stepped the form of a tall, dark-haired man wearing white robes that seemed to shift and shimmer with all the colors of the rainbow. He paused in front of the television, blocking that bogus message about a "feed interruption," then folded his arms and gazed at all of us.

Persephone got to her feet, eyes wide. "*O-Otto?*"

She sounded incredulous, and I didn't blame her. Yes, I knew that Otto had been her spirit guide, once upon a time, but from what I could tell, she hadn't heard from him since that cold December night twenty-five years ago when my aunt drove the aliens out of Sedona and Otto sentenced Martin to exile here for interfering in human affairs. That exile hadn't turned out to be particularly onerous, but still, Otto's judgment had pretty much landed him on everyone in our group's shit list, for obvious reasons.

His gaze flicked toward Persephone, but he didn't smile, nor offer one word of greeting. Instead, his brows drew together as he surveyed the rest of us for one long, painful moment, his gaze, for some reason, pausing at Callista before it continued to sweep around the room. Like Martin and Gabriel, Otto was extremely good-looking, but there was almost something preternatural about those good looks. I didn't see one pore or one speck of stubble. No wonder some people thought the Nordic aliens must be gods.

Then he crossed his arms and said, "We need to talk. Time is running out."

And I knew this was far from over. In fact, it had only just begun.

The Sedona Files series continues with Callista's story in *Falling Angels*.

Darknight

Darkmoon

Sympathetic Magic

Protector

Spellbound

A Cleopatra Hill Christmas

Impractical Magic

Strange Magic

The Arrangement

Defender

Bad Blood

Deep Magic

Darktide

Books 1-3 and Books 4-6 of this series are also available in two separate omnibus editions at special boxed set prices. Chronicles of Cleopatra Hill includes the series' two "back in time" novellas, *Bad Blood* and *The Arrangement*.

Or get the entire series in one enormous, specially priced boxed set! (Not available on Amazon.)

THE DJINN WARS

(Paranormal Romance)

Chosen

Taken

Fallen

Broken

Forsaken

Forbidden

Awoken

Illuminated

Stolen

Forgotten

Driven

Unspoken (June 2019)

Books 1-3 and Books 4-6 of this series are also available in two separate omnibus editions at special boxed set prices!

THE WATCHERS TRILOGY*

(Paranormal Romance)

Falling Dark

Dead of Night

Rising Dawn

The Watchers Trilogy is also available in a specially priced boxed set!

THE SEDONA FILES*

(Paranormal Romance)

Bad Vibrations

Desert Hearts

Angel Fire

Star Crossed

Falling Angels

Enemy Mine

Get the first three books of this series in an omnibus edition, or read the complete six-book series in one super-low-priced boxed set!

––––––

TALES OF THE LATTER KINGDOMS

(Fantasy Romance)

All Fall Down

Dragon Rose

Binding Spell

Ashes of Roses

One Thousand Nights

Threads of Gold

The Wolf of Harrow Hall

Moon Dance

The Song of the Thrush

Books 1-3 and Books 4-6 of this series are also available in two separate omnibus editions at special boxed set prices.

––––––

THE GAIAN CONSORTIUM SERIES*

(Science Fiction Romance)

Beast (free prequel novella)

Blood Will Tell

Breath of Life

The Gaia Gambit

The Mandala Maneuver

The Titan Trap

The Zhore Deception

The Refugee Ruse

Books 1-3 of this series are also available in an omnibus edition at a special boxed set price!

———

STANDALONE TITLES

Hearts on Fire

Sympathy for the Devil

Taking Dictation

Night Music

Golden Heart

* Indicates a completed series

ABOUT THE AUTHOR

USA Today bestselling author Christine Pope has been writing stories ever since she commandeered her family's Smith-Corona typewriter back in grade school. Her work includes paranormal romance, fantasy romance, and science fiction/space opera romance. She makes her home in Arizona.

Don't miss out on any of Christine's new releases — sign up for her newsletter today!

Christine Pope on the Web:
www.christinepope.com

facebook.com/ChristinePopeAuthor
twitter.com/ChristineJPope

*9 7 8 0 6 9 2 3 5 8 4 4 3 *